PANGS

PANGS

Jerry L. Wheeler

Queer Space

New Orleans

Published in the United States of America and United Kingdom by
Queer Space
A Rebel Satori Imprint
www.rebelsatoripress.com

Paperback ISBN: 978-1-60864-178-9
Ebook ISBN: 978-1-60864-179-6
Library of Congress Control Number: 2021947488

To Duncan, who slept at my feet while I wrote most of this and who now sleeps in my heart. I miss you, my beamish boy.

CONTENTS

A THIRST FOR TALENT

knew from the moment I sensed the prey that Seth and I would end up fighting over it. We always did. We were the oldest and the strongest of our kind left, except for the Old Man. But he hadn't walked in centuries. We couldn't even feel him anymore. But I felt Seth's desperation. Neither of us had fed in a long time.

Unlike the Blood Brethren, our needs are different and cannot be fulfilled by just anyone walking the street. Our prey is rare, which is why we must compete to feed. Only the strongest and smartest survive, and Seth is a formidable opponent, especially when desperate.

I knew he was already in New Orleans before I stepped off the plane, but I was in no hurry. I caught a cab to the bed and breakfast where I always stay in the Marigny, dropping my bags in my room and heading out into the courtyard. I sat down and closed my eyes, letting the hot afternoon sun steam the grimy travel stench of the airport out of me until sweat rolled off my brow and soaked my back. When sufficiently acclimated, I napped, showered, changed, and headed into the Quarter as the twilight dawned.

New Orleans is one of those places, along with Memphis, London, and New York City, where I can always find a less talented musician to tide me over until someone worth feeding from comes along. The quality we seek is in abundance here, but I could never move back to the Quarter—too many memories, too many close calls, too many who still bear grudges. I might be able to alter my appearance a bit and change my name, but my presence is far too well-known for more than a brief visit. I don't fear competition, but I embrace anonymity.

On Friday and Saturday nights, the tourists on Bourbon Street are layered as thick as powdered sugar on a beignet, weaving sloppy, drunken patterns in their cargo shorts and flip-flops. They take up space at the bar, laughing too loudly so as not to feel the ghosts of the city shuddering past them. I love those spirits. I've known many. But I follow my nose and my instincts rather than the tourists.

And those lead me to a small doorway off Royal and Tolouse. It's painted black and has no sign outside, but I know it's the Club Du Monde. And I know Seth will be inside, waiting for the object of our search. When I open the door, a cold blast of air conditioning shocks me. I sigh, remembering when the city was not chilled for tourism, and I remind myself that change is neither good nor bad. It is simply change.

A jazz quartet is on the small stage, the saxophone player riffing a sweet, slow twilight song as the bass and drums structure the beat and the guitarist drops in a Wes Montgomery run now and then. They are adequate appetizers. Nothing like what will be on stage later, but I'm not looking for *hors d'oeuvres*.

Others of our kind are here, but they know Seth and I have

first claim on the real prize. They will settle for the quartet because they are used to those meals. Seth, of course, is sitting alone at the front table, but he is not wearing the unshaven, sallow, snaggle-toothed visage I'm used to seeing. He is the woman this time—what is her name? Laura? Laurene? No matter. He's probably changed it again.

His eyes, however, are the same deep green, and I know the scalp beneath that long blond hair still bears the scars of our last encounter. He is wearing a crisp, light blue strapless summer dress, showing off his ample cleavage. I have to smile. He thinks a female form will give him an advantage, but such artifice only expends energy. Besides, he obviously does not sense what I do about the quarry.

He drained his drink as I slid into the empty chair at the table. "Hello, Seth."

Munching an ice cube, he grinned. "Warner—how lovely to see you again. Please call me Laura."

"I'll try. I might forget. What are you drinking?"

"Amaretto on the rocks."

I signaled the waiter for another round as the band left the stage to a smattering of polite applause. "You look marvelous. All healed?"

"Ah, yes. That *was* a nasty blow. Did you enjoy our jazz man?"

"I did, indeed. I fed from him for five years until his gift dissipated. After that, I had no reason to hold on to him."

Seth clucked his tongue. "Even the most talented eventually run dry." He tossed his hair and smiled as the waiter brought our drinks. "However, five years is a long time. I imagine that has sustained you for…what, ten years or more?"

"Twelve. I don't waste energy on frivolities like useless shape-shifting."

"Useless? This shape will win the prize, I guarantee."

"If you say so," I replied with a shrug, "but take care not to overestimate the power of your breasts." I sipped the too-sweet drink and grimaced. "For argument's sake, since I already assume your answer, let's say you *are* the victor this time. Would you share the prize? Properly nurtured, his gift could last us both decades. We could be sustained for several lifetimes after that."

Seth shook his head. "Dear Warner. I appreciate the sentiment, but you know that's not my way."

"I suppose not," I said, sighing. "Your way is all death and destruction. Do you feel no remorse for the talent you've denied the world time and time again? Billie Holiday, Janis Joplin, Hank Williams, and so many others—you could have sipped slowly from them for years instead of sucking them dry and letting them kill themselves with drink or drugs trying to figure out how they lost such an essential part of their beings."

"Don't lecture me, Warner. It's tedious. You know perfectly well if I don't take them, someone else will try to. We don't all have your sense of fair play and cooperation, and I refuse to share my meals with others. That's why I feast quickly and leave them." He shifted and I saw his true face for a moment. "Nurturing your prey," he said with scorn. "I'm a vampire, not a wet nurse."

"Being a vampire doesn't make you a creature without conscience. That's your choice."

Seth raised his head high and sniffed the air, a look of rapture in his eyes. "Conscience?" he said. "How can you even think of conscience when you smell something like this? Our quarry is in the building, if you hadn't noticed."

I had. The scent was overpowering—a splendid *melange* of murk and musk that conjured visions of a vast, limitless sea of talent, heady with the rich, briny funk of Delta blues, all swampwater moonshine and bitter greens in bacon grease. But that was just the topnote. I also smelled undercurrents of the lush, heavy cream of Seventies soul, sweaty cocaine-fueled disco, hip-hop's pungent relentlessness, and the bitter, regretful smoke of late-night jazz.

As I drank in the amazingly complex influences that comprised the aroma of his singular talent, I vowed Seth would not win this prize no matter what the cost. I would fight as I had never fought before. And as I watched Seth, I knew he was making the same vow.

"You must go," he said. "He should not see us together."

Seth was correct. I left both him and that horrid drink and got a good seat at the bar, ordering a very dry martini as I waited for the first show to begin. Looking around the shabby dive, I formulated a plan. His massive talent rested on the twin supports of ego and ambition, both of which I could also smell. Clubs like this would not hold him for long.

With my industry contacts, I could give this one a career he'd only dreamed of. And as his manager, I'd be closer to him than anyone. He'd be vulnerable to me in so many ways and I would, indeed, nurture him. Seth would, of course, attempt to entangle him emotionally, but even if he got to the boy first, the greedy bastard couldn't take all his talent as quickly as he'd done with others. He'd explode like an over-engorged tick. He'd have to take this one slowly whether he liked it or not. And time would not work to his advantage here. Neither would his breasts.

"Laaaaydies and gennnlemen," a disembodied voice slurred into a microphone somewhere, "the Club DoooMonde is proud to present, from Lafayette, Louuuusiannna, the sennsaaaational Missssstah WADE DIXON!" The applause was enthusiastic enough for the rather sparse crowd. The others of our kind had gone in search of the opening act, leaving the main course for us. As the booming voice faded, Wade strolled out on stage.

He was somewhere in his early twenties—short, dressed in a plain white t-shirt and jeans with a pair of expensive yet well-scuffed snakeskin cowboy boots. His dirty blond hair fell in a careless wave over his forehead, nearly obscuring a pair of powder blue eyes, and he wore a delightful three-day scruff of beard. He carried a stool and an acoustic cherrywood Gibson with a pick-worn scratch plate around which was printed THIS MACHINE KILLS. I grinned. How Woody Guthrie. He plopped the stool down in front of the center stage mic, perched and grinned.

"I hope y'all like blues out there," he said in a slow drawl as he hoisted the guitar up on his lap, "'cause that's what the next hour or so's gonna be about. If that don't suit ya, come back for the eight o'clock show when my rock and roll band'll be with me."

He struck up a standard eight-bar blues run with a twelve-bar break before it became Sonny Boy Williamson's "Bring It

On Home." His phrasing was derivative, drawing on the original as well as Van Morrison's take. The boy had clearly taken cues from the classics and the master interpreters but was not yet confident enough to put his own stamp on the material. No matter. That would come in time.

His playing was not astonishing, but his potential was. I heard not how he was but how he could be, given room to grow. Seth never understood that. You can't just *take* an artist's talent. You have to grow it in order to get all there is to get from it. Otherwise, it doesn't nourish you the way it should. It's the difference between eating a green apple and a ripe one.

And there was something else Seth didn't understand about Wade Dixon, at least not yet, and that was how little his disguise would impress him. I had felt it all along, but seeing him in person confirmed it. Not that it was Seth's fault. When he was mortal, he was not a man who loved other men, so he couldn't be expected to recognize that quality so quickly. Feeding from them—*kissing* them—was a taste he'd had to acquire or cut out fifty percent of his food supply, the same as I had had to do with women. By the time he realized his mistake, the advantage would be mine.

I listened to Wade run through a virtual catalog of bluesmen, from Robert Johnson to Charley Patton to Big Bill Broonzy, but I did not stay for his whole set. I'd gotten the information I'd come for. And the next show with his band, who were far less talented than he, else I would have felt them, would consist of Lynryd Skynyrd and Springsteen covers for the tourists. My eyes watered from the smoke in the club, and the martinis had given me a headache. I longed for the quiet of Washington Park near Elysian Fields.

Giving up so soon? Seth asked inside my head as he watched me from across the room, a grin on his painted lips. I shook my head ruefully. Yet another energy-expending talent he insisted on using constantly. I merely grinned back at him and walked out of the club.

☙

heard the high whine of the mouth harp long before I saw the player. I was at the corner of Frenchman and Dauphin next to Washington Park, but he was inside the fence close to a stand of bougainvilla. Street musicians rarely stray far from the Quarter. I thought perhaps this one had decided to work the Marigny arts district, which had less competition. The music lured me, but I was also hungry. Smelling Wade's talent had unleashed an inconvenient appetite in me, and it needed to be sated, if only by a busker's snack.

When I entered the park, however, I knew it was a trap. I saw no one around the musician, but I felt the presence of at least two other men nearby. It was almost dark and passers-by were few. No one would see what would happen. I smiled. Let them set upon me however they wished. I would have my snack regardless.

Sitting cross-legged on the grass, the bearded musician vamped a brighter, more sprightly tune as I approached. His aroma wafted toward me, quickening my steps. I put my hand in my pocket as if to dole out some change and felt the other men stirring. They were about ten or fifteen yards away, but my meal would take only seconds. I'd be finished and ready to deal with them long before they arrived.

A battered, bright yellow slouch hat lay before him, already containing some bills and change. As I tossed my offerings in, I caught his eye. That was all I needed to charm him. He rose at my silent command, and I stepped close to him, hearing the clink of the spilled change as my foot upset the hat.

I grabbed his face with both hands and drew him to me, his beard rough on my palms. It smelled of soap and cleanliness, so he wasn't homeless. Up close, he looked all of twenty-one or two, just a suburban kid out to relieve a tourist of a few dollars, as were his compatriots, I'm sure. I looked deeply into his brown eyes and brushed my lips against his. They parted easily, and I pressed into him.

His breath was stale at first, then sweet as I drank in his essence. It tasted sharp and acrid, a hallmark of the marginally talented. It's like drinking chemically aged swill instead of fifty-year-old scotch. I could have taken all he had and still been hungry, but I took only a few breaths worth. I wanted to leave him at least able to play his instrument.

As I finished, I felt two men coming up behind me. I did not hurry. Their hatred and scorn were palpable even though my back was turned to them, but I expected no less. They were young and far too foolish to feel anything else.

"Jesus *Christ*, Ryan, are you letting this faggot *kiss* you?"

Rough hands grabbed my arms and wrenched them behind my back, spinning me around to face a man wielding a knife. I could have told them Ryan wouldn't answer for a while. He was still entranced. I hadn't released him, but it would wear off in time. He wouldn't remember a thing.

"Empty your pockets, faggot."

I chuckled. "That's going to be hard to do with my hands behind my back."

"Stick the cocksucker, Shaun," the one holding me hissed.

"You boys haven't done this a lot, have you?" I asked. "The idea is to keep your identities secret. I know two of your names already."

"*Stick* 'im!"

"Oh yes," I said. "By all means, *stick* me."

The boy with the knife lunged forward and drove it into my stomach. The look of shock on his face when I didn't crumple to the ground was priceless. Even better was his astonishment when he withdrew the weapon and I began to laugh. He stabbed me again with the same result. I laughed again and broke the hold behind my back, twisting my assailant's arm as I forced him to his knees in front of me. I snapped his wrist and he screamed, his companion dropping the knife and turning to run.

Before he could get away, I grabbed his shoulder and pulled him close, putting my arm around his neck in a choke hold. I didn't smell any talent, which was a shame. I would have drained that one dry. I tightened the hold, relishing his struggle as he clawed at my arm and gasped for breath.

"Don't play games you cannot win, Shaun," I said evenly into his ear. "I'm going to let you go in a moment, but you mustn't be foolish enough to let revenge cross your mind. That would be counterproductive. Help your friends instead. Ryan will be fine in an hour or so, but that other boy will need a trip to the emergency room. Count yourself lucky I didn't kill you. Are we understood? Stop struggling and nod your head."

He did as he was told and when he was calm, I let him go. He fell on the ground and stared up at me. I felt his unblinking glare on my back as I turned and walked away.

"Who *are* you?"

"Ask me no questions," I said over my shoulder, "and I'll tell you no lies."

CB

What makes you think I need a manager?" Wade asked, barefoot and shirtless as he scratched the patch of thick blonde hair between his navel and the top of his jeans. We were standing on his balcony overlooking Dauphin, the early afternoon smell of the Quarter drifting up to us. Birds were singing, but I couldn't say what kind. I don't know much about birds except that they're too pretty.

"What makes you think you don't?"

He didn't reply, so I continued. "You're an extremely talented man, Wade. Anyone can see that, but you need shaping. You have to hone your abilities to become what I know you want to be."

"What's that?" he asked with a sly, toothy half-grin that made me giddy.

"The best."

He read me up and down, his blue eyes strangely inexpressive. For a moment, I thought he was going to ask me to leave, but then he chuckled and leaned close to me, throwing his arm over my shoulder as he walked me inside. His very air thrilled me. "Well, now if you'da said you were gonna make me a star, I'd have toldja you were a lyin' motherfucker. But the best? That's somethin' else."

"And it's well within your grasp."

"For how much?"

"Nothing at first. If you like what I do for you in the next two months, we can make an arrangement. It won't be painful to you. I won't bleed you dry." I had to grin. "But there's always a price to pay, Wade. You know that."

Seth appeared in the doorway leading to what I assume was the bedroom. I was not surprised to find him here.

"Now, you got to watch out for men who talk about prices," he said. "They always get raised in the end." He was wearing the same dress from the night before, obviously having spent the night. But I could still feel his hunger. Indeed, an odd silence hung in the air on his entrance. I had the distinct impression that whatever had happened last night had not yielded the result Seth expected.

"Sorry," Wade said, remaining at my side. "Did we wake you up? Warner, this is Laura. I met her at the gig last night. She had a little too much to drink and, well, kinda passed out."

I nodded. Seth nodded back. "Pleased to make your acquaintance," he said.

It was most certainly a ruse. Seth could out-drink any

mortal. Yet he hadn't fed last night. I was certain of it. "Likewise,"
I replied, "but you must forgive us. We have business to discuss."

Wade scratched his left nipple. "Warner is my new manager."

Seth smiled. "Really? Well now, don't let me interrupt you.
I'll just get a cab home."

"I could drive you," he said.

"No, no—a cab will be fine, sugar." He sauntered up to
Wade and reached for his hand, clasping it with both of his.
"Wonderful to meet you, Wade. You're a very sexy guy, and I
enjoyed the show last night. Thank you for rescuing me and
putting me up for the evening. We'll talk again soon, I promise."
He faced me and smiled.

Dear Warner, he said inside my head, *did you think I was
going to pounce on him like a mouse? This one is different. Thus,
the hunt must also be different. I am not desperate enough to be
foolish. For now, I am satisfied to drink from his aura, but rest
assured he will be mine in the end.*

"It was lovely to meet you, Mr. Warner," he said aloud.
He turned and walked out the door, the clicking of his high
heels echoing down the staircase. We both stared after him a
moment, apparently lost in our own thoughts.

"Weird girl," Wade finally said. "She sat at the front table all
night long looking like she wanted to eat me up. We barely got
finished with the last set before she came bouncin' up on stage
and followed us to the dressing room. I was hopin' she'd go for
our drummer, Dave, but she goes straight for me."

He stopped to light a cigarette he shook out of the pack
on the coffee table. "Now, I don't do the groupie thing," he said,
exhaling. "Never have. I don't wanna end up with herpes or

warts or some shit like that, but she's sweet and she won't take no for an answer, so we end up havin' breakfast at the Clover Grill and pretty soon we're back here talkin' on the couch. She's askin' all kinds of questions about me, and all of a sudden, she's sound asleep. I carried her into the bedroom, tucked her in, and slept out here."

"That doesn't sound so weird."

He gave me a grin that could break hearts. "I guess not, but she was so intense. I can't describe it, man—it's like she wanted to *consume* me."

"Did you get her phone number?"

"That was the other weird thing," he replied, stubbing his cigarette out. "I don't even think she *had* a phone. Or a *purse*. Crazy, huh? But I think she'll find me again even without one."

"Not in the next month she won't," I said. "You'll be in St. Louis."

"St. Louis?"

"That's right. Then Los Angeles for a bit. Perhaps New York."

"Wait, wait—I've got a gig *here* for at least two weeks. I can't just up and go to St. Louis."

"You mean at the Club DuMonde? I know the owner quite well. If he won't let you out of your contract as a favor to me, he'll do it for money. Either way, I'll make it work."

"What about the band?"

"What *about* them?"

"I can't just leave 'em. That wouldn't be right."

Sometimes I took Seth's point. Principles were such an aggravation. "I'm not managing the band," I said with a firm sigh. "I'm managing *you*. They will be left behind at some point. Why drag it out? If you're too nice to do it, leave it to me. Part of a manager's job is delivering bad news."

"Lemme think a minute," he said as he flopped down on the sofa, interlocked his hands behind his head and propped his bare feet up on the coffee table. I didn't see what there was to think about, but a forced decision is easier to renege on, so I let him consider his options in silence. After a minute or two, however, my curiosity was getting the better of me.

It wouldn't hurt to pop into his head for a second, I thought. Just to see which way he was leaning and give him a bit of a push in the right direction if need be. His furrowed brow and flatlined mouth indicated difficulty making a choice, and I expected him to be envisioning an angry confrontation at the very least, perhaps considering means of avoiding potential violence. To my astonishment, that was not the scene playing in Wade's mind.

His thoughts were of a more pornographic nature. The vision he conjured was of me on the sofa, him kneeling between my spread legs. My pants were down about my ankles, and his head bobbed up and down on my prick. His fantasies were more generous as to its length and girth than reality deserved, but I took it as a compliment. And just as I had fathomed that scenario, his thoughts switched our places, me with my head between his legs, cupping his balls while I gobbled his cock.

My knees grew a bit shaky as I withdrew from his head and sat down on the sofa next to him. He shifted slightly, keeping his eyes closed. I looked down at his crotch, watching the bulge in his jeans expand until the length of his shaft was clearly outlined. My own prick grew in response, my hunger increasing as my defenses lowered.

Seth was right. His aura was strong, exuding enough of his essence to tantalize me. I leaned a bit closer and tried to take in as much of it as I could. It rose in my senses, fragrant and masculine as my cock hardened and my will softened. I drank it in deeply, feeling it nourish each cell it touched. Instinctively, I reached out for him but stopped myself.

No, I thought. Now is not the time.

His eyes popped open. "I'll do it," he said with abrupt conviction. He shifted the hard dick in his jeans and stood up, turning his back to me. I could see the flush creep up the back of his neck. "Just let me tell 'em," he said. "They shouldn't hear it from anyone but me."

"That's fine," I assured him. "Don't let them talk you out of it, though."

"Nope. Not a chance. But now that I don't have a payin' gig anymore, what am I supposed to do for money? I lead a pretty hand-to-mouth kinda life, y'know."

"Let me worry about that. My pockets are deep, and you'll be earning your own way soon enough."

He turned to me, his eyes shining with a curious mix of glee, avarice, and ambition. "Y'know, I think I been waitin' all my life for somebody like you."

"The feeling," I replied with a smile, "is completely mutual."

☙

don't got to ask where you found this one," Stacks said. "I smelled him too, but I knew you and Seth'd be on him like stink on shit." He flipped the studio intercom switch and leaned forward. "Okay, Wade boy—try it again, only use that open tuned National."

Stacks sat back in his tattered leather swivel chair, pushing a few sliders up and some others down on the battered 16 track console as Wade switched guitars. We'd been friends since 1925, when he was Robert Johnson, not Stacks Jackson. Contrary to the legend, however, he hadn't sold his soul to the devil that night near Dockery Plantation in exchange for the blues. I'd taken it. But I'd given it back to him and so much more with it. What happened after that was a shame.

"Yes sir," Stacks said, smiling though his chipped, nicotine-stained teeth as he lit another cigarette. "He's powerful talented, that's for sure. Reminds me of myself back in the day. You gonna take him all the way, ain'tcha?"

"I'd like to try," I said. "That's why I brought him to you. But to teach, not to feed."

Stacks wheezed out a laugh. "Sheee-it," he said, "I'm done feedin'. Ain't got long left on this earth, and I'm glad of it. 'sides, I ain't fool enough to step between you and Seth. He comin' for your boy there, y'know. I can feel him."

"So can I. That's why we need to hurry."

"I can't teach him no faster'n he can learn. But he's quick. Don't take him no studyin' at all to pick somethin' up. He just goes ahead and does it." He stubbed the half-smoked cigarette out in the full ashtray with rough, callused hands. "You stayin' here? All I got's a spare room upstairs and a sofa. Like this here studio—nothin' fancy but you're welcome to 'er."

"If it's no trouble. Wade needs to eat and breathe this stuff, and he can't do that in a hotel."

"No trouble. I owe you my life. Ain't your fault what I done with it." The whites of his eyes were yellow with age-old regret. "Anyway, old Seth be sniffin' around, but he ain't found us yet. We'll do what we can."

"I'd appreciate that, old friend."

He put a hand on my shoulder and grinned. "Your 'preciation gonna get you in trouble some day." He flipped the intercom on again. "You wanna lay one down, Wade boy? Go on over and getcha a beer from that cooler in the corner and we'll try a little 'Dust My Broom' once you wet your whistle. This time lean in close to the mic and don't be poppin' your p's. Nasty habit."

"Yes sir, Mr. Jackson."

"That's Stacks, son. Mister Jackson's my daddy and he been dead almost sixty year now. C'mon, let's lay this down."

⁂

tacks tucked a wad of mashed potatoes and gravy into his cheek. "You got to walk out on stage like you *own* that motherfucker. You got to feel it *here*," he said, tapping Wade's chest. "If'n you don't, it ain't comin' out nowhere else." He grinned and resumed eating. "You readin' me?"

Wade smiled and saluted him with a chicken leg. "Like a

book, my brother. Like a book."

If either one of them were exhausted by two and a half weeks of sixteen-hour days in the studio—playing, tuning, writing, talking—neither showed it. Stacks worked like a man half his age, and Wade rode a palpable adrenaline high most of the time. He only slept a few hours a night, spending most of his time staring out the window of our small room as he listened to the day's work on headphones.

We were yet again having dinner at Stacks' favorite all-you-can-eat buffet restaurant. He claimed to enjoy the variety, but the food all looked the same to me—salty, greasy, slathered in sauce or gravy and pawed over by a particularly obese segment of society. But I could hardly refuse my old friend, and I always managed to find something to eat.

Eat? Of course we eat. Unlike our Blood Brethren, we can savor the same repasts we used to as mortals. We don't *have* to eat. However, many of us do. Not only does it mark a fuller, more enjoyable life, but it allows us to blend in and gain the confidence of our victims. Disappearing Dracula-style while the guests in your castle are left to their own mealtime devices is a bit off-putting, if not altogether rude. The problem is that food doesn't really nourish us. We could eat three times a day and still starve without feeding.

I picked at my pasta salad, feeling unaccountably distracted as I took in the bright lights, bland music, and clashing of cutlery from nearby tables. Stacks and Wade debated some obscure tuning question I only half understood, but I didn't mind being left out of the conversation. Anything that helped Wade was fine with me.

That's when I saw Seth sitting across the room.

He was at a table by himself and *as* himself. None of this Laura sham. He wore a dark green workshirt, jeans, and workboots with a Cardinals baseball cap turned backward. But his "regular guy" look couldn't hide his long face and sharp nose, his oddly spaced teeth, his sallow complexion and mean muddy eyes. He smirked as he put his fork down and blew smoke toward the ceiling fan.

I knew I'd find you here.

I looked at Stacks, but he was still engrossed in his discussion with Wade and showed no sign of feeling Seth's presence. Either Seth had learned how to hide himself from others or Stacks's powers were failing.

Seth answered my question. *He doesn't know I'm here. And if you're depending on him to help protect your protégé, your faith is sorely misplaced. He has nothing left. He'll be dead soon, by his own choice as much as anything. But I'll help him along as much as I can. You may count on it.*

There is, however, a solution, he continued. *If you give Wade up to me, I can ensure the safety of your old friend. I might even give him the gift of a second chance. He'd like that, wouldn't he? It's a shame you never made a study of our kind—what we can do if we apply ourselves. You don't even know how to kill one of us, do you? You were always too busy playing with the prey to bother about such things. But you won't give this one up. Not even for your friend.*

I would not be baited. I kept my mind blank.

I thought as much. He stubbed his cigarette out, pushed his chair away from the table and turned to leave. *At least I've made the offer. I'll see you when you least expect it, Warner. Or I'll see your friend.*

And I knew he would.

CB

A in't afraid," Stacks said, staring off in the distance as we rocked back and forth in the old caneback rockers on his front porch. "Been ready to go for a while now. He can't do nothin' to me I wouldn't welcome, and dyin' for a cause? Well, that's just about the best way a man can go."

"Cause? What cause?"

He stopped rocking and took a long swig of sweet tea from the glass on the windowsill. "Wade. That boy's got the biggest gift I ever seen. You *got* to win this over Seth. He won't treat the boy right. But you'll see to it the world gets to hear him, and I can die knowin' I helped pass on what I learned from my betters."

"There *is* no better than you, my friend."

Stacks wheezed out a chuckle. "You hush, now. They's lots better'n me. I just been lucky."

"Forget lucky. You need to be careful."

He shrugged and squinted, looking down the street. "Here comes your boy with our libations. I hope he got somethin' a little finer than that horse piss he bought last time. Micro-brew, my ass."

The Jack Daniels in the bag Wade brought back was more

than acceptable to Stacks, and we poured healthy slugs in our sweet tea, sipping and talking as the sun went down. Wade didn't bother with the tea, preferring to drink his straight. Thus, his conversation quickly passed from reasonably coherent to a maudlin muddle.

"All I ever wanted to do's play guitar," he said from his seat below us on the porch steps, "and I'm lucky—*damn* lucky—to meet up with you guys. We're gonna go places, boys—and I mean *go* places." He lifted another shot into the air and knocked it back, his torso weaving.

Stacks smiled and got up from his rocker, tossing a half inch of watery tea and Jack out of his tumbler onto the grass near the porch. "I think the only place this one better go is to bed. We got a long day tomorrow, and he gonna be sufferin' enough as it is. You need some help with him?"

"I think I can handle it." I shook his shoulder, and he swiveled his head slowly towards me. "Let's pack it in, Wade. Time for bed."

He nodded silently and almost stood up. I grabbed his hand and put him on his feet, helping him shuffle his way inside. Stacks followed.

"See you boys in the mornin.'"

"Remember what I said about being careful."

He waved me away as Wade stumbled on a throw rug and fell on me to keep himself upright. His smell was so enticing, I could barely restrain myself. I could feel his emanation feeding me, making me stronger. I turned my head away, but I was still tempted. It took an eternity to reach our room, and we fell heavily onto his bed—him face up with me on top of him.

His eyes were closed, and I thought he must have passed out. I slid my hand out from underneath his back, intending to retreat to the safety of my own corner cot. Maybe I'll just take his boots off, I thought, so Stacks' sheets don't get ruined. I pulled off his well-shined snakeskin cowboy boots, inhaling the delicious, faintly leathery aroma of his socks and feet as I took them in my hands and swung his legs into bed.

I should have stopped there, but I couldn't let go. I sat on the edge of his bed and ran my hands slowly up his jeans-clad shins, past his bony knees to his firm, warm thighs. My prick grew hard at once, and his crotch began to bulge as well. He emitted a soft moan and arched his back slightly. I kneaded his stiffening cock, exulting in the rush as his dick lengthened at my touch. Untucking his t-shirt, I ran my fingertips over his treasure trail and worked my hands up the warmth of his hairy chest, flicking his nipples when I reached my destination.

He jerked awake and sat up quickly, his eyes wide. He grabbed my shoulders roughly, and my heart sank. I had been betrayed by my worst instincts, but I could not turn back or undo what I had done. Before I could speak, however, he pulled me close and put his lips to mine.

His essence exploded into me with so much force I had no chance to savor it or experience it as anything but a flood. A deluge after months of drought. It washed over me instead of seeping into me. Nourishing, yes, but without pleasure. And then it simply became too much. It crushed me against its wave, taking me under, rendering me helpless and short of breath. I had to break the kiss or drown.

The look on Wade's face was devastating for both of us—

shame, regret, and rejection all flashed through his eyes and leaked from his parted lips like the steam of his essence. I knew instantly I had erred. I should have embraced him and begun the kiss anew, my own discomfort be damned. But in that moment of hesitation, that fleeting second upon which everything hinges, he bolted from the room.

"Wade!" I shouted. "Wait!" Hot on his sock-clad heels, I followed him through the house and out the front door. He quickly sprinted away from me, running silently through the neighborhood. I could have easily overtaken him but I hung back, allowing him time to exhaust himself. He did so as he reached a small park tucked away between blocks, falling on the grass near a bench.

He was in tears when I approached him, sitting up and hugging his knees as he sobbed. I slowed to give him some additional privacy, but he sensed my presence and looked up, standing as if to start another sprint. Before he could escape, I rushed to him and took him in my arms. He put his head on my shoulder and started to cry again, choking out indecipherable words.

I held him for a long time, listening to the sound of sirens in the distance as I tried to calm him. He quieted in a while, his emotions subsiding. When he tried to pull away, I held on to him. He did not resist. "Stay close to me," I said into his ear. "I must share some private thoughts, and I would rather do so with you in my arms." I expected to feel reticence, but he clutched me tighter instead.

"You must never feel shame or disgust at who you are," I said. "These matters are out of your control, despite what others may tell you. The long run will find you happier if you simply acknowledge it and move on to the great accomplishments you have before you. I accepted it when I was a young man and have not thought much about it since. Let me also say that the attraction you feel is entirely mutual, Wade. I have wanted to kiss you for some time."

I let him raise his head from my shoulder. "Then why did you…"

"Break away from you?" I had already formulated a response and merely had to make it sound plausible. "Although your run has sobered you considerably, you were quite drunk, Wade. You must have realized by now that I am an honorable man in my business dealings, and I try very hard to extend that honor to my personal affairs as well. Unfortunately, I have failed. I have violated your trust by letting my lust overcome me. For that, I must apologize. But to continue that episode while you were compromised would have compounded my error beyond reason. I could not do so, for the loss of your trust would be inestimable. I can only hope you will forgive me."

He wiped his eyes and gave me that half-grin of his. "Forgive you for thinkin' I'm sexy? Yeah, I can do that. Warner, I gotta tell ya, I think you're…well, I never met anyone like you before."

Smiling, I put my arm around his shoulders and began to walk us back to the house. "Thank you, Wade. I feel the same way. And I assure you, this incident changes nothing between us professionally. In the years to come, we will make a formidable team, and I would be loathe to see anything prevent that. I hope you agree."

"Absolutely," he said. "If it wasn't for you, I'd still be at the

Club DuMonde wondering how I wanted to get where I want to be. I owe you so much already. You and Stacks."

"We shall owe each other much more by the time the final cards are played," I replied. "Let us speak no more of it. This adventure is just beginning. Who may say what will happen?"

Seeing he was able to walk on his own, I withdrew my arm, and we ambled side by side for a few blocks. "So, when did you find out you were...you know?" he asked.

"As I said, when I was a young man."

"Did your folks kick you out when you told them or what?"

Careful, I thought. You must not be too candid. "I was at university," I replied. "My first love was a linguistics instructor, but he was too bold. There was a scandal. He was discharged, and I was disinherited. I have been on my own since then."

"My dad purt'near broke my arm when he caught me and my cousin Joe messin' around out in the hay field. Told me he'd chop my pecker off and stuff it down my throat if he ever saw me doin' somethin' like that again."

"Charming."

"But I'll tell ya somethin'," Wade said. "I like girls, too."

"I have sought female companionship at times myself," I admitted. "We're lucky to be living in an age where making a choice between the two is not always necessary. If we..." The flashing red and blue lights ahead stopped me from saying anything else. They looked as if they were right in front of Stacks' house. Wade saw them as well.

"What the..."

We ran the last few blocks, my worst fears confirmed as we reached the house. It was blocked off with yellow police tape, with an ambulance parked out at the curb and uniformed policemen crawling in and out the front door, crowding the front porch. Neighbors and passers-by were gathering across the street. Wade took off and began questioning every officer in earshot.

I had no need for the details, but when they carried the body out of the house, Wade beckoned me over. The EMTs laid the gurney down on the bumper of the ambulance and pulled back the sheet. Stacks's face was puckered and wrinkled, as if the life had been sucked right out of him. His mouth was twisted and his eyes bulged, but the terror was not confined to his face. His limbs were contorted and his back arched, as if in eternal pain. He had not died a quiet death.

"That's him," I said. "Stacks Jackson." They nodded, covered him up again and drove off.

"What the fuck *happened* to him?" Wade asked.

"You know as much as I do," I replied, even though it wasn't true. But why were Wade and I the only ones who seemed to see the horrible way in which he died? Everyone else seemed to take this as an ordinary death.

When I looked up, I saw Seth standing on the fringes of the crowd, grinning at me. He said nothing in my head, but what was there to say? He had kept his promise in spades, adding pain and a horrible death in the bargain. My relationship with Seth changed at that moment. We were no longer engaged in a mere competition over prey. I vowed then that he would die, just as terribly as Stacks.

Even if I perished as well.

ymns are not my favorite type of music, I'll confess. The lyrics are almost uniformly puerile, and the tunes are insipid. There is, however, something to be said for the fervency of the performance, especially live Baptist gospel. The sweaty, exuberant perfume of talent rose from the choir in a heavenly offering of "Abide With Me" and "Amazing Grace."

I'm sure Stacks would have enjoyed it immensely. However, it was hot in the church, and the sermons had been long. The mourners stuffed in the pews fanned themselves restlessly, knowing more was in store at the graveside. I wondered if they would have been so eager to bury him in hallowed ground had they known what he really was. Then again, as I looked around, I realized that many *did* know, for many of us were in attendance.

Considering what we subsist on, I suppose it's not surprising that the music business is rife with our kind acting as producers, managers, agents, A&R men, or just *entrepreneurs* like myself. And we would, of course, turn out in droves for Stacks, who was loved by all.

But I also believe many had gathered at the funeral to personally witness the next episode in the drama playing out between Seth, Wade and myself—for Seth was there in the church. He sat in the back, once again masked as Laura, which meant he intended to approach Wade in some fashion, either here or at the graveside. Let him come. I had no intention of stopping Seth's game. Indeed, I had to *see* his next move to counter it.

The prayers concluded, we rose respectfully and filed out of the church into waiting limousines and private cars. Stacks had no family left, and as I was the executor of his will and both Wade and I were there the night he died, we were accorded *de facto* main mourner privileges and were in the first car. Wade looked a beautiful wreck. His eyes were soft and vulnerable and he was unshaven, his blond stubble melding with lines of grief to etch a sad masculinity into his boyish face.

Wade had not said much since Stacks's death, bearing it with a blank stoicism as attractive as it was frustrating. I could have peeked into his head to see how he was handling the affair, but such matters should remain private no matter how curious their shielding may make others.

If Seth wanted to gain an unfair advantage by poking around and seeing which of Wade's thoughts might be useful, he was certainly free to do so. In my experience, such subterfuge only results in knowledge ripe for misinterpretation and, thus, will backfire when all is said and done. The disconnect between thought and action is rarely taken into account.

"Is he happier, d'ya think?" Wade asked. "Y'know, like the preacher said?"

I sighed. "Who can say? Perhaps there are things the living should not know lest it affect the way they lead their lives. The solution may be less satisfying than the mystery itself."

He nodded slowly then went back to looking out the window. Even though I was not in his mind, I could hear it whirring, and it wasn't being driven by grief alone. He was creating.

He was writing—either music or lyrics—applying the lessons Stacks had taught him about making art with what life hands you. The old man would have been proud.

The trip to the graveyard was mercifully short, and the graveside service was also brief. The cemetery, however, was packed. Not only had most of the church attendees showed up, but many of Stacks's fans were waiting for us as we drove in. The gravesite was so festooned with wreaths that finding a place to stand was difficult. After the service, I found myself pressing the flesh, working my contacts, and setting up Wade's next move. And everyone, it seemed, wanted a piece of him.

The only person who was currently getting that piece, however, was Seth. Wearing a tasteful black sheath and pearls, he was speaking earnestly and quietly to

Wade in the shade of a large tree. I had no idea what he was saying, but I knew he was laying his own groundwork. By the time I worked my way over to them, I had two potential bookings of professional studio time Wade could choose from. I'd surprise him with that.

"Ah, there you are," I said as I approached them, "and I see you've found your friend from New Orleans. What a surprise— Shirley, isn't it?"

Seth smiled sweetly. "Laura, Mr. Warner."

"Just Warner," I replied. "It's my first name. I doubt you'd be able to pronounce my last. What are you doing in St. Louis?"

"It turns out she was a big fan of Stacks," Wade said, a grin splitting his face. "She came just for the funeral. Wasn't that sweet?"

"I simply *had* to pay my respects," Seth/Laura said. "His

music meant so much to me, but seeing you both here is an incredible coincidence."

"Isn't it?" If my voice betrayed any annoyance, no one seemed to notice.

"We were just going to grab some lunch," Wade said. "You wanna come?"

I smiled and sighed. "I think not. Thank you for the offer, but there are still some people here I should speak with. You two go ahead—and when you're done, why don't you bring Laura back to the house, Wade? You can show her the studio." I wasn't about to be cowed by Seth's presence.

"I'd *love* that," Seth/Laura cooed. He crooked an arm and offered it to Wade. "But let's stop by my hotel first and let me change. My car's just over there. Shall we?"

Wade took Seth's arm and grinned at me. "We'll be home in a while—got some good news for ya, too. We'll talk later."

"I have news for you as well. Have fun at lunch."

I smiled and sighed again as they walked away. After our ill-fated kiss, Wade would naturally swing towards the distaff side. He was not yet certain of his proclivities, thus his need to brag about "liking girls." But his needs would win out in time. Besides, what could I do? Any attempt to interfere with their budding affair would only drive Wade away from me. So Seth would feed from Wade in the interim. *C'est la vie.* There was more than enough to go around. Let Seth have his moment. Let him drown in Wade's essence. The race was not yet over.

CB

s I suspected, Wade's good news was that he had some song ideas, his first original work. He also wanted to pick out a few of Stacks's guitars to keep. A blues museum in Mississippi had also requested them, but I saw no harm in letting Wade have what he wanted and giving the museum the rest.

The next month saw us living at Stacks's place while I had his possessions packed, sold or otherwise apportioned out and settled the details of his will as Wade worked on songs. He spent mornings on the sun-soaked front porch, playing snatches of melodies again and again, adding or changing notes. Sometimes he wrote in a battered spiral bound notebook, scribbling down lyrics he'd been mumbling in a maddeningly indistinct tone.

At first, he went down to the studio unobserved, usually when I was out on an errand. When I came back and settled down in the booth to listen, he'd stop and either go back to the front porch or sit there quietly humming until I left. After a few weeks, however, he grew more confident of his material and let me help him in the booth, even asking my opinion occasionally.

Nights were spent with Seth in his Laura guise. Seth would pick him up around dinnertime, and Wade would not return until later. Oddly enough, Wade never stayed with Seth the entire night. I have no idea why he declined or if Seth even offered, but Wade was always home by two or three in the morning, back at his post on the front porch once the sun came up.

As a result, Seth looked very well-fed at month's end. However, he was tired and irritable, quite the opposite of what I would have expected. He seemed increasingly nervous, casting his eyes about furtively when he came to pick Wade up, and he scrutinized me closely during our chance encounters. Once I felt him clearly inside my head. He wasn't saying anything; he was just there. Waiting for something. It was most curious and a bit disconcerting.

I had been competing with Seth for centuries and can honestly say nothing he did surprised me. Even Stacks's murder, as reprehensible as it was, was wholly in line with Seth's behavior. He said he would do it, and he did. If nothing else, he was a creature of his word. He would pay for that, make no mistake, but that particular bill had not yet come due. His next move, however, shocked and puzzled me beyond measure.

Wade was in the studio and I was behind the controls in the booth. He played a tune he'd been fiddling with for days, but now he picked it confidently, adding a snatch of lyric:

When I play this dead man's guitar/Whose music will it
*   turn out to be?*
Should the change feel this strange to my fingers?
Do I even know this key?
My head swims with all his ideas/And places that I've
*   never seen.*
If I become a star/playin' this dead man's guitar
Will it be him or will it be me?

"Did you want to put that down?" I asked.

"Not yet. Hang on a sec."

He bent over the Gibson and began strumming lightly, mumbling as he worked out the next verse or a break or something. I felt a disturbance in the booth and suddenly Seth was sitting next to me, in his own body. The effect was just as disquieting as I'm sure he intended it to be. He smiled at me and winked.

"Afternoon, Warner."

"Good afternoon, Seth," I replied, returning his smile thinly. "Another party trick, I see. Quite amusing. That must take a great deal of energy."

He shrugged. "I have energy to burn, thanks to Wade. He has nourished me well these past few weeks and seems to have suffered no ill effects."

"In sharp contrast to yourself."

"Whatever do you mean?"

"To use the vernacular, you look like shit, Seth. Your face is drawn, the skin sags beneath your tired, red eyes, your complexion is even more sallow than usual, and…well, I needn't go on."

He was quiet a moment, listening to Wade strum with his back to us. "You're right, of course. That's part of why I'm here. Have you felt anything *odd* lately?"

"No. Why?"

"I suppose you wouldn't be as attuned to it as I. After all, you were not made by the Old Man."

"The Old Man? He hasn't walked in centuries."

Seth shook his head wearily. "You're wrong, Warner. He's walking now. Toward us. Toward *Wade*. I feel him. I've dreamed him. He wants what we have, and we are all in danger. Don't scoff. I see that look in your eyes. Think about it. Our entire race feels Wade's essence. How could have it escaped the Old Man's attention? It's awakened him, Warner. And he's famished."

I felt a chill. "Don't be daft."

"You know I'm right, Warner. And you'll know it further when I tell you I've a proposition."

"I'll strike no bargain with *you*," I insisted.

"Because of what I did to your friend? Your loyalty will be the undoing of us all. Put that aside for a moment. You can punish me for that later, provided we survive the trials ahead of us. First, we must share Wade."

"Share? But in the Club DuMonde, you—"

"The situation has changed dramatically since the Club DuMonde. In order to do battle with the Old Man, we will both have to be well-nourished and at the top of our form. That is one of the reasons Wade will be coming to you tonight."

"*One* of the reasons?"

"He has also confessed to me—to Laura, rather—his attraction for you. I don't understand it, myself," he said with a disdainful sniff. "Oh, I suppose you're handsome enough. How old were you when you were made? Thirty?"

"Twenty-five." Wade's natural instincts are winning out, I thought. Is the Old Man really walking, or is Seth bargaining so as not to lose him entirely?

"You have not aged much since. Your profile is not as noble as mine, but…" He waved one gloved hand in the air. "There is no accounting for taste. Besides, he insists on taking me from behind every single night. It's most unsettling."

"Poor Seth," I said, grinning. He started to say something, but I held up my hand to stay him, listening to Wade pluck, strum, and mumble. "There is more to your proposition, I assume."

"I will also teach you some defensive strategies—words of binding and the like—but you must be a quick study. I will be unable to shield such activities from the Old Man for long. And you must agree, for the time being, to use them only on him. I understand you have a grievance with me. Fair enough. Once we have defeated him, if that is possible, you may use anything I teach you in subsequent battles, but I must know that we are on the same side until then. Are we so agreed?"

"'Scuse me," came Wade's voice from the studio. "Warner, is there somebody else up there in the booth?"

I flipped the intercom switch. "Yes, Wade. One of the producers I was telling you about dropped by to see how the demos were coming along."

Wade put the guitar in its stand and stood up from the stool. "Um…I don't mean to be fussin', but this is a closed session. No visitors, okay?"

"Of course, Wade. I apologize. Give me a minute, then we can get back to work." There was an audible click as I flicked the switch off again. "You'll have to go now, by the door this time."

"But are we agreed?"

"Give me a day to think about it. I'll let you know."

His face darkened. "A day. No more. The longer you delay, the greater the danger we'll all be in, your precious Wade included." With that, he vanished. I looked quickly to see if Wade had seen, but he was bent over getting a drink from the cooler.

The Old Man walks and Seth bargains. Even after four hundred years, life still has surprises in store.

y six that afternoon, "Dead Man's Guitar" was a finished demo, joining "Front Porch Blues," "On the Horizon," "Spark," and "Jesus Doesn't Even Know You're Dead" as Wade's first completed songs. The first two had gone slowly but the last three were all done in a day each. His confidence in his own abilities was growing, and he was becoming more assured with every session in the studio.

"I think that's gonna be the title track," he said as put the Gibson down and got up from his stool. "And I even know what I want the cover to look like—a picture of Stacks's National down here in its stand. Over there by the chipped acoustic tile. Yeah…kinda like that Yoko Ono album cover with John Lennon's broken, bloody glasses. Think you can make that happen?"

"Not a problem," I said, leaving the intercom open as I finished up some paperwork. "I'll set the shoot up before we leave."

"When do we have to leave?"

"In a few weeks, probably. The realtor is bringing some people by to look at the house tomorrow. I'll try to minimize the time they're down here so you won't have to stop working for long."

"I'd 'preciate that. I think I'm done for today, though. How 'bout we order a pizza and kill the rest of that beer in the fridge?"

I feigned surprise. "You're not seeing Laura tonight?"

"Nope," he said, using that wicked half-grin on me. "I

thought I'd stay home and see what kinda trouble we can get in around here."

"I could do with a bit of trouble," I replied, trying to match the salaciousness in his voice.

"No doubt. So could I."

"Are you sure we have enough beer?"

He chuckled. "I don't plan on gettin' that drunk."

"Good."

Wade exited the studio and bounded up the few steps to the booth. "Let's hear the playback," he said as he walked in. I queued it up and hit the button, Wade's crystalline picking filling the room. I expected him to take a seat beside me, but he stood behind my chair, put his hands on my shoulders and began to rub them. He leaned over to nuzzle my neck, and as we listened to "Dead Man's Guitar" for the thousandth time that day, his lips brushed my skin, and I breathed in his nectar.

My thirst rose, and my prick stiffened. I couldn't decide which appetite needed to be sated more. Wade spun my chair around to face him, then he closed in for the kiss. The smell of him was everywhere, making me dizzy. He put his mouth on mine and unlike before, I did not flinch or back away. This time, however, there was no suffocation, only the bliss of his essence filling me evenly and steadily.

His taste was warm and sweet with a slight pungency, like the bayou air after a cleansing rain. I felt myself rising to gain more leverage, the kiss becoming serious and passionate. My hands went to his face, caressing the stubbly roughness of his cheeks as I pressed myself into him. Wade snaked his arms around my waist and drew me close. We could have kissed for an eternity. I was lost in him.

He gently broke away. "Jesus," he breathed into my ear as he held on to me. "I've wanted to do that ever since that first day you came to my apartment."

"Was it as you thought it would be?"

His grin as all the answer I needed. "But," he said as he stepped away from me, "we better get that pizza ordered. We're gonna need some strength. You make the call, and I'll grab a shower." He headed for the door. "Get anything you want on it, just no green peppers. Can't stand 'em. Breadsticks, too—don't forget the breadsticks." I watched his ass as he left.

My cock deflating, I savored his lingering aftertaste as I reached for the telephone and ordered our meal. I finished up my paperwork, but my mind was elsewhere. I considered Seth's proposition, trying not to feel jealous that he'd had Wade to himself as long as he had. I castigated myself at such an unproductive emotion at first, but I had to let it wash over me so I could rid myself of it. It was only natural. To not feel it would have been less than human.

Well, you know what I mean.

As far as what Seth told me, I hadn't felt the Old Man walking and I considered myself fairly sensitive to such matters. However, he probably *was* better attuned since he had been made by him. Such a bond would indeed enable Seth to feel his presence more keenly than would the rest of us. Seth's sharing of prey also alarmed me. He wouldn't be taking that measure without a good reason. Seth never did *anything* without a good reason.

I collected my things and went upstairs to wait for the

delivery boy. I heard the shower running through the bathroom door as I passed, leaving the papers on the desk in the living room. At length, our meal arrived but Wade was still in the shower. I paid the boy, took the pizza into the kitchen, got plates and napkins from the cupboard and sat down at the table. Wade finally emerged from the bathroom, appearing in the doorway clad in only a pair of thin boxer shorts.

I'd seen Wade in his underwear often, but this was the first time he was so accessible—so *mine*—that it seemed as if I'd never before examined his flat, hairy stomach, the patch of fur across his chest, his strong, naturally muscled arms, and his fuzzy, well-formed thighs and calves. The light from the living room window silhouetted his tantalizing genitalia through the threadbare fabric of his cotton boxers. I knew I was staring but couldn't help myself.

"Too formal for pizza?" he asked wickedly.

"I think it's just about right," I replied, grinning.

He slid around the back of my chair and leaned into it, his meaty cock grazing my shoulder through his boxers. As I looked down to admire the bulge, it began growing and tenting the fabric out until finally the bare head poked through the fly. I took it between my fingers and guided it to my lips, sucking gently as he grew to full hardness in my mouth. He arched his back slightly and ran his fingers through my hair, murmuring curses of endearment.

Even his prick leaked the sweetness of his essence. I lapped hungrily, searching inside his boxers with one hand and cupping his balls as he fell back against the wall with a moan. I rose, stroking his slicked cock as our lips met and I once again began to drink my fill. His hand clutched the crotch of my slacks, grasping my stiffness and drawing a sigh from me. It had been a long time since another man had touched me there.

He broke away, smirking as he ducked away from me, grabbed my waistband and led me into the living room. "The food can wait," he said, throwing me down on the sofa as his prick bobbed in the air. He knelt on the floor and began unbuttoning my shirt, kissing my chest as he freed it. Unbuckling my belt, he unsnapped my pants, eased down the zipper and pressed his nose into my crotch. "God, I love your smell," he breathed. My hips rose as he tugged down my pants and shorts, my dick slapping my belly as it came free. I threw my head back in ecstasy as he took me into his mouth, caressing my balls with his hands.

I grabbed his head and brought him to me for another kiss, our lips never parting as his boxers and my clothes came off. I landed on top of him as we rolled off the sofa onto the floor. I kissed and bit his tiny nipples until he writhed beneath me, then I sucked his cock until he was within a hair's-breadth of shooting, but I would not let him come. So he always took Seth from behind? We were going to change that.

I flipped him over and beheld his marvelously fuzzy ass, running my tongue down his crack until I reached his deliciously wrinkled hole. I traced it with my tongue and teased it with my lips, inhaling his musk mixed with soap from his shower, gently sucking and nibbling as he grunted low, guttual joy. I even found his essence there, which only increased my ardor. Then I wet my index finger and pushed inside.

"Easy," he groaned. "I've only done this once before."

"We can stop if…"

"No," he insisted, raising his ass higher. "I want you to fuck me."

My prick was aching for him, but I worked him with my fingers until he sighed with satisfaction. I positioned my cock then slowly pushed in. He let out a small cry and I stopped, allowing him to relax for a bit before I continued. When I was fully inside him, he threw his head back. "Yeah," he moaned, "that's it, dude. Fuck me."

His ass was hot and tight, slick with spit and sweat as I slid in and out with ease, but I was not satisfied. I wanted to see his face. I withdrew and turned him on his back, kissing him long and slow before I went back to fucking him. "Do it, man," he breathed as he stroked his own hard cock. "Fuck your boy." Dripping with sticky sweat, I pumped in and out until my balls began to tighten up and I whimpered with helpless lust. "Fuck yeah," Wade said. "You got it, dude—come in my ass."

I exploded into him, shuddering as I spurted. Wade closed his eyes and frigged himself faster and faster until he also came a long, ropy shot that nearly went up to his chin. Instinctively, my tongue went to his chest and belly. Even his come tasted of essence. When I had finished feasting on it, I fell on top of him, kissing him even though we were both out of breath. "Jesus," he said. "That was incredible, man."

I nodded, laughing. "It was indeed."

"Okay, *now* I'm hungry."

08

stood naked on the beach of a vast ocean, staring at the light of the full moon reflected off the waves. In the improbable manner of dreams, a figure stood atop the water, waving to me as it came closer. I smiled, thinking it a friend or acquaintance, but as it drew nearer to me, my smile vanished.

Its face was a grotesque white with sunken cheeks, sparse hair flying in all directions. Its tattered sleeve flapped about its elbow with every wave. Its thin, red lips parted to show teeth stained yellow, some broken, some pointed, and some missing. Dark and disgusting matter drooled from the corner of its mouth. Its eyes were black and deep—no white or iris to be seen. They were malignantly vacant, even more shocking set against the unnatural whiteness of the face. The creature called my name as it neared the beach.

Before I could flee, it was on me. Its foul, mouldy breath assaulted me, but maddeningly, there was essence in it. I couldn't help but breathe it in no matter how repulsive I found it to be. And I felt nourished. It gripped my shoulder with clammy, chill hands as it held me fast.

"So," it said in my head, "*you and Seth seek to overthrow me. That will not happen. I will have your prize no matter how well you prepare yourselves. All you shall be left is the black ruin of the grave, if I am kind enough to kill you. In your own words, 'do not play games you cannot win.'*"

Laughing, it pushed me backward into the water. I staggered and fell, swallowed up and sucked under by the sea. Instead of a mouthful of brine, I swallowed the foulness of his essence instead, but it pulled me farther down. I closed my eyes against the water's salty sting, but all I could see was the Old Man's loathsome face. I sank until I awoke.

I was lying next to Wade, my pillow wet with nightmare sweat. His steady, calm breath soothed me, decelerating my rapid heartbeat. I breathed in his sweet essence and felt refreshed. Still, I could not get the Old Man's face out of my mind. It leered at me from every corner of the room when I closed my eyes. I drew back the covers and sat on the edge of the bed.

This could not be one of Seth's parlor tricks. The Old Man had mocked me personally, bringing back what I had said to the boy who assaulted me in New Orleans. Seth could not have known that. As difficult as it was to admit, Seth was right. The Old Man *was* walking, bent on our destruction. And even more difficult, I had no choice but to accept Seth's proposition. I was not foolish enough to think I could fight him on my own. I *needed* Seth, damn him. Very well. I would work with him for now. And kill him later. If we survived.

"Warner? Are you okay?" Wade's sleepy voice brought me back from my thoughts.

"Fine," I replied. "A bit of indigestion, perhaps. It will pass." I laid back down and drew the covers over us. Wade snuggled into my chest, his essence rising up to my nostrils as I drank it in.

"I could get used to this," he said.

"Used to what?"

"Sleeping with someone. Not fuckin' or anything, but just sleeping."

"You mean you've never slept in the same bed with anyone?"

"Nope."

"I'm truly honored to be the first, but I must say I'm surprised. A man as handsome as you surely must have disappointed many."

He chuckled. "Well, I ain't so sure about the handsome part, but I know Laura gets kinda pissed off about it. It's like I told her, I can't do somethin' if it don't feel right. This feels right."

My heart swelled, beating so fast I thought it might burst. "Yes," I said. "It does." I scooted us down, burrowing under the covers as I held on to him. "You'd better get some sleep. Good night, Wade."

"'Night, Warner."

In six hundred years, I have been companion, friend, and beast to many men and women. I have badgered and nurtured prey, lectured it, held its hand, drunk with it, gotten it to the show on time, and applauded after it performed, but until that moment, I had never fallen in love with it. I had gone out of my way to avoid such sordid entanglements, but with a smile and a confession, this one had captured my heart.

I had yet to see how dangerous that would be.

છ

The next two months bordered on the most surreal I'd had for years, an observation which struck me on a plane from one gig to another, a snoring Wade slumped on one of my shoulders whilst Seth gripped the other, expecting me to flawlessly repeat a centuries-old

Etruscan incantation for repelling evil after having heard it only once.

Seth traveled with us as Laura, much to Wade's surprise. He had temporarily dropped Laura after we began sleeping together, but I knew he'd want a change eventually. As long as he came back to our bed—and he *always* did—I had no problem with letting him have his way with Seth whenever he liked. Wade hinted at a *menage a trois* once, but our refusal was so adamant, he never brought up the subject again.

Consequently, Seth became less an enemy and more a comrade. I tried to become comfortable with this new role, but I could not allow myself to trust him completely. His smile always carried a hint of disingenuousness that alerted me to study anything he said carefully, analyzing it for potential untruths or misdirection. His frantic, hurried lessons in spells, magic words of binding and other defensive strategies did not add to his credibility, either. I did, however, learn many useful tactics at his hand.

Both of us now dreamed of the Old Man regularly. Seth did so more than I, but his tether to the Old Man was much shorter than my own. For my part, the creature seemed to be taunting us. He knew full well where we were. Wade's tour schedule was Tweeted and Facebooked and Instagrammed regularly, but he never showed himself at the gigs. Only in dreams.

But what dreams they were. I do not know what nighttime realms Seth dwelt in, but mine were dark and horrifying—full of vivid splashes of blood, sharp teeth rending tender places to shreds and puckered corpses sucked dry of life and essence, leaving shriveled husks behind. The danger and sense of dread increased daily.

As did Wade's fame. We polished the demos done at Stacks's house in various studios whose owners were friends of mine. The CD dropped in late October. The video of "Jesus Doesn't Even Know You're Dead" went into heavy rotation on a couple of country outlets, leading to a *Saturday Night Live* spot where Wade premiered "Dead Man's Guitar," which ascended the country charts quickly and began rising on the pop ones as well.

Wade coped admirably with the brutal tour schedule, always obliging and friendly to fans and supporters, ready to break out his guitar and sing in airport lounges or sign autographs during meals. He was even writing on the road in whatever spare time we could cadge away for ourselves. He thrived on the activity, which only sharpened his essence. And I fed daily, becoming as strong as I had ever felt in my life. Let the Old Man come. I'd be ready for him.

"When he comes," Seth had said, "he will come quickly. There will be no warning and no chance for mistakes. We must be on our guard at all times, each ready to come to the other's defense, for he will try to defeat us singly. Even he would not chance to fight us simultaneously."

Or would he?

A promoter I know had gotten Wade a weekend gig at the Beacon Theatre in New York City. We had been scheduled for that time off before the next leg of the tour, but this was an important venue with some well-placed people to be in attendance. My friend had called in some favors to win us the slot, so we could hardly refuse.

And I could hardly refuse Wade his chance to stay at

the Chelsea Hotel, host to Leonard Cohen, Bob Dylan, Jack Kerouac, Janis Joplin, and Sid Vicious among other icons, especially when he read it was soon to be closed for remodeling.

I was no stranger to the Chelsea, having already encountered many of the ghosts Wade so eagerly sought there, but I was not enthusiastic about once again negotiating its threadbare carpets, antiquated plumbing, and stifling rooms. I warned him that historic hotels often have less than luxurious living conditions, but he would not be swayed. No matter that the knob fell off in his hand when he opened the door, he was—as he confessed—"jacked."

"This is so fuckin' *cool*," he said, looking around the tiny room and pointing at two mismatched chairs around a marred table under the window. "I mean, Bob fuckin' Dylan could have been writing right *there*."

His zeal did not spread to Seth, who yawned and stretched, his cleavage on display to whatever spirits happened to be looking. "I'm going to my room for a lie down," he said.

Wade made a grab for him as he left. "Don't get too comfy. I'll be in to see you after a little nap myself."

"Make it a couple of hours." The door beside ours slammed shut.

"I'll unpack later," I said, putting my suitcase into the doorless closet. "There are a couple of people I should see, and I want to check out the theatre."

"When will you be back?"

"Not for a while, I think." I grinned. "Don't worry. You'll have enough time for Laura." He smirked at me. "And I doubt you'll take a nap. If I know you, five seconds after I'm gone, you'll be sitting in that window with your guitar, strumming and looking down five floors to 23rd Street."

"You're probably right about that." He walked over to the window, looked down then over to the left. "Hey, I can even see the pigeon shit on the sign."

"This is New York—seeing pigeon shit isn't noteworthy."

Wade chuckled, then crossed over to me and took me in his arms. "You don't mind about Laura now and then, right?"

The musky scent of his essence always overwhelmed me, but now it made me hard as well. "Wade, we've been over this."

"I know, I know. I just…"

I stopped him by brushing my lips against his. They parted, his tongue searching for mine as we kissed in the open doorway. Nothing new for the Chelsea, I'm sure. My hand went to his crotch, kneading and tracing his fattening prick. "You'll need to save that for Laura," I said with a smile. "And I have things to do. I'll see you in a few hours."

I took my leave, truly regretting Seth's presence. The waiting for whatever encounter was to take place was becoming interminable, and I found myself wishing something—anything—would happen, so we could get it over with and move on to who would be the eventual winner of Wade's heart. I was sure it would be me, but Seth was probably as sure it was him. Who knew what promises were made when I was not with Wade?

Putting the affair out of mind so that I could do business, I saw a promoter to finalize details of a new Eastern and Southeastern leg of Wade's eternal tour. I also took a meeting with a representative for a digital radio station who wanted

Wade to be a guest DJ. I knew he'd love the latter. Wade liked to talk about music almost as much as he loved playing it. Then, I stopped at the Beacon, where my contact showed me around the theatre.

I rarely use cabs in New York City. I prefer using the subway or walking as both modes of transportation are far less frightening. So, by the time I got back to the Chelsea, night had already fallen. As I approached the hotel, I saw the lights were off in our room but on in Seth's. Most likely, they were not yet finished with their tryst. I stopped on the sidewalk beneath our windows.

At length, I saw a bare-chested Wade cross the room and draw the curtain. My heart leapt, then fell back down again as I stopped to consider he was being bedded by someone else. At that moment, I despised both Seth and the situation we found ourselves in. I wanted to burst in and kill him right then and there—I now knew how. And I would have done so had I been more impetuous. However, life had taught me the value of patience early, and I had never forgotten the lesson that rash acts often result in unwanted consequences. I quashed my impulse and stood on the sidewalk, looking up at the draped window.

My foot went slightly forward, brushing a grate in the sidewalk, which gave beneath the toe of my shoe. I immediately stepped back as pebbles and small chunks of concrete from around the edge fell and clattered below with a deep echo. Exploring its surface with a light tap of my shoe, the whole grate—approximately six feet square—pitched and shuddered.

Damn dangerous, I thought. They should have this blocked off. I cast my eyes around for orange warning cones or something to place near the precarious grate but could find nothing. Since I had some time, I decided to speak with the hotel manager about it. As I bounded up the steps and entered the revolving door, Seth burst into my head.

"Warner! For the love of Christ, come quickly! It's…"

A curtain of silence descended, shocking me even more than his voice. I ran past the desk and up the stairs, taking them two or three at a time. Other than the abhorrent vision of that foul white beast with his mouth pressed to Wade's, I have no memory of thinking anything else. All the spells and incantations and words of binding were gone, supplanted by blind anger and fear.

The door was partially open, and I had no idea what I would see when I entered. I thought briefly of a *tableaux*, perhaps two muscled Greek warriors engaged in hand to hand combat, the prize recoiling in horror in a corner. Instead, I saw Seth on the bed, his head bent at an unnatural angle with a figure covering him, its mouth pressed to his. The figure had no shirt and wore Wade's boots, but it looked up at me as I entered and saw the disgusting white visage that had haunted my dreams.

It returned to sucking at Seth's mouth, and Seth's limbs shriveled into emaciated appendages then disappeared altogether. His trunk shrank and then finally his head, until all was subsumed beneath the victor and nothing remained of Seth except a spot of smoldering shadow on the sheets.

"This one was easy," the Old Man said. "I made him. I knew his weaknesses and his flaws. Exploiting them was the most natural way to get rid of him. I appealed to his vanity and his hunger."

"What have you done with Wade?"

He laughed. "Don't you know *yet?*" His leering countenance changed to Wade's handsome boyishness. He gave me that heartbreaking half-grin one last time before it flickered and faded back to its previous hideousness. "There *is* no Wade, you fool. There is only my deception. My beautiful lie."

I shook my head dumbly, disbelieving him even though I knew in my heart what he said was the truth. That's why his pool of essence seemed inexhaustible. It was the body from which we all came. "I...I..."

His mirth echoed throughout the room. "Has all your cleverness been reduced to stutters? How flattering I inspire such fear in you. Allow me to answer the question you appear unable to ask, and that is 'Why?'"

"Yes. Why?"

"I knew you'd find your tongue," he said, smiling. "As to why...well, you and Seth were becoming far too powerful. You felt too many ripples, became too well-known. It was only a matter of time before you both felt you could challenge my supremacy. Oh, *you* might not have had the idea. You have a streak of decency I find repellent but fascinating. Exploiting that enabled me to deceive you. But such an act was not unworthy of Seth's hubris. He would have lured you into cooperating eventually. See how easily he enlisted you against me this time? I am merely culling the herd of the most powerful opponents to serve as a warning for the rest."

"But why would either of us want to overthrow you?"

"You really don't know?" He chuckled again. "Seth was correct regarding your lack of curiosity about our kind. Let me be plain, then. My powers give me access to another realm, which contains a never-ending, self-sustaining body of essence, the All-Ocean. You have tasted of it and have sensed a part of its vastness."

"That first night...the first time we..."

"Yes. I should have killed you then, but I must confess I was having fun. I rather enjoyed making music again, not to mention the thrill of acting a role to achieve my purpose. I have not felt as alive or invigorated in centuries. But the endgame is at hand. I am ready to finish this."

An invisible force grabbed both sides of my head and drew me slowly, inexorably, to his vile mouth. I smelled mould and brine, as if being dragged into a beachside grave. I struggled to recall even the simplest tactic Seth had taught me, but fear and horror crowded out all else. I reached his arms, embraced by his chill grasp, and then his cracked lips were on mine.

To my surprise, I felt an onrush of essence similar to that I had experienced the first time but just as I began to feel drowned, it rushed back like a tidal force, sucking out all I had been given. Then, the tide came back in once again and rushed out. At last I understood. He was gathering strength and momentum for a final draining, the technique Seth had taught me. I struggled him off the bed and we fell onto the floor, but the impact did not loosen his hold. I had to find a way to break his kiss.

Once more, essence blew in until I felt I could hold no more, then drew back with a monumental force. My time was short. Unconsciousness crept up on me. I felt weaker and more limp with every wave. I got us to our feet again, and we staggered around the room in a deadly clinch. Then a sudden thought seized me. I dug down, summoning reserves I did not know I had, and ran us toward the fifth-floor window. If the fall did not break his hold, I would be lost.

We crashed through the glass, still locked together as we hurtled to the sidewalk below. As we fell, I began to lose consciousness once more. But I was not so drained that I did not feel something. A force, like an invisible hand—Seth's hand, my imagination told me—guided our fall. It pushed this way and that, as if aiming us at a precise spot below. And then it was gone.

My shoulder and right side crashed into the sidewalk, on the very lip of the loose grating under the window. The collision with the cement broke his grasp on me. And then *he* was gone. Screaming in frustration, he had fallen through the grating and into the hole, chunks of concrete and sharp sections of broken metal chasing him into the depths below. One of Seth's words of binding came into my head, and I hurled it as well as a few other accompanying incantations.

I was free, but I did not know for how long. I had to escape while I could. I struggled to my feet, ignoring the gasps from the startled onlookers who had just witnessed two men plummet five stories and watched one get up. A few souls shouted encouragement and whipped out their phones to document the event, but they would not see me on their screens, again thanks to Seth. I needed a place to hide and think, so I ran. I ran as fast as I could from the crowd, from the hotel, from whatever had happened to the Old Man, not knowing how long the word of binding would hold. I could not feel him in my mind, but my strength was severely depleted.

I do not know how long I ran, but the cool night air recharged me somewhat, and the physical exertion brought some clarity back to my thoughts. I reached the far western edge of Central Park and took refuge on a bench in the night shadows of the trees, keeping watch up and down the path as well as in my head.

I was both heartsick and heartbroken. My narrow escape meant nothing to me alongside the knowledge that Wade—*my* Wade—had never existed, and any fantasies I had entertained about making him one of us, spending the rest of eternity together, were foolish schoolgirl nonsense. Who was I to believe I deserved love? I felt gulled. Cheated. And I had lost both my best friend and my worst enemy in the bargain.

The role of worst enemy, however, had been recast, the new player far more deadly and devious than Seth had ever been. But I could not ignore the enormity of my losses. The Old Man would find me a force with which to be reckoned in future. I would have that which he most feared to lose. I would be master of that vast, unending sea, consigning him to eternal torment on its shore.

His power was great, and I would have to learn much to vanquish him. But it could be done. I had to seek out the knowledge—make it my life's work, for without that work my life might end. Until that knowledge was mine, I would have to be very, very careful.

Very, very careful indeed.

PANGS

t was, perhaps, only fitting that I ended up at the Club du Monde again. I feel a sense of kinship with New Orleans even though it is not the place of my birth. That event predates the city's founding by at least a century. Sometimes I find it difficult to remember my life before I became what I am. It becomes more remote, more indistinct every time I try to recall it, not that its recollection is high on my list of priorities.

What is high on that list, however, is feeding. Not a full meal, of course. I have not been able to partake of one since... since the incident. I can only dream of such a possibility in the foreseeable future. But my future is long and offers no hope of returning to my earlier patterns before the—damn it, before Wade. Or *not* Wade.

I have neither seen nor sensed the Old Man since that night at the Chelsea. His vision still haunts me in many ways, but the nightmares ceased once he crashed through that gate to whatever befell him below. The uncertainty provoked by his silence unnerves me and prevents me from moving forward. Perhaps that is his wish.

I had my eye fixed on the keyboard player of the three-piece combo on stage. The jazz they played was meek and unchallenging, too derivative to be of any consequence. This has not gone unnoticed by the other patrons, most of whom are tourists talking and drinking too much. They are both a blight on the city and its lifeblood. Such contradictions are not uncommon here.

The drummer is the most talented of the three and would make a far superior meal. However, he resembled Wade too much. His eyes may be muddy brown instead of blue, but his shaggy blonde hair and two-day scruff are too close to the mark for my comfort. I would only waste his talent anyway. I can no longer indulge myself in more than a few mouthfuls before my gorge rises and I must turn away, leaving the essence to evaporate between us. No, I will be better off settling for the less talented keyboard player whose dark hair and swarthy complexion cannot remind me of past conquests. Or past mistakes.

This diet of mere subsistence has, of course, depleted my powers and makes even the simplest seduction somewhat difficult. Were it not for my rather formidable reputation among my fellow creatures, I fear someone would have attempted to vanquish me some time ago. Only the Old Man knows how vulnerable I am, which is why I am surprised he has not made his move.

The band wound up the number and the set with a particularly amateurish flourish and a rather dispirited exit. The shockingly bad guitar player headed offstage, and the drummer struck out for the bar, but I directed the keyboard player outside. Wearing a confused look, as if not quite sure why he felt compelled to go out in the rainy night without a jacket, he walked past my table.

Trembling slightly, I followed him. This was yet another new experience for me. I found myself afraid to feed. The feeling was not as pronounced as it was immediately after that night at the Chelsea Hotel, but I had to steel myself to follow through. It was not the most desirable side effect, I grant you. I could do little about it, though. One must play the hand one is dealt or leave the game, and I am determined not to throw in my cards. Not yet.

By the time I reached him, he was already leaning with his back and the sole of his right foot flat on the front of the building, his untamed black hair ruffled by a gentle breeze off the Mississippi, watching the people walking by as he smoked. I inclined my head in greeting, pointing to the cigarette in his fingers. "Do you have another?" I asked. "I left mine in the car."

Of course, I neither smoke nor drive. I have never even attempted the latter as the machine confuses me. But I find being able to feign the former puts some men at ease and provides a reason to talk to them. I really don't like the smell of it and couldn't abide being addicted to it. Thankfully, that is not possible given my constitution. The keyboard player smiled at me, shook out the pack he retrieved from his pocket and handed me one.

"Light?" he asked.

"Please."

I cupped my hands around the lighter as he put the flame to the cigarette. Leaning toward him, I drew the smoke in my lungs my mouth and gazed into his eyes. This one was easy. I saw I had him, but I made no move to draw him into the alley.

No one would think twice about two men kissing a block off the Quarter in New Orleans. I blew out the flame and held his eyes.

Completely immobile, he was mine. Our lips pressed together. He tasted of smoke and some indefinable spice. Curry, perhaps, or nutmeg. I could not tell, for as soon as I sensed it, his essence came forth and drowned it. It was acrid and somewhat bitter, as it always is with the less talented, but I had to feed.

I gulped, taking only a few hasty mouthfuls before I began to sense the brine. It crept into my nostrils then tainted the essence until that hideous taste flooded my consciousness. And with it came the memory. The sight of the Old Man, his pasty lips attached to mine as the essence from the All-Ocean—for I now knew its name—filled me then emptied me. The fear built and grew until I had to stop. I hungered with frustrated deprivation, yet I could not feed further. My terror was larger than my need, and I had to break away before it overcame me and sent me screaming into the night. It had happened before.

Dispirited and defeated once more, I slunk into the shadows of the alley and leaned my forehead against the brick building, feeling its rough surface bite into my skin. The helplessness overwhelmed me, and I began to weep yet again. As I did every time I attempted to feed. It had become part of me. I despised and resented it, but I could not prevent it any more than I could abide the hunger.

Through my tears and self-pity, I was dimly aware of a noise behind me. I assumed it to be the musician stirring from his seduction at first, but the footfalls came closer than I was comfortable with. Still, I did nothing. Damn my frame of mind and the attendant sloth. I realized too late the other being in the alley was *not* my conquest, but one of my own kind.

As I moved away from the wall readying myself for battle, I glimpsed a figure in jeans and a dark hoodie. I could not see its face, but I persisted in the attempt despite the tinny clinking noise I heard coming from its hands. Its swiftness astounded me, for no sooner had I decided on my plan of attack than it struck.

Before I could react, an unseen force jerked my wrists upward, and the figure clapped a pair of silver handcuffs around them. It held me roughly, pulling me close enough to smell its essence. I detected no hint of brine, so it was not the Old Man. But whoever it was had intimate knowledge of me; I felt it as strongly as I have felt anything. It leaned into my ear and whispered with contempt.

"You are *pathetic.*"

Then I mercifully lost consciousness.

woke to find myself in a bed in a dark room. I no longer had the handcuffs on my wrists. Neither was I bound, but the very situation reeked of captivity. My thoughts naturally turned to the Old Man, but he would not have captured me. He would have killed me outright. Granted, that hadn't worked well for him last time, but I envisioned him as an enemy more likely to plan the next attempt rather than dwell on past failures.

Still, my instincts told me he was not my captor. I had no idea who could be, but instead of agonizing fruitlessly over the possibilities, I rose and looked around the room, believing I might find some clues that way. If not, I was certain to find out sooner or later. It might be one of my fellow creatures who rightly sensed I was weak. Yet, he would find he was wrong. I had learned much.

The room was well-appointed. It was spacious, clean, and furnished with both a love seat and an overstuffed easy chair as well as the almost-too-soft bed I had been lying on. A flat screen television was on a desk in the right-hand corner along with a computer and monitor. Ambient light seeped in through a heavy curtain, which I parted with some caution.

The sun was setting outside, so I knew it had to be late afternoon. I even recognized the corner of Prytania I saw from my perch, so I knew I was somewhere in the Garden District. The window was not barred or obstructed, so I opened it wide and breathed in the heady scent of jasmine and honeysuckle. I smiled grimly. Captive, yet not captive. Did this same ersatz freedom extend to the door? My curiosity overwhelmed me.

Making no effort at being quiet, I walked across the creaking floor and tried the knob. It was indeed unlocked, and the door opened easily if somewhat noisily. I stepped into a carpeted hallway, sinking into the plush Oriental rug beneath my feet. The afternoon sun lit the area through a marvelous white, scarlet, and violet stained glass window at the end of the hall where a stairwell awaited me. Seeing no reason not to, I walked to the stairs, again not disguising my intent with stealth.

In the manner of all older homes, the stairs groaned

mercilessly as I descended. The sound was deafening in the silence. Surely my journey had not gone unnoticed by whomever brought me here. My jailer was either incredibly careless or contemptuous of my abilities. Remembering that he had called me pathetic before I lost consciousness, I assumed the latter to be the case.

Reaching the bottom of the stairs, I found two rooms to either side of me and a doorway straight ahead. It would be easy enough to reach the door, but my inquisitiveness proved to be more of an impediment to escape than bars. To my left was a small drawing room with fussy chintz draperies, brightly colored carpets, and furniture of gleaming blonde wood with overstuffed cushions. It looked very feminine.

To my right was a more masculine-looking library. Bookshelves lined three walls of the room floor to ceiling with sturdy, seemingly important volumes. A large bay window let in the sun, which illuminated a cloud of cigar smoke surrounding a chair whose high back hid its occupant. I took a step toward the room, a floorboard squeaked, and a head popped around the back of the chair.

"Ah, Warner," a man said, "you're awake. Please come in, won't you? May I pour you a cognac?"

"Yes, please." My curiosity was almost uncontrollable, but I displayed nothing. Revealing one's emotions in a situation of this nature is often dangerous. My host poured from a crystal decanter on a small black lacquer table in front of him. He gestured me into a chair facing him on the other side of the table. I tried to recall his face as I sat, but he did not look familiar to me. This, of course, means nothing as some of us can shapeshift, but even so, a vestige of the shifter's original appearance can be seen. Perhaps my powers had diminished even more than I thought. Still, I felt certain this was the same being that had captured me so easily last night.

"Did you rest well?" he asked, handing me a snifter. "Do you find your quarters satisfactory?" His dark brows were knit, as if he had a genuine interest in my comfort. He had rather longish brown hair tied back with a gold ribbon. Clean shaven and more tanned than is usual for our kind, he blinked his lustrous blue eyes lazily and brushed a stray hair behind his ear with long, tapered fingers. He sat on the edge of his chair, awaiting a response.

"Most satisfactory, thank you," I replied, settling back so that he could do the same. "However, I *do* have my own rooms in the Marigny."

"Not anymore. I have taken the liberty of dispatching some men to pack that lot up. They should be here later this afternoon. Perhaps your belongings will put you more at ease."

"I see," I said as evenly as I can. My temper was rising past my curiosity, and I found it difficult to remain seated. I sipped my cognac and pursed my lips. "Who *are* you to take such liberties, not to mention abducting me? And I'll warn you to be quick with an answer while I am still stunned by your presumption."

His smile turned to a smirk. "Presumption? My dear Warner, if your oldest, dearest friend and enemy cannot presume to make you whole, then what is this world coming to?"

Only one person matched that description, but it was not possible. Or was it? I could no longer mask my feelings. "Seth?"

I asked, not caring what my face betrayed.

"In the flesh," he said. "Somewhat different flesh than when we last saw each other, but yes. It is me."

"But how? I saw your death, shriveling up beneath the Old Man as he sucked the essence from you."

Seth frowned, tenting his fingers together and putting them to his lips. "Ah, yes," he said at length. "What an ugly situation. It is complicated, but I survived due to a spell I learned on an excursion to Europe many years past. Your entrance distracted the Old Man, enabling me to separate my soul, for lack of a better term, from my body. It was then imbued into the only contiguous surface available, the mattress of the bed on which we struggled. When the gentleman you see before you rented the room and laid on the mattress, I inhabited him."

His story sounded plausible enough. Seth's knowledge of such lore was esoteric enough that he probably had that spell at the ready all along. He had not, however, taught it to me at the time. No matter. Past is past, if this indeed *was* Seth. "How do I know you're who you say you are? You speak of that night, but you could be the Old Man."

He drained his glass and poured another. "Your wariness is tiresome, Warner. However, it is understandable for our first meeting since the Chelsea. Let me give you a detail about that evening not even our opponent knows. Do you recall jumping out the window locked in a deathly embrace with him?"

"Of course I do."

"Do you think it was mere coincidence that when you landed, *you* happened to hit the sidewalk while *he* crashed through a loose grate and fell into the bowels of the New York

City sewer system? Or did you feel my push? First left, then right, then left again as I aimed you toward the ground. I saved your life, Warner."

"How could you have done that if you were inside a mattress?"

"As I said, it's complicated. Really, Warner, this suspicion... this hesitance, this *fear* that prevents you from feeding properly has to stop."

"Have I not tried to stop it?" I said, more to myself than to him. "Night after night, week after week, month after month. I steel myself. I try to block out the stench of the ocean and feel the essence, but my memory brings the scent of that foul beast to me no matter how I attempt to keep it away. Do you know how to stop it?"

He remained silent, staring at me with an expression I could not read. His silence was more than I could bear. He had opened up a floodgate, and I was unable to contain the deluge.

"*Speak,* villain!" I shouted, standing up. Somewhat dramatically, I must admit, I threw my snifter of brandy against a wall of books. It shattered, soaking a number of volumes. "You would not tell me if you knew. You have always wanted me dead, but more than that you have always wanted to see me suffer. Well, look upon it. Look upon it and laugh. Kill me if you think you can." The possibility he might accept my offer left me weak-kneed. I sat back down.

He pointed two fingers at the bookcase, then crossed them. The spilt cognac beaded up and flew back into the regenerated goblet, which was suddenly in my hand once more. The look in his eyes changed, and he seemed genuinely puzzled.

"Kill you?" he said. "Is *that* what you think I brought you here for? My dear Warner, that is the farthest thing from my mind. You're much too valuable for that. And you're compromised. If I wanted to kill you—which I assure you once again I *don't*—I'd want you at the peak of your powers. To take advantage of you in your present condition would be churlish. Though I am many things, I am no churl."

"Why have you brought me here, then? And sent people to fetch my things?"

He sighed and rolled his eyes. "Because you are *broken*. You're weak, and you fear to feed. You even walk as one cowed, not like the opponent I once knew. It pains me to see you this way. I have no other choice but to help you."

Seth rarely lacked choices and never did anything without reason. It didn't take long to understand why he wanted me whole, but I needed to hear him speak it. I leaned forward and took a sip of cognac. "Why?"

"The Old Man must be vanquished, and I cannot do it alone. He has failed once, but that has only strengthened his resolve to see us *both* dead. We have our own quarrel, I realize. You wish to avenge the death of your friend, Stacks, but we also have a common enemy who must be our priority before we settle our differences. You need to be healthy for that battle, and I can help you."

My snort was immediate and derisive. "Help me? How can you help me?"

"I cannot do it alone," he said, narrowing his eyes at my insolence. "You need to help yourself as well." His voice rose as much in anger as fear. I could smell it on him. "And we do not have time for childish petulance or tantrums. Even now his emissary walks among us."

"What emissary? Why would he not come himself as he did the last time?"

"Don't be a dolt, Warner. He has suffered defeat in this world and wishes the advantage of fighting in his own. He will have us there, at the shore of the All-Ocean. One approaches who will bring us to him."

"How do you know this?"

"*Everyone* knows it," Seth said. "You would know it yourself if you were whole. Do we start tonight with your first full meal in ages, or will you continue to sulk like a child?"

Did I dare hope to rid myself of this curse? Putting myself in Seth's hands was dangerous, yes, but I had no reason to suspect he was not telling the truth. To feel strong again, to feel whole… "Yes," I said. "We will start tonight."

☙

The sparsely bearded young man was tall and sunburned, his pale skin as red as the dreadlocks peeking out from underneath his green knit cap. His dirty jeans were worn white in spots, but his scuffed work boots seemed sturdy enough, and his black t-shirt fit his trim chest snugly, pulled tighter by the strap of the guitar. "Umm, my name is Chet. I came about the Craigslist ad. For a guitar player?"

He looked nothing like Wade, but he had talent. I could

smell it. And that smell both enticed and revolted me. I'm afraid I hesitated longer than I should have. My face must have betrayed something, for he suddenly shrank into himself.

"I didn't know this was going to be such a fancy place," he said. "I came straight from work, but I should have dressed up some. I could change and come back if you want."

Unable to decide, I stood on the threshold like a fool. From the way he scrutinized me, I could tell my mouth was opening and closing but nothing was coming out. Damn my indecision and my wavering. Seth was right. I *was* broken. I only hoped I wasn't beyond repair.

"No, no, you're fine," Seth said from behind, easing me out of the way. The setting sun glinted off the rooftops as he ushered the boy inside and I stepped to the side. "Thank you so much for responding," he told Chet, putting an arm around his shoulders as they walked through to the library. Falling in behind them, I felt jealousy rising within me. I once had those skills, but my tongue was tied .

"...oh, you know," Seth was saying, "something classical. Some Tarrega or Vivaldi or perhaps Bach. Some lovely dinner music. Sit right there, dear boy, in that chair and let us hear a sample."

Dreads fell over his shoulders as he bent down and took a beautiful yet very used Martin from the weathered, stickered case that had plastered his t-shirt to his back. "Are you sure you don't want me to go home and change? I mean, how many people are going to be here?"

"Just Warner and myself," Seth said, "so you see it's not necessary to be all dressed up. We're more concerned with how you sound than how you look. Please play on."

Chet ran his fingers up and down the neck a few times, adjusted the pegs a bit, then began picking a beautiful melody. Essence flowed from him as strong and sweet as the notes he played. His eyes closed, and I could tell any shame he felt at what he wore had fallen away. He was inside the music, and I could have wept with regret for what was to come later that night.

"That's exquisite," Seth said. "Carcassi, isn't it?"

I shook my head. "No. It's Robbie Basho."

"Who?"

The young man stopped playing and smiled at me. "I had no idea you'd recognize him. I *do* know quite a few classical pieces, but I thought…I mean, I really like Basho."

"So do I," I said, my heart breaking at his smile. It was wondrously wide and innocent, inflected by his joy of playing. "I'm also a fan of John Fahey."

"*Who?*" Seth said again.

"They're contemporary guitarists," I explained.

"Oh. Well, it's fine. I rather liked it. Very good, Chet. We'll need you for the next couple of hours to play during dinner and afterwards back here in the library. Just some lovely atmospheric music." He reached into his pocket. "I believe the advertisement said one hundred dollars?"

"That's right."

"Give him five," I said.

"Oh Warner, five dollars is hardly—"

"Five *hundred*."

Chet's eyes grew wide.

"For goodness sake, why?" Seth asked. My look explained all he needed to know. The boy would not leave the house the same way he came in. He needed compensation, no matter how paltry. Seth shrugged and peeled off five bills from his money clip. "Very well," he said, handing it to him.

"Just for playing for a couple hours?" Chet asked. "That's all?"

"Yes," Seth replied.

And no, I thought.

You are lucky he cannot hear us, Seth said. *Of all the traits you've lost, your sentimentality is unfortunately intact. I would have thought you'd learned your lesson.*

"So, this must be a special occasion for you guys to hire someone to play guitar during dinner for this much money. Is it your anniversary?"

"No," Seth told him, "but it *is* a special occasion. If you'll come this way, I'll show you where you'll be playing. There's a cozy little anteroom just off the dining area that will be perfect." Chet shouldered the guitar, picked up the case, and followed Seth. "What kind of lighting will you need?" Seth asked.

He shrugged. "I'm not reading music, so not much."

"No music? You must be very talented."

And he was. I could smell it as Seth led us back through the house to the dining room. And his was no cheap street musician talent, either. It was clean and pure and heady in its strength. I hadn't had a meal like this in ages. Yet I could have wept. I had been living off dregs for so long, I had become used to it. In the face of a real meal, I was somewhat guilt-stricken.

Even at the best of times, I would only feed until I was full.

I had no desire to drink someone dry and render him unable to ply his trade, for that is what would happen. Seth, however, would not allow that with this one. He would insist I bleed the boy of all talent, leaving him unable to play after our encounter. I knew I had to do so as well, for my own sake. And I hated it.

I hated it so much I could not concentrate on the meal at the table. The serving girl came and went, depositing bowls and plates in front of me then taking them away again. I couldn't remember eating anything from them, and I certainly didn't enjoy any of it. I was too apprehensive about what was to happen. Could I finish? Would I smell the brine of the Old Man again? And then I must face the aftermath of my meal. The dread was almost too much to bear. I wanted to run away, but I had fled too much of late. And Seth would never have permitted it.

Dinner was finished at length, and the deed had to be faced. I delayed it a bit longer with cigars and brandy, but Seth guessed my game. He grew impatient, cutting my attempts at conversation short with a brevity he had not embraced during our meal. The music continued, deft and agile melodies tumbling in the air like lithe acrobats, their creator hidden from view in the small alcove.

"You cannot put this off any longer," Seth said with some finality.

I hated him for being right, but that did not change the facts of the situation. My second brandy untouched and my cigar smoldering in the ashtray, I rose from my chair and poked my head into the small space. "You played magnificently," I said to him.

He raised his head, smiling widely as his eyes sparkled. "Thanks. You paid pretty magnificently, too."

"Talent deserves its due," I replied, nearly wincing from the irony in my words as I fixed my gaze on his eyes. Charming him was a simple matter, really. The guitar slid from his grasp and almost fell to the floor. I caught it and leaned it gingerly against the wall. He would never play it again, but I had respect for a fine instrument and did not want to see it damaged.

"You have him," Seth said from behind me. "Were you not in such a weakened state, I would have you share him. He is quite a meal. One isn't often so lucky with Craigslist ads. They are, as is said, a crapshoot. Still, he is yours and yours alone. I shall hunt on my own later. Please, Warner. Feast."

I was actually frightened to begin, and to have Seth witness the event, not to mention constructing it solely for my benefit, was more than a little disconcerting. I was unused to this level of scrutiny and wished he would simply go upstairs. But I knew he would not. I also knew I needed him by my side in case something went wrong.

Easing closer to the boy, I was surprised at how my hunger overcame my hesitation. I grabbed either side of his head tenderly, though I don't know why as he was unable to feel anything. His dreads were bulky yet yielding under my palms. I tipped his head up and pressed my lips against his, savoring the purity of his essence. I already felt nourished, but I had to drink.

I took his sweetness deep into my lungs, astonished at the complexity of his taste. This was a rare meal indeed, especially considering what I was used to. I drank deeply, still I felt tentative and nervous. My rational mind told me not to worry. As odd as it sounded, I knew Seth would protect me. He needed me too much to let anything happen. I tried to put everything out of my mind except my hunger.

For a brief time, I succeeded. I felt nothing but the enormity of his gift, the warmth of his lips, and the scratchy stubble of his cheeks as I pressed my face into his. His vitality flooded every cell of my body and for the first time in many months, I felt normal. Powerful. But even as nourishment poured into me, the sickeningly familiar taste of the Old Man's brine asserted itself. Seth must have sensed it. He moved in closer. Instinctively, I hunched over the prey, keeping him mine despite my rising disgust at what I tasted, but Seth stopped just behind us.

It is not real, he said inside my head. *The Old Man is his lair at the shore of the All-Ocean and cannot interrupt you. What you taste is memory, and it is false. It is imprinted deeply on your consciousness, so let your mind go. Do not think. Do not plan. Do not stop. Do nothing except drink, for only essence will make you strong. There is no ocean nearby. There is no danger. All is well, and all shall be even better the more you drink.*

Amazingly, the salty tang and the accompanying disgust abated somewhat. It was still there, but its presence was not overwhelming. I wished it were gone. Would it always…

Do not think, Seth said again. *Be mindful of only the essence flowing into you.* The boy hung limply in my hands, enervated. I would usually stop at this point, leaving some essence so he could, in time, recover the talent he had. Once it had grown to its former glory, I would have another meal. I had survived that way for centuries. *You cannot stop*, Seth insisted. *You must finish*

*him. I know how distasteful this is to you, but you have no choice.
You must be strong. We must be strong.*

I detested the necessity as much as Seth's veracity, but if I
dwelt on it, I would risk yet another mental lecture. No matter
how much it pained me, I had to strip him of all he possessed.
I broke from our embrace, exhaled breath and essence—Seth
immediately swooped in to gather what I expelled—put my lips
to his once more and inhaled with all my might.

The last of his essence rushed into my lungs, the final wave
as fresh and bracing as the first breath of a winter's day. The joy
of its taste was accompanied by sadness at the manner in which
he slumped in my hands. It was over. His talent was gone. He
would play no more. Perhaps enough of a vestige remained that
he could partially recover his abilities, but he would never be as
he was before. Moreover, he would never know why. The loss
might consume him; it had others.

"But you feel marvelous, don't you?" Seth crowed. "He will
find his place in the world, Warner. Of that I have no doubt. He
still has a part to play, as do we. Do not debate. Do not regret.
It is our way."

I nodded, unwilling to speak at first. I put the limp figure
back on his stool, propping him up against the wall. Forcing
his eyes open, I was going to uncharm him enough to send him
home. He would not remember what had happened. But in the
end, I could not. "Let him go," I said to Seth as I walked toward
the stairs. "I no longer have the stomach for it."

"Warner," he said quietly. "I know this has been difficult for
you, but you see the right of it, don't you? And you know you
are not yet whole. This will have to be done again."

Putting my hand on the bannister, I steadied myself and looked at him. "Yes. Perhaps it will get easier, perhaps not. In any case, I must thank you for your efforts. The road will be long, but it is good to be on it at last."

He nodded and turned to the young man to instruct him how to get home as I mounted the stairs to my room, simultaneously feeling better and worse.

⁣☙

het was only the first of five. The other four were not as fruitful, but they were good meals in their own right. Bobby was a chunky, blond buzzcut accordion player we found near my old place in the Marigny; long and lanky Jeffrey played bass guitar in one of the many dives on Bourbon; Joseph, dark-haired and hawk-nosed, was a drummer working for change in Jackson Square, and Marilyn was a keyboard player we found in the lounge of a Holiday Inn in Slidell.

Thanks to me, none of them play anything now. I have no idea how they earn their livings after our encounter, but Seth believes this is not our concern. We sent them on their way with generous sums of money, and that alone is supposed to ease our conscience. Well, *my* conscience. Seth is unfamiliar with the concept, but after these five, he assured me this portion of my cure was complete.

"I think you are ready to hunt on your own," he said over

breakfast the morning after Marilyn. "That way, you may do what you wish with them. You certainly didn't look as if you had any difficulty with Marilyn last night." He grinned, availing himself of the boyish charm he'd found in this body. It was definitely better looking than his last. "Are you switching teams, as they say?"

I nearly choked on my coffee. "Hardly. But my feeding is no longer impeded by the smell of that damnable brine or thoughts of the Old Man. I must admit your therapy worked. And I'm grateful for your assistance, Seth. I…I could not have done this alone. I know I've been a less than ideal patient."

Seth shrugged, doling out scrambled eggs to us both from the chafing dish on the table. "You have scruples, Warner. I find it baffling, personally, but your convictions are your own, and I reluctantly admire your adherence to them. You are a man of principle. Too honest for your own good, but then again, we all have faults. However, I cannot fault you for your courage or your fortitude. I know it was not easy for you to do what you have done."

I sighed, accepting my plate of eggs and getting a piece of buttered toast from the platter. "It was not. I understood the necessity, but I will enjoy getting back to my own hunting routine alone this evening."

"Not *quite* alone," he said with a smile. "I'll be going with you. Not to either hunt or assist you. You will be perfectly free to hunt as you please, but I will be standing guard."

"Standing guard?"

He ate smugly, if that was possible. "You were rather occupied last night with pursuing prey you are not accustomed to, so you likely did not notice the being who followed us—indeed, has followed us on our last two outings."

I was dumbstruck. How could I not have felt such a thing? My senses are so easily overrun lately. What was wrong with my focus? I had to get myself right, else we would be lost. And the thought of being pursued chilled me. "A being? Not…"

"No, no. Not the Old Man. If you will think back to our first conversation after you arrived here, I spoke of his emissary."

"And he is watching us. What does he look like?"

Seth put his fork down and pushed his plate aside. "I don't *know* exactly. It's maddening. I feel him nearly on top of me sometimes, yet I see nothing and no one."

"Is he invisible?"

"It's most likely a simple spell of misdirection," he said with a sniff. "The feelings I get are so vague, it's no wonder you have not felt them as well. But he is definitely present, and I have a feeling he will show himself sooner than later, which is why I would like us to go together. Perhaps nothing untoward will happen, but we should be on our guard."

We were enough on our guard to go to my old neighborhood, the Marigny, to cruise the small clubs around Frenchman Street rather than venture out on Bourbon on a Friday night. I wasn't even certain I needed to feed, but Seth insisted. To argue would have been futile, and he was probably right. In retrospect, however, I wonder if he had using our excursion as a means to draw out the Old Man's emissary. Such subterfuge would be typical of Seth.

After dinner and a browse at the bookstore, we strolled down Frenchman to LaPage, a small club whose open door let out a beat so big I thought the chalkboard advertising their drink specials might rattle right off the window. The talent we smelled was not coming from the band as much as its vocalist, a lithe blond boy nearly as thin as the mic stand he was twirling about. He had big green eyes, and his longish hair was plastered to his forehead with sweat.

He crooned, he growled, he sang behind the beat, then in front of it. He snapped the meter in half and spliced it together again with sheer bravado. He was marvelous. I don't usually get much of a meal out of singers, but this one entranced me, and his essence rose high above the pedestrian band behind him. He must also have some talent for an instrument. Guitar. Definitely a guitar.

"It's the singer, isn't it?" Seth asked.

I nodded.

"That's a mark of your recovery," he said into my ear. "He almost looks like Wade."

In fact, he did. I was stunned to find I hadn't noticed. Even more stunning, it seemed to make no difference. Maybe my cure was more complete than I thought it to be. I felt empowered by the ability to overlook his resemblance to Wade. I was stronger and more assured. Enough confidence crept back into my being that I was able to dismiss Seth.

"I can take it from here," I said to him.

He grinned. "I have no doubt. I'm going to get a drink. Would you like something?"

"No thank you."

Seth moved away from my consciousness. I felt his presence, but no more than that of others around me. I concentrated on the singer, now crouching low at the front of the small stage, enticing the young women crowding its edge, the mic stand thrust behind him in a rather phallic manner. Perhaps it was just the mood I was in. I could have waited for him to look my way, but in games of power one must establish one's superiority as soon as possible.

I did not enter his mind. That would have been presumptuous. Instead, I continued to stare at him as he ended the song and stood up to take his bows. He found me at length, his gaze not leaving mine once I met it, until I let him go. I saw the slight shake of his head and a look of puzzlement cross his face. He announced a short break and jumped off the stage.

He was looking around for me as he landed, crowded by ladies who shoved CDs at him. Signing as he walked, he handed them back to whomever was closest. I caught his glance once, then walked out the door and lit a cigarette as I leaned up against one of the date trees lining the other side of Frenchman and waited for him. I didn't have to wait long.

Coming out alone, he barely checked traffic before he crossed the street. I held out my pack of Marlboros as he approached. He looked at me and looked at the cigarettes before he took one and tamped it against the bark of the tree. I cupped my palm around the flame of my lighter, and he leaned into it. Smoke and essence rose from his nostrils as he spoke.

"Who are you?" His speaking voice was huskier than his singing voice.

"Just a fan," I replied, staring into his eyes as I began my charm in earnest.

"I'm not…"

"A homosexual?" I chuckled. "Nobody's perfect. Come, my friend. Walk with me a moment." I put my arm around his shoulders and steered him toward the dark alleys down Chartres Street. He walked without argument. He was mine. Seth watched, backlit from the open doorway of the bookstore, with his arms crossed. It was too dark outside to read the expression on his face. I expected him to shout some parting comment in my head, but I heard nothing.

We did not speak as we walked down Chartres. Nothing needed to be said. I was not in the mood for small talk, and he was dizzied by magic, unable to initiate any conversation on his own. I don't know how or why, but with each step I seemed to grow stronger and more self-assured. By the time we reached Voodoo Music, an aptly named business for what I had in mind, I felt as if nothing could stop me. I had finally regained my former self.

The streetlights shone faint and ghostly, casting a sickly green light so nauseating I was glad to shepherd him into the darkness of the alley. I took a quick look around to make sure we were not observed by anyone except Seth, who lingered across Chartres, then I peered down the alley to ensure we weren't stumbling on a crime or a drug deal. Others use these passages for nefarious purposes, but thankfully we were the sole occupants.

I waited until we were halfway down the alley, totally enveloped by the shadows, and I pinned him against the wall. Looking deeply into his eyes, I bent him to my will. His lips parted, and his essence flowed forth, warm and spicy-sweet. Covering his mouth with mine, I drew deep draughts from him.

His eyes closed reflexively, then another instinct of mine took over.

Reaching down, I cupped his crotch with my hand. Feeding is not necessarily a sexualized action, but it is not unheard of for the two to happen simultaneously. And it had been a long time since I'd had a man. Seth's constant presence made such contact impossible, but this boy was too delicious to resist.

He may not have been a homosexual, but his cock had no difficulty stiffening beneath the denim. I stroked its hot, hard length, flattening my palm out as I rubbed my finger over the head and pressed my hand into it. He sighed, releasing even more essence from deep inside his body. The atmosphere grew heady and sensual, both of us lost in hunger and need and satisfaction and inchoate desire, at least on his part. I could tell he had never experienced this level of intimacy with one of his own sex, and the knowledge inflamed me. I kneaded his prick roughly as he ground his hips into my arm.

I sensed Seth inside my head. His presence indicated no command or suggestion on his part, merely observation. I pictured him leaning up against the wall of my cerebral cortex, his arms folded and a quizzical expression on his face. He never understood my attraction to males, but he wasn't judging. He was making sure I could keep the brine at bay on my own.

He had no worries on that score. The smell was a distant memory, though I did not want to linger on the thought of it for fear that bringing it to the forefront of my consciousness would cause its return. I closed my eyes and continued to feel the young man's cock as I sucked in his essence. Suddenly, the taste grew very, very sweet, and I knew he was about to be exhausted.

You should finish this one, Seth encouraged.

But I had no intention of doing so. I had had enough of destruction and wished to leave this one a kernel of his gift so it could grow and flourish again. Perhaps I would come around to harvest him once more. As his essence reached the apex of its sweetness, I took my lips from his.

I resisted the urge I always have to blow a breath or two back into him, but that would make him one of us. That's not to say being one of us isn't a good life. We are immortal without many of the nasty drawbacks the blood brethren have, but I think it exceedingly rude to force someone into our ranks without permission. Besides, we have enough competition for a small pool of individuals talented enough to make a meal.

Seth's disapproval was plain. *If you'd have…* he started, but then he was jerked out of my head forcefully enough to cause me pain. I dropped the young man on the damp concrete of the alley. I had last seen Seth across the street, but that corner was now empty and my head was full of incomprehensible chatter rising in volume.

As I darted toward Chartres, a scream pierced through the chaos. The voice, however, was not Seth's, and it carried no fear or horror. It was a cry of rage. I looked up and down the street but saw nothing other than lost tourists and loitering locals. However, blue flashes of light illuminated the brickwork of the alley across the street.

Quickly checking for traffic, I ran across the street. The noise in my head subsided, but the blue flashing lights continued in the alley. I couldn't imagine what those lights heralded. I knew no magic that could produce such pyrotechnics, but Seth was far better versed in that sphere than was I. I hoped the bolts were coming from him. What I saw when I entered the alley, however, chilled me.

Seth was at the far end, held at least ten feet aloft and pinned to the side of the building by a jagged blue arc of energy. His head lolled to the right as if he was unconscious, but his eyes were open and flashing anger. His mouth worked, but I heard nothing with my ears and felt nothing in my head.

The figure whose hands originated the arc was no more than ten or fifteen feet away from me. I was able to distinguish his dark topcoat, superfluous in the New Orleans heat, and a pair of spindly legs beneath its hem, but the angle and the moment prevented closer examination. I had to free Seth.

I ran at the thing as quickly and quietly as I could, my hands clasped to deliver a two-handed blow to the back of his neck. Fearing he might step aside or otherwise escape such an attack, I was surprised my attempt was successful. My strike landed exactly where I had planned with the desired effect. The bolt ceased and Seth plummeted to the ground. I wished his landing had been gentler, but it was unavoidable.

I half-expected to see the visage of the Old Man when he faced me, but I did not smell his telltale brine. However, this figure's resemblance to the apparition that had haunted me until all too recently was similar enough to startle.

His skin was as white as the Old Man's, but his features were vastly more human except he had no nose. He was tall, and the absurd, battered top hat he wore made him taller. Wild tufts of straw-yellow hair stuck out from under its brim, and his mouth was a cruel, downturned line. He chose not to open it to speak but instead forced his way into my mind.

Ah, so here you are, he said, the voice low and raspy. *You must be fully healed. Or do you still pine for your lost love? What a fool*, he chuckled.

My anger overcame me, and I reached out to strike him once again. He raised his hands, but before he had fully extended his arms, a blue bolt similar to that which had held Seth aloft came from behind me. It snaked around the figure, wrapping him tightly in a cocoon of light. As he now rose in the air, I looked behind me to see Seth upright, his hands emanating the force that held our enemy.

Seth nodded at me. "Thank you, Warner, for disrupting the spell. I was marshalling my energies for a countermove, but your assistance was timely, to be sure. Had I not been concerned and overprotective at your feeding, he would not have caught me off my guard."

"As if it was my fault you weren't watching?"

He smiled and shrugged.

Listen to you. Seth turned toward the grinning figure wrapped in light, so I assume he heard what I did. *Your enmity is delightful. It will, no doubt, serve you well in battle. Bicker away.*

Seth squeezed his hand, tightening the bonds of light holding the Old Man's emissary. The constriction seemed to bow the sides of his head, his wild hair bulging out even farther under the top hat, which looked as if it might pop off any second to relieve the pressure. But nothing stopped his infernal grin.

Is this the extent of your abilities? he said to Seth before turning my way. *We shall see. Our conflict is in the future, though not as far off as the future I now present to you. Behold your end.*

His grin vanished as he opened his mouth wide, producing a stream of black vomit that gushed out of his face, spattering the split and broken concrete of the alley until it collected in a smooth pool of darkness at our feet. He then disappered into thin air, the strands of Seth's light clutching nothing before they also dissipated.

We were on opposite sides of the dark pond, and I caught a whiff of the brine that heralded the Old Man. The black fen reeked of it. I felt as if I might swoon, but I ignored the feeling and inched closer to its edge. I was compelled to peer down, though I did not want to. I looked up at Seth, who was already staring raptly at whatever vision was there to behold. I could read nothing in his face. I wondered if we were being shown the same future or something designed to pit us against each other. My heart in my throat, I gazed down into the pool.

I saw only my own reflection at first, but then it shimmered as if I had dropped a coin in the murk. I held my breath as the scene rearranged itself into a setting straight out of many of my nightmares, the shore of the All-Ocean as viewed from some distant vantage point. Its dank, briny stink mingled with essence as relentless tides broke on the black beach.

A group of objects sat far back on the shore close to an obsidian mountain. I could not determine its height, but it seemed immense. As I drew closer to the objects, I saw four glass boxes—two tall rectangular ones and two smaller squares. Closer yet, and I could see shapes inside them. Still closer, and my blood ran cold.

For Seth and I were inside the boxes. Our bodies were inside the taller ones. Sitting neatly beside them were the smaller cubes containing our heads. Our eyes were open, looking around and out at the All-Ocean as it lapped the shore. Mesmerized by the gaze of my own imprisoned head, I could not look away.

The face of the Old Man suddenly filled my vision, blocking out all else. His withered, wizened visage spoke to me, but I couldn't hear what it said with either my ears or my mind. It began to laugh noiselessly, its mouth wide open showing his sparse, jagged teeth, then all was blackness once again. My reflection returned and the pool receded, drying up as if absorbed by the hot New Orleans night until it was no bigger than a drop. Then it, too, was gone. Seth stared at the spot for a few seconds more, then looked up at me.

"And so it begins," he said.

❦

We walked home in silence until we approached Elysian Fields. "What did you see?" Seth asked me as we waited for the traffic light to change.

Even relating the vision brought the smell to me. "The shore of the All-Ocean," I replied. "And our demise."

"Our demise?" He sounded surprised. "If you're speaking of the separation of our heads from our bodies, both placed in containers of glass, that hardly represents our demise. That is merely *cha'lan.*"

"Cha'lan?"

"The Punishment, in the ancient tongue. Have you learned

nothing since our last encounter with the Old Man? Done no research? Damn your laziness, Warner. Your willingness to be ignorant astounds me."

"Forgive me. I was a bit preoccupied with not being able to feed without a psychotic break from reality. *Mea culpa.*" The light changed, and I gestured him across the street, letting my sarcasm sink in for a moment. "We apparently saw the same thing."

"Apparently. However, that outcome is only one possibility. I know the spell he used, and it merely shows that which might come true. There is no reason for alarm—well, not on your part anyway."

"What do you mean?"

He slowed his pace a moment, as if considering his words carefully. "It grieves me," he began, "to see that your last battle with our enemy did not prompt you to give our lore any serious study. We will only be victorious if we have the power that comes from knowledge. I have much of that knowledge and am gaining more every day. You, however, remain blithely unaware of what we can and *must* do. This a serious problem, Warner. You have a fine mind and keen instincts. Now is the time to put them to use."

I hated that he was right. But I am not so unaware of my own deficiencies that I refuse to acknowledge an error. "How shall we begin?"

His pace quickened as he grinned at me. "Are you serious?"

I returned his smile. "Yes. But don't expect either contrition or an apology."

"I would ask neither of you. The course of study will be

rigorous, you understand."

"I'm sure of it."

"What do you know of the ancient tongue?"

"Nothing."

He sighed. "No matter. I can teach you spells phonetically until you have mastered enough to read the text on your own. You can practice either in the house or in the back garden. We should start with defensive spells first—no, no—some general lessons in lore before anything. The stakes are much too high to assume you know something elementary that you may not." A light I had not seen before seemed to shine from his eyes.

As we came up to the iron gate of the house, I paused and smirked. "I thought you were a noble when you were made, not a schoolmaster."

His eyebrows flew up like windowshades. "Please," he said, "there's no need to be *insulting*."

☙

O nce the last syllable left my mouth, I raised my palms as Seth instructed. They tingled slightly, then a faint white light emanated from them. I was so intent on watching the progress of the rays my attention faltered, causing them to flicker and die before they really got started. Seth groaned softly behind me.

"That was *marginally* better," he said, disappointment raging under his encouraging grimace, "but you must concentrate. Find the center of the energy within you and move it forward. Out through your palms. Look at the target, not your hands. Do it again, and this time try not to stumble over the spell. That's not helping you."

I paused a moment, listening to the birds and the steady hum of the cicadas in the garden as I cleared my mind. When I had calmed sufficiently, I repeated the spell and again raised my palms, focusing on the empty wineglass Seth had placed in the middle of the dry birdbath. I went inside myself and visualized my energy in earnest. Suddenly, my surroundings slipped away from me. The birds, the insects, Seth, and the feel of the sun on my back all faded, replaced by a powerful warmth within.

I cannot say how, but I seemed to get underneath that warmth and pictured myself pushing it forward slowly and steadily as I gazed at the glass, enraptured by the starburst the sun created on its rim. And as I gazed and pushed, two strong arcs of white light reached into the periphery of my vision. I kept my sights on the glass, however, continuing to force the energy out of my body. The bolts of light pressed on toward the glass until they converged on its bowl.

I felt a thump in my chest, as if I'd hit an actual solid mass. The sensation surprised me enough that the rays again flickered, but I redoubled my efforts. I felt the weight of the glass. Its heft. My emanations danced over its smoothness and grasped it at the join of the stem. Lost to everything except the glass and my energy, I tugged upward with my mind.

The glass wobbled and rose a few shaky inches, wavering in the sunlight. I could no longer sense its weight. It traveled lightly on my beams as if it wasn't even there. It would not still itself, however. Its path grew erratic no matter how hard I tried to steady it. A loud horn blast from a passing vehicle in the street shattered my concentration. The rays dissipated, and the glass fell and broke inside the birdbath.

The headache came on me before the pieces finished clattering. I breathed deeply and rubbed my temples.

"That will do for a start," Seth said. "It will become easier with time and practice."

"How much time do we have?"

He shrugged. "Impossible to say." He sat down in one of the lawn chairs and indicated I do the same. Pouring a nice Chardonnay into two unbroken glasses, he picked one up and saluted me with it. I did the same. "However," he said. "If I were to hazard a guess, I would say we have all the time we find necessary."

"Why would you say that?" The headache was easing off, and the wine was delicious.

"Because the Old Man loves his sport," Seth replied. "If he simply wanted to get rid of us, he could take the advantage in any number of ways. I don't believe he'll do that. He wants to feel as if he's actually won something should he be the victor, and that means getting you up to speed. His emissary could have killed you and crippled our efforts, but I believe he had instructions not to do so. As to what will happen next, I have no idea."

"I trust your instincts. After all, you were made by the Old Man. That must make you one of the oldest of our kind."

"Yes, but this new body has rather given me a new lease on life." He set his mouth as if to continue speaking, but he stopped.

"I don't believe you've ever spoken of how you were made. Did you know him when he made you, or was he a stranger to you?"

He shifted in his chair, obviously discomfited and silent for so long I thought he would not reply. At length, he reached over to the bottle of wine and refilled his glass. "I find myself somewhat embarrassed," he finally said, the bottle poised in mid air. "I I have not been entirely truthful with you."

"You *were* made by the Old Man, weren't you?"

"Yes, yes," he said, waving his other hand, "of course."

"Then where is the lie?"

He finished pouring. "I would not exactly term it a lie. It's more of an omission than anything else—a small detail I left out, of no consequence really. It certainly doesn't alter our present situation, and I hope it doesn't color our relationship."

"Stop dancing around," I said, my curiosity now tempered with annoyance. "Out with it."

"He is my father."

"Your..." The glass nearly slipped out of my fingers. I searched his face for any trace of a joke, but Seth had no sense of humor. He was being truthful. My first sense was one of betrayal. I considered that scene in the Chelsea and wondered if he had manufactured the mattress story, the Old Man instead sparing him out of some sense of familial obligation. I felt Seth try to enter my mind but blocked him. I knew how to do that now.

"You've learned that much, at least," he said with a rueful smile. "But the suspicion is written on your countenance,

Warner. Hardly a challenging read."

"Do you blame me?"

He sipped and sighed. "I suppose not, though I am unused to explaining myself to others. It's bothersome."

"I believe you owe me that much."

He grinned slightly, set his glass down and rose. "Yes, of course. But come, let us walk while I relate the tale. I find such chores easier while on a stroll."

We exited the small garden through the back gate, which opened onto Octavia, close to the Audabon Cemetery. I was curious but did not wish to hurry Seth. Such personal details were apparently difficult for him to disclose, so I contented myself with the sight of the lush greenery and the smell of the bougainvillea. At length, he began.

"We were, indeed, of noble birth. Roman nobility, I'll have you know. My father was a quite famous senator. Any antiquities scholar worth his salt would know the name immediately, but it bears no relevance here. What *does* matter was his talent, both in rhetoric and music. His skill with the cithara was well-known in many circles, and it is said he was one of Gaius Octavius's favorites, often requested at funereal gatherings such was his ability to soothe and comfort on the instrument. That proved to be his undoing. Shall we stroll through the cemetery? I find it most diverting."

"Of course. So, if I am reading between your lines correctly, your father was not the first of our kind?"

He stopped in his tracks and glared at me. "You may stop calling him my father and continue to refer to him as the Old Man," he said before resuming his pace. "The origins of our race are lost in the beginning of time. The All-Ocean has had many masters and even more names. Your supposition, however, is correct. Another smelled his considerable gifts. One named Marcus."

"What happened?"

Seth shrugged. "What usually happens. But Marcus was looking for more than a meal. He wanted a companion, so he turned my father. And *that* proved to be *his* undoing."

"How so?"

We were now in the cemetery. Seth paused and leaned against the masonry of a monument, lighting a cigarette. He held the pack out to me, but I refused. Vile things. I only affect them when I hunt. He blew out blue smoke and gazed off into the distance. "You have, of course, seen corpulent men and women for whom food is more than sustenance or even enjoyment. It becomes an addiction. Thus it was with my father. He could not stop indulging in essence. He drained most of his friends, even the most modestly talented, and when he had raced through them, he began to feed on his own family."

"And that's when you were turned."

"Not at first. He left my sister utterly without her skills at oratory and bled my mother so dry, she could not even bring herself to pluck the lyre. But I had overheard some of his conversations with Marcus and got a glimmer of what they were. I escaped his scrutiny at first by pretending to be a dullard without talent at all. He was not yet sensitive enough to pierce that guise, but my ruse eventually failed. He turned me because he wanted my assistance."

"In what?"

"In supplanting the master of the All-Ocean." He blew out more smoke and crushed the butt under his heel, crossing his arms as if warding off a nonexistent chill. "He learned of its shores from Marcus, whom he killed accidentally during a mutual feeding. Or, rather, he *said* the murder was accidental. I have my doubts. Regardless, the possibility of an unending supply of essence consumed him."

My suspicion grew alarmingly. "And you helped him accomplish this task?"

He uncrossed his arms and began walking once more. "Do not anticipate the tale," he warned, looking back as I followed him, "nor make assumptions about my complicity. I never intended to fulfill his fiendish request. My goal was knowledge alone. We organized and studied the morass of scrolls left in Marcus's library. Such an untidy man. I learnt much, as did my father. However, he kept some information from me. I saw him tuck several items inside his robe."

"Items?"

"Yes. Something which resembled a compass, I remember, and a few amulets. I thought nothing of it at the time, but those implements not only guided him to the shore of the All-Ocean, they helped him defeat its master. At least, I believe this to be the case."

"And how was this done?"

"I truly have no idea. I never reached that realm.. I have only seen it in dreams, as you have. Although he sought my aid, he simply vanished one night without notifying me. We were to meet at Marcus's quarters of a midnight, but he never showed up, and the place had been cleaned out. Not a scrap of parchment was left. I heard nothing for several days and thought he had failed in his search or been defeated himself."

"How did you find out otherwise?"

"He came to me in my sleep one evening, possessed of that wretched face he now bears. 'It is mine,' he said, then he vanished as I woke up in a cold sweat. Dreadful. I still shiver when the image comes to mind."

"As do I." I had not beheld that terrifying visage for some time. However, as the thought came to my mind, the stench of brine rose in my nostrils, borne by a gust of breeze off the river. But the wind was blowing the wrong direction. My gut shrank.

Seth looked up and around. He had smelled it as well. He opened his mouth to say something and even managed the first utterance before he stopped. Off to the left, we both saw the Old Man's emissary leaning in the doorway of a mausoleum. It was still dressed in top hat and coat, its legs like black matchsticks and a hole where its nose should have been. It swung a shiny object at the end of a golden chain.

I believe this is yours, Master Seth? Your father bade me return it to you. He hung the chain on a spike of the wrought iron fence surrounding the tomb. *Don't worry. It won't bite.*

It howled with laughter, then it vanished.

Seth frowned and changed direction, striding wordlessly off down the center of the path toward the fence. I followed him, keeping a watchful eye to our backs lest the emissary reappear behind us. His long limbs covered the ground in no time, and he bent down to examine the object before plucking it from the fence.

"It is the very compass of which I spoke," he said. "He is

playing games with us, but at least the next move has been made."

"May I see it?"

"Do not open it," he said. "Not here." He paused a moment longer before dropping into my hand.

The instrument itself was light, barely heavier than the chain itself. It resembled a pocket watch with a cover and a clasp. The face of the cover, however, was mutable. The bas-relief on its surface shifted and wavered, its lines and sculpted elements in constant flux as it nearly settled in an image then flew apart again, swirling in an unceasing motion. The effect was altogether mesmerizing.

Seth took hold of the chain and snatched it back. "Do not look at it for too long," he warned.

"What will happen?"

"I have no idea. I was never able to study it closely enough as it was always in his possession. Its properties are unknown to me, hence my caution." He put it in the pocket of his jacket and looked all around us once again. "Are your curiosity and suspicion satisfied with my tale?" he asked.

I nodded.

"Then let us strike for home," he said, shouldering past me. "We have much to ponder."

CＳ

ur pondering took place in the library amongst the volumes Seth had surrounded himself with. He had taken down a few immediately upon our return and was now engaged in thumbing through them, the artifact from the emissary face down between us on the heavy oaken table.

"Nothing," he said, closing the one he had been reading. "If only I had Olafsson's diary, we might have the clues we need to utilize this compass."

"Olafsson's diary?"

He lifted his snifter of brandy and swirled the amber liquid around in the glass. "Yes. Olafsson was one of our scholars, who penned a unique and altogether rare book detailing his journey to the All-Ocean and back. I have sought it for millennia and have come close to acquiring it a few times, but it always eludes me at the last." He pointed to the object. "I'm certain this is a part of that journey."

The waiting, the inaction, the explanations, and the unceasing lessons were all taking their toll on my nerves. It was time to do something. "Well, if we do not have it, we do not have it. We shall have to glean what information we can from direct examination." I snatched it up from the table and held it by the chain as Seth looked on in horror.

"Do not—"

Before he could finish his warning, I undid the clasp and opened the damned thing. It looked like any other compass save that it bore no directional letters on its white face. The arrow pointed straight north. Its mutable outer covering felt warm in the palm of my hand. I even felt its surface shifting against my skin. "There you are," I said.

Seth put down his brandy and peered closer. "It appears quite ordinary," he remarked. "Odd that it has no letters, but I suppose directions are universal."

"But what if those are *not* simply directions?" I thought aloud. "At least not in the usual sense."

"Whatever do you mean?"

"Think of it," I said. "The inside face is unremarkable and apparently fixed, but its outside is singular and ever-changing. Suppose they work in concert with each other?" An idea glimmered in my head. I grabbed Seth's brandy, placing it far to the right. I then closed the compass and, without looking at the snifter, tried to fix the shape of it in my imagination whilst staring at the swirling golden circle. It shimmered a moment, then resolved itself in an exact picture of the glass. That remained long enough to register, then it was replaced by a bas-relief of the table on which it sat. When I again opened the compass, its arrow pointed dead right.

"Brilliant!" Seth said, beaming. "What a marvelous deduction! Of course, it would have occurred to me sooner or later, but I knew you would prove your worth."

"Indeed," I replied with a polite smile. Even Seth's compliments contained a modicum of self-congratulation, but I overlooked such nonsense. Through trial and error, we determined that North was forward, South was backward, East was right, and West was left. It also showed gradations of direction. Seth's housekeeper interrupted us to tell us dinner was laid and cooling in the dining room opposite, but he waved her away.

Another thought struck me as I recalled the earlier part of our conversation. "Do you know what your tome looks like?" I asked.

"My *tome?*"

"Yes, the diary of which you spoke."

"Olafsson's book? Of course. I nearly acquired it at auction on two separate occasions."

I must admit I looked at him with some amazement. "You were that close and did not take extraordinary means to secure it?"

"My funds were limited, and I was unaware of its importance at the time else I would have strived harder to obtain it. What are you getting at, Warner?"

"What did it look like?"

"It was shaped like every other book on these shelves," he said, glancing around the library. "Neither oversized nor odd in any manner."

"What color was it?"

"Color?" He frowned at first, then his forehead smoothed out. "Ah, I see what you're about—but this artifact has no means to determine color."

I shook my head. "It's a *magical* artifact," I countered. "Who can say what it can or cannot determine? You've spent the last few weeks schooling me, now take a lesson yourself. See the book in your mind's eye. Consider not only the color but the texture of its binding, its age, how the pages seemed."

He regarded me curiously, almost skeptically, but then his aspect said he'd decided to indulge me. Perhaps he even believed me. One cannot ever be sure with Seth. In any event, I could feel him concentrating until, at length, the roiling depths of gold formed a book. As soon as it had appeared, it vanished, forming a picture of a room. We both recognized it at the same time, looking at the dining room. When I opened the compass, it pointed directly ahead.

"Well, there's the fault then," Seth sniffed. "Either it or you are wrong. I do not have the volume, and it most certainly is not in the dining room."

"All the same…" I said, taking the compass by its chain and striding across the hall. What I saw brought me up short, Seth uttering a strangled cry behind me. For the emissary was sitting at table, indulging in a leg of chicken.

My compliments to your cook. Admittedly, I have not tasted earthly comestibles for some time, but this is quite tasty. Of course, my enjoyment is limited as the sense of smell is as important as that of taste, and…well… He gestured at his absent nose and threw the bone on the floor, wiping his fingers on his lapel.

He reached inside the breast pocket of his topcoat and produced a reddish-brown book he laid carefully on the table. *This is your lucky day. I bear yet another gift from the master—one you have been seeking. The time, however, was not right for you to possess it. Besides, it would be rude of us to invite you to our home and not provide directions.*

Seth said something under his breath I did not hear. Perhaps I wasn't meant to. In any event, he shouldered past me into the room, unafraid or unheeding of the emissary, and retrieved the volume from the table.

"It's the very one I nearly purchased in Amsterdam," he said, his voice curiously flat. "I now remember the scratch along the binding."

It's a claw-mark.

Seth grinned. I could not determine if it was false or genuine, but Seth was quite good at that sort of deception. He twisted an emerald ring off his little finger. "You must thank the Old Man for us. Two presents in one day is quite generous. Please accept this in exchange for such a handsome gift."

He tossed it to the emissary, who frowned and raised two fingers, halting the piece of jewelry in mid-air. *Do you think me a fool? This bauble is undoubtedly charmed, designed to lead you back to my warren. I thought better of you than that.* He snapped his fingers, and the ring fell into the gravy boat.

Seth lowered his head, feigning contrition. This much I knew to be a sham. Seth was never contrite about anything. "Forgive me," he said, a polite look in his eye. "A feeble attempt, to be sure, but my talents are limited. All I can do is try, as you would in my position."

The emissary glowered. *Study the book carefully. It will tell you much you need to know. And much you don't. I hope you are wise enough to recognize the difference.* And then it vanished.

I felt Seth's shielding spell immediately. Then he started to laugh and clutched the volume to his chest. "Misdirection, Warner. It is always your ally and often stronger than the magic you use."

"I knew you and he were playing different games. What did I just witness?"

"The spell I used was on his magic, not on the ring. When he held it in mid-air, I caught his scent, so to speak." His smile was wide and his laugh hearty. "We can follow it any time we wish and beard him in his own den—or warren, as he put it. But come. Let us eat, and then we shall peruse the book. We have much study ahead of us. Olafsson's downfall will be our boon."

☙

The ancient tongue exhausted me enough during spells, never mind reading it. The language was ugly and had far too many consonants and glottal stops strung together to be spoken smoothly. Seth advised me I would attain a facility with it once I practiced, but after a somewhat enervating day, I hadn't the patience.

He, however, sat himself in the library immediately after dinner and pored over Olafsson's diary, finishing it once then starting it again. When he had read it a second time, he slammed it shut, putting an end to my drowsiness.

"If any of this is true, Olafsson was a fool," he stated flatly. "His hubris was his unmaking. He had no plan or thought other than the same obsession which drove the Old Man to find the shores of the All-Ocean in the first place—addiction. No wonder he could not beat him. They played the same game."

"What happened to him?"

"That's the specious part. Even though he was mortally wounded, he supposedly built a raft and simply floated back to this realm unconscious. It smacks of Jules Verne. He had no materials, no tools, and there is no place where the All-

Ocean touches our world, believe me. I would have found it. The rumor is that he died a lingering, painful death, but I have no firsthand knowledge of this. I'm sure the Old Man and his emissary have circulated the story to discourage others from attempting a similar journey."

"What else have you learned?"

He scowled and pushed the book in my direction. "It would serve us *both* well for you to read it rather than listen to my summary. The language is plain enough for your understanding, and you might notice something I have not detected. If nothing else, it will improve your skill with the language."

I bristled but understood his meaning. The next morning when I was fresh, I set to work. The task proved easier than it had appeared the night before, and I actually finished before lunch. I attempted to speak with Seth about it during our meal, but he requested I go through it once more before we discussed it. He even cancelled our session for the afternoon. By the time I concluded the second pass at the table in my quarters, twilight was upon us.

"Ah, *there* you are," Seth said as I strode into the library. He put down his afternoon snifter of cognac and poured another for me. "I was about to check on your progress. How are you coming along with our friend Olafsson?"

"I don't believe a word of it," I said, handing Seth the book and taking the glass in hand as I sat down in the chair facing him. "There is no more detail in the book about the realm than we have already seen ourselves in dreams and visions. He provides no actual spells to gain entrance to the place, and I wouldn't trust the spells he claims to have used in battle. They sound useless to me."

"Why, then, do you suppose his emissary gave it to us?"

"For that very reason, perhaps. Were we gullible enough to believe in them, those empty spells would surely render us impotent before the Old Man and work to his advantage. As you said, misdirection. At the very least, we should try them beforehand and see if they work—and even that may be a waste of time."

"Your skepticism is heartening," Seth said, smiling. "I have come to much the same conclusion. Due to my efforts, entrance to the realm will not be a problem, and I am also heartened by the fact you recognize those spells as bogus. We shall, of course, try them, but I expect little. As for myself, I am most lucky the Amsterdam deal fell through. I would have been out several thousand dollars for a schoolboy fantasy."

"Even the supposed claw mark seems manufactured," I said.

Seth looked at me, then laughed aloud. He did not do that often. "Indeed, it does," he agreed. "And while you have been deconstructing Olafsson, I have been making preparations for our meeting with the emissary."

With that, he opened a drawer in the table and withdrew a small, ancient dagger, perhaps of Roman origin. Its plain white handle appeared to be made of pearl. He rose, touching the tip of the sharp blade to his index finger as he twirled the weapon in the light of the window. It glittered meanly in his grasp.

His proud grin was replaced by a mask of grunting anger as he suddenly whirled around as if to bury the blade in my chest. His actions were so swift I had no chance to move. I cried out in surprise, but the blade disappeared on contact with my shirt, the hilt of the dagger barely touching me. He grinned once more and began to laugh as he straightened from his attacking crouch.

"I was rather hoping that would happen," he said as he sat back down, tossing the knife to me. I caught it by the handle, lifting one eyebrow in response. "Actually, I knew it would. The tether binding it to him has now been concentrated into the metal, which has been attuned to his magic. The blade will track and harm him only."

I touched the tip to the skin of my palm, feeling its sharpness until it began to cause pain. Then it vanished, leaving no temporary mark or even indentation. "Ingenious," I said. "Did you charm an existing item or is it entirely magical?"

"That is the delicious part," he said, his smile gaining a faraway aspect. "It is the dagger the Old Man used to carry with him for protection before he met Marcus. I've kept it for centuries. We shall leave it sticking out of the body of his emissary for a calling card. It might not strike fear into his heart, but it will prove our mastery of the situation."

"Do we indeed *have* mastery of the situation?"

"The first part of attaining such mastery is assuming it exists."

"You have a plan for the Old Man, then?"

"For his destruction, yes. The method of luring him to that destruction is proving more elusive. My instinct tells me *not* to have a plan. The Old Man has always had a facility for figuring out the most complicated of schemes. Thus, that aspect of the plan may have to be on the fly, so to speak."

"How, then, do we bring about his destruction?"

He again shrugged. I hated his doing that. "Use the research you have done," he said, sounding bored. I hated that as well. "How does one of our kind kill another?"

"Various ways. Draining one of all essence, paralytic spells that prevent feeding, fire—"

He sat forward with a smirk. "Death by fire is the only way to ensure no resurrection takes place, remember? Other methods are possible to reverse. In your dreams of the All-Ocean, have you noticed the mountain at its shore?"

"Just its base."

"If only your powers of observation were a bit keener."

I was tiring of lectures and chidings and planning. I knew it needed to be done, but studying Olafsson's diary had been wearisome and useless, and I longed for the sort of peace and quiet I was unable to find in Seth's company. "My time there is usually spent avoiding being drowned by the cursed being guarding it. Pardon me for not looking up and noting the mountaintop. What is its name, anyway?"

"What?"

"The mountain."

He reached back for his brandy, sighed, and took a long draught. "Must *everything* have some doom-laden name? May we not simply call it a mountain? In any case, the top of that mountain has trees."

"Trees? Are we to bring axes to the All-Ocean and play woodsmen, felling trees for a vampire-killing conflagration? We might as well be Olafsson and build rafts."

"Your droll side is not at all appealing, Warner. And the less equipment we carry, the better. However, I can see your mood grows foul. I believe we need some time apart, so let us feed separately tonight." He drained his brandy and stood up. "I would ask you to drain whomever you feed on. Your damnable conscience will, of course, not allow this, but I ask it anyway. We shall need all our resources for the emissary tomorrow."

"Tomorrow?"

"Of course. I see no reason to delay, do you? You are as prepared as you will ever be. Feed, then rest. Our journey begins."

I usually enjoy the life and vitality of the Quarter, where I fed, but Seth's continual presence was particularly irritating for a solitary creature such as myself. After my meal, then, I opted for the relative peace of the Marigny. Of course, since Katrina and the influx of opportunists tragedy always brings, peace was becoming difficult to find anywhere in the older part of the city. After leaving my prey, I found my way to a small neighborhood place I remembered on the far side of Elysian Fields called—what else—The Neighborhood Bar.

I noticed him immediately when I entered, but he was difficult to miss. His lime-green board shorts and white-soled flip-flops were nearly luminous even in the dim light of the bar, but moreover, his features were exactly like Wade. His hair was the same shade of blonde, and his eyes the same color blue. Even the pattern of hair on his legs and chest, exposed by his open Hawaiian shirt, were the same. He also had the same tufts of blonde hair on his toes.

Momentarily startled, I hesitated the slightest bit then headed straight for him as he broke out in a wide grin. This could be no coincidence. I smelled no brine, so it was not the

Old Man, but neither did I smell Wade's scent. Instead, a curious bouquet of must and old paper came to my nose, as if the being had just emerged from research in an ancient library. I say being because he was not a man. He confirmed that as I approached his table.

Dude, he said in my head, *you're all better*. He signaled for the girl serving drinks by hoisting his pilsner glass in the air. "Another beer for me, honey, and bring a round of absinthe for my bro, here," he said aloud. "Your favorite, right?"

"Indeed," I said, sitting down. "And you are…"

"Eddy with a 'y,'" he replied, extending a broad hand. As we shook, a faint meow came from the black backpack hooked on the back of his chair. He continued grinning, pulling down the flap to reveal a black cat with blue eyes. "That's Pluto."

As absurd as it sounds, I nodded in greeting to the cat, unsure if it was a shapeshifter of some sort. I leaned closer to him. "And *what*, exactly, are you?"

"Same as you, bud." He never stopped smiling.

"I *do* sense a similarity," I admitted, "but a difference as well."

He nodded so enthusiastically, the sunglasses nearly fell off their perch on his shaggy head. "*Now* you're catchin' on. You're all about the music, but I'm all about the words. Words and books."

"You don't appear to be much of a reader," I said without thinking.

Eddy stared at me for a half second, then laughed heartily and clapped me on the shoulder. "Good one," he said. "I *knew* we were talkin' to the right guy. Your *amigo* Seth seems kinda snooty."

The waitress brought our drinks and carried away his empty glass. He picked up his beer up and extended it to me. "Here's to your success, my dude," he said, clinking glasses with me.

An odd toast, I thought as we drank. "You seem to know a great deal about me," I said. "And Seth."

He licked the foam off his lips. "Yup," he said. "And we're kinda interested in what happens to your Old Man."

"We?"

He pursed his lips—or at least I thought he did. The beard made it difficult to be certain. "That would be me and my boss, but we ain't your problem right now. Your Old Man stole a book from us. Bad manners, dude. Not only that, but he's a greedy little fuck. No way we're gonna put up with that shit."

"Greedy?"

"Uh-huh. He's, like, gotten hooked on our essence. It tastes different on our shore."

"*Your* shore?"

"Dude, the Big Sea is just that—big. And a Big Sea's gotta have more than one shore, right? Since you're not the only kahunas ridin' the waves, there's gotta be more than one kind of essence, y'know what I'm sayin'? Well, his don't satisfy him no more, so he's movin' in on our turf. Now, it's not like we got none to spare. Hell, there's a whole ocean of it. But it's the principle of the thing, man. Plus, he stole our book. So, when we heard you were gonna give him the beatdown, we were all about that."

My head hurt. The old tongue was difficult, but this was equally exhausting. It only made sense, however, that different beings of our kind existed. I'd just never met any before. "Let me see if I understand you correctly. Outside of stealing from you, the Old Man has intruded on your territory and intends on usurping your portion of the All-Ocean, so you and another being have come to this realm to…to do *what*, exactly?"

"Well, not *both* of us. I drew the short straw, so the boss stayed home."

I nodded toward the cat. "This is not the…boss?"

"No. That's a cat."

"I see. But you're here to fight alongside us?"

"Aaaahh, no. Not directly. This could be part of the prophecy, and we don't want to fuck that up."

"Prophecy? What prophecy?"

"It's in *The Big Book of Prophecies*," he said, "which your Old Man swiped . Can't remember the whole thing, but it ends up with The Big Sea being ruled by The Wounded One—or Ones—we're not sure. And you're the only wounded one we know about."

"How was I wounded?"

"C'mon. Everybody knows you couldn't feed and almost died. That's gotta be it."

"I hardly—"

"And Seth is *not* your friend." He pointed one long finger at me for emphasis. "Not now, not ever. He's gonna fuck you over big time."

"Is that also in your *Big Book of Prophecies?*"

He drained his beer and brought the backpack up to his lap. "Naw. That's just common sense, dude. Anyhoo, I brought somethin' you might need—s'cuse me, Pluto." I heard the cat purr as he rummaged around in the bag and withdrew a metal box about the dimensions of his palm. He laid it on the table.

"It's a tinderbox."

"For?"

"Regular fire won't light the trees on the mountain, but the lucifers in here will."

"I hope our plan isn't as transparent to the Old Man."

"It's not. He's distracted by our essence right now. He ain't lookin' at shit. But he knows you're comin' for him. That much he can tell. If you'll open your mind up to me for just a sec, I got some spells that might surprise him. And you."

My hesitation must have shown on my face, because he frowned for the first time since I sat down.

"Trust is not easy for me," I said. "Much of what you say appears true on its surface, but I have been gulled before. And you will admit that for a being who claims to survive on literary talent, your usage of slang and idiom are such that your words may belie their meaning."

He rolled his eyes and flickered, and I caught a glimpse of the figure beneath. Not enough of it registered for me to recognize, but I knew it was neither the Old Man nor his emissary. It certainly wasn't Seth. The pentimento, however, brought me a measure of unaccountable comfort.

He leaned over to speak low, in a different voice. "I should not have to tell you how deceiving appearances can be. I have gifts which may save your life and that of your erstwhile friend. I beg you to do me the honor of accepting them."

I nodded, barely noticing his entrance and withdrawl. I could not even tell he had left something behind.

"A couple more things. First, if you get to the Realm and kill him, you might find it a tetch hard to get back here. His absence will kinda fuck up the vibe, you dig? The boss might have somethin' for that, but I don't know for sure. Ain't my pay grade."

"Noted," I said. "And the second item?"

He grinned broadly. "You gotta be the hottest thing I've seen in centuries. Somethin' about your dark eyes and them fine, full lips gives me some serious wood, dude." He reached down to adjust his board shorts. "Mind if I kiss you?"

Before I could think, I smiled. "I'd like that very much," I said.

He embraced me with great tenderness and kissed me sweetly and fully. His lips were soft and yielding, my own erection rising in response. He brought his hand to it and kneaded me as I did the same. I tasted his essence, similar to what I was used to, but with a spicy piquancy different from ours. I could have languished in his embrace for an eternity. We both sighed with satisfaction as he broke the kiss.

"Oh, maaaan," he said. "I'm gonna' dream about that until I see you again."

"Likewise. And I *will* see you again."

"Count on it, my dark dude," he said, straightening up with a smile and flashing me a peace sign. "Watch your back. Peace out."

He and his backpack were gone, leaving me with the tinderbox. And the check.

CB

B ut which of these is the *real* dagger?" I asked Seth the next morning, looking at the two identical weapons on the library table.

Seth closed his eyes and shook his head. "They are *both* real," he said, a tired disgust in his voice. "Are they not both solid? Do you not feel the magic emanating from each? It does not matter which you take. I merely created another and split the spell between them."

I knew what he had done and understood his reasoning, but I was being purposefully dense because it pleased me to vex him now and again. "But why?" I again said to him.

"Again, distraction. The emissary might not expect us to both have the same weapon."

"But I refuse to go into battle with a weapon which does not have the same properties as yours."

He snatched them both up and plunged each toward his chest, the blades vanishing as they touched his skin. "See?" he said loudly, his anger resounding in the quiet of the library. "*Damn* you and your suspicions. Now, take one and conceal it somewhere on your person. We must be underway."

I grinned inwardly as I gestured toward the dagger in his right hand. He held it out, but I snatched away the one in his left and put it in the pocket of my waistcoat.

"Thank you," he said disdainfully as he secured his own weapon. "I hope you'll be less hesitant to use it when the time comes."

"I assure you I'll do what has to be done. Do you have any notion of what happens after the spell is spoken?"

He stepped into the circle chalked on the floor. "I have no

idea whatever, but I would be prepared for anything. Join me, and we shall recite the spell together. Do you know it? If not, I have it written down for you." He reached into his pocket, but I waved his efforts away

"I know it."

"Very well, then," he said. "Are we ready?"

"Ready." I strode into the boundary and we jointly spoke the incantation. No sooner had we finished than the room seemed to tilt. The library around us grew darker until we were surrounded by pitch blackness, yet my stomach felt as if we were in a rapid descent. I took Seth's hand as he reached for mine, but I could not see him in the dark.

We could have fallen for seconds or for forever. My sense of time was as dulled as my sight. My other hand went to the dagger in my pocket, and I wondered if I should draw it. Caution prevented me from doing so. Seth would not have created a second one unless it was to be kept in reserve. His would be the first thrown, of that I was certain.

At length, my stomach stilled and, very second it stopped roiling, the room appeared around us. We were no longer in Seth's library. We stood in a hobbit-hole of a warren, the walls lined with books and papers, light from an unknown source, and a desk heaped with more volumes. And seated at that desk was the emissary, behind a wall of glass. Or so I thought.

I looked to my side and saw Seth also encased in glass and then knew we were in the boxes I had seen in the dark pool the emissary had cast in our initial meeting. *Cha'lan*—the punishment. Except our heads were still attached. For now.

Did you think I was unaware of your intent to track me? That

I would not be ready for an attack?

Seth intoned a spell, then he raised a hand and his *cha'lan* shattered into pieces that flew in all directions, clattering against the side of my own prison. As the emissary frowned, Seth reached for his dagger and threw it with lightning speed. But his target circled one finger in the air, creating a windstorm around Seth that halted his weapon.

The storm intensified the faster the emissary twirled his finger. Still, the dagger remained in mid-air, buffeted by the loose papers and books the storm had dislodged from the chaos of the room. I then heard a voice in my head that was neither Seth nor the emissary.

Has'mich te broma, it said.

I repeated the words, keeping as close to the inflection as I could under the circumstances. Nothing happened.

Step through, it said.

I remained rooted, helpless in my cage.

Conquer your fear, it urged, *and step through.*

Holding my breath, I stepped forward into the room. The barrier was no more than a spider web, a brush of gossamer and then nothing. I was free. Seth's explosion had earned a frown from the emissary, but my escape brought a full-on scowl.

"Damn you," he said aloud. He stopped twirling his finger and clapped once, the windstorm dying down. The dagger clattered to the floor and skittered toward the desk out of Seth's reach. Seth muttered a few words, but before he could finish, the emissary spread the fingers of both hands wide, pointing an arm at each of us.

Blue bolts of the kind we had seen in the alley during our

first match shot out from his palms, encasing us in jagged bonds that squeezed tighter as he curved his fingers inward. Seth grimaced, struggling to raise his own hands to no avail. The emissary then lifted his arms, elevating Seth off the floor of the warren.

Has'mich te weima, the voice said.

Once I repeated the spell, I felt a definite pressure girdling me, but the bolt did not encase me, stopping about a quarter inch from my body. My arms, however, were trapped. I could have freed them, but I had a plan in mind. Intent on making him believe I was suffering as badly as Seth, I screwed up my face in mock pain. The bonds moved up when he attempted to lift me, but I remained on the ground. He did not notice at first, so intent was he on punishing Seth. The bonds were nearly half a foot above where he initially cast them before he caught on.

The emissary's scowl turned to fury, and he snapped his hand into a closed fist. My bonds grew tighter, but only pressed into my clothing. I attempted to portray agony. However, when he again began to raise the arm controlling the bolts, they found no purchase, as if I had been lubricated against their effect. The ruse was up, but his fury and anger resolved themselves into confusion. His attention was so disrupted that Seth began to dip toward the floor.

My chance had come. I slipped my hand into my pocket, freed my arm, and threw the dagger as best I could, not bothering to aim. The weapon was supposed to have been charmed, after all. One would hope it would find its own way to the target, and it did. It struck him in the right side, burying itself up to the hilt.

As the emissary clutched his side, the bolts faded away and Seth dropped to the ground with a surprised grunt. Before I could assist him, he scrambled to his feet and ran to the emissary's body. I met him there, wary of any last-minute trickery on our enemy's part. I saw his ash-white, noseless face gradually fade, replaced by a boyish countenance in turn changing to an Asian man, and then a dark, swarthy female face.

"*B'ren mach*," Seth said. "The parade of faces he has worn in his lifetime."

On and on the faces changed, going so fast I was unable to register one before another took its place until at last they stopped on an adult male in his forties with short blond hair and green eyes. Seth gasped.

"Marcus," he said. "I should have guessed."

The body then began to shrivel, puckering in on itself until its desiccated limbs were drawn askew, and its face was no more than horrible wrinkles. A faint mist rose from it, a cloud of being that dissipated as soon as it gathered and was no more. The dagger lost its hold and clattered to the floor. "Is that what happened to Stacks?" I asked.

"Yes."

That reminder of Seth's perfidy, long undiscussed between us, hung in the dank air of the warren for some moments as we both sank into our own thoughts.

"You did well to duplicate the dagger," I said at last.

"How did you free yourself from the *cha'lan*?" he asked, ignoring the compliment. "You recited a spell, then walked through it as if it wasn't there. I did not teach you that. And his bolts slipped from you like loose ropes."

Before I could respond, I felt his rough intrusion into my mind, prodding and assaulting me like some back-alley rapist—then he was gone. He sat back on his haunches and regarded me suspiciously. "There is a part of your mind I cannot reach. A box I cannot open. What is inside, Warner?"

I drew myself up. "What is inside is none of your damned business," I said. "You have the effrontery to ask me that after forcing your way inside my mind like an enemy? This only serves as a reminder that we have business to conduct once our common goal has been achieved."

He also stood, the conceit of contrition in his eyes. "I saved your life, you ingrate."

"And I just saved *yours*. The only reason you did so was because you needed my help. I have known you for centuries, and I have never seen you act without a motive other than the one you speak. I appreciate you bringing that to my attention once more. Should you again attempt to access my mind without first seeking my permission, I will consider it an act of war and deal with it accordingly. Are we understood?"

He raised his eyebrows, then grinned widely. I knew that grin well and also knew the extent to which I could trust it. "We are, Warner. My apologies. I meant no harm. I must confess to being quite envious of the prowess you've shown in this battle, and I wondered how you managed to acquire your newly found skills."

I felt it best not to confess that or to speak of the conversation I had with Eddy at the Neighborhood Bar, for I was sure it was him—or perhaps even Pluto—who was speaking in my mind. Seth already knew far too much about me for my tastes.

However, he continued to regard me expectantly, waiting for me to explain myself. I declined by changing the subject.

"Perhaps our time would be better spent looking for the door to the All-Ocean," I said with as much finality to the matter as I could muster.

I could not fathom the odd look he gave me before he shrugged his shoulders, apparently relenting. "A girl must have some secrets, eh? You're right, of course. I have the means to find the door, unless you possess a more efficacious way."

"No, no," I said. "Please continue. I have no alternative." None that I knew of, anyway.

"Fine." He then began a recitation of some sort—or incantation—I had never been able to discern the difference.

Look past him, the voice came again.

As Seth concentrated on what he was doing, I did as the voice asked. I focused on a point beyond him when suddenly I saw a change in the air at a certain intersection within the room. It seemed to slide a different way somehow.

There is your door.

Would it be wise to reveal what I saw or withhold it in hopes Seth would come to the same conclusion as to where it was? I'd then not have to reveal I already knew, for surely if we just walked that way, the All-Ocean awaited us. I could almost smell it. Before I could decide, however, Seth pointed to exactly what I saw.

"It is there," he said. "See where it shifts?"

"I do sense some disturbance," I agreed, "but nothing as clearly as you, I'm sure." I tried mightily to keep the sarcasm out of my voice. "Lead on."

The way he fairly strutted forward told me I'd made the right decision.

The wall we faced was difficult to describe. Perhaps the best I could manage was the unhinging of a crosshatch, its edges blurred and distorted. Although the voice did not say so, I felt an urge to enter as I stood in front of it. I'll wager Seth felt the same pull.

"Shall we walk forward with linked arms?" I asked, grasping his.

He gave a me a weak grin. "It couldn't hurt."

We stepped through.

∞

The smell of the brine brought back some unpleasant memories, as I had expected it to, but nothing more. My fear was gone, replaced by a curiosity at the scenery before me. Everything was black, yet somehow delineated and differentiated. A three-dimensional ebony, if you can imagine a myriad of shadings and distinctions within a single color. For truly, I saw nought but black, but I saw life within it.

I saw stars in the sky. I saw the sand on the beach. I saw the foam on the waves of the essence rolling in on its glistening shores. And it was all black. Every single detail. With the greatest of anxiousness, I lifted my hands to my face nearly afraid of what I might see. And I beheld the hair on each knuckle—all black and moving against blackness.

As was Seth. His very form and outline. The face of my savior yet my greatest enemy in its most exacting distillation. And yet as black as that which surrounded him. I was astounded, but the whole made as perfect sense to my brain as would any earthly landscape. Made entirely of black.

I could have wept for its beauty.

Seth appeared to be looking around, lost in the same wonder. "What world could this be?" he said, the awe resonant in his voice.

"Ours," I said, becoming accustomed to the brine the more I beathed it. "Does it not feel like home?"

He shook his head. "I'm not certain I have a home any longer."

The sound of the surf washed softly under all, and I saw the All-Ocean. Its vastness was inestimable, its waves as graceful as a dance of life. And behind us rose the mountain, immense and foreboding. A gentle breeze stirred.

"Where do we go?" I asked.

"You have the artifact, do you not? You were the one with the affinity for it."

I fumbled in my pocket, finally feeling the warmth of the compass in my palm.

"We have no idea where the Old Man would be, so I cannot visualize anything like his lair. I suppose I shall have to think of him." I swallowed my revulsion and fixed an image of him in my mind, beholding the swirling surface as it resolved itself into the depiction of my worst nightmare. That soon vanished, replaced by the image of a cave outside a wood.

I opened the compass, which pointed to the right. We both looked in that direction, discerning the beginnings of a trail up the side of the mountain. "There is a trail to the right," I said.

"I see it."

I started out, but he held my shoulder and sought my gaze. "Please understand how grateful I am for what you did during our battle with the emissary, no matter the origin of those skills. You have become a formidable magician, Warner. One I regard as an equal."

I'd hoped for better than that, but I accepted his sentiments as well as his compliment with a smile and a nod. "Let's go," I urged.

&

The path meandered up the outside of the mountain gently at first but then grew steeper. More than once during our ascent I stopped to gaze out at the All-Ocean for a moment, always taken aback by its immense volume and how merely being within its sight was as refreshing as a month's feeding in the earthly realm. I knew not how I could ever leave it or even why I would want to.

"Once the Old Man has been deposed," Seth said alongside me, the path sometimes being wide enough for us to walk abreast, "this will be our land to rule. You know that, don't you?"

"Who says it needs to be ruled? Why may it not simply be—and us with it? Your need for possession is alarming."

"It is land," Seth dismissed. "It must be ruled. Who better than us to do that?"

"Careful not to plan too far ahead of yourself. Our task is not small. Do you have any more specific idea about how to accomplish it? But even before you answer that question, let me pose another. Do you even *feel* his presence? Shouldn't we?"

He stopped as if to sniff the air. "I take your point," he replied after a moment. "It feels…unguarded. Is he absent? Where else would he be?"

Feeding his new thirst, the voice told me. *But he knows you are here.*

"I cannot say," I told him. "I only know if we both feel it, he must not be here. Perhaps if we hurry we might gain the top of the mountain before he returns. I feel exposed on this cliff."

"What does the artifact show you?"

I pulled it out as he looked back and drew close. Once again we saw the cave in the wood on the cover before it resolved into a tableaux wherein a path much like the one we were following blended into the trees at the top. When we opened it, the arrow pointed straight ahead. "Ahead, then," I said.

In less than half a mile, we came upon the very site. I will admit to some relief at being able to duck into the trees, yet I regretted losing view of the sea. I had grown quite attached to it.

The trees, however, were another matter. As we could see no color other than black, the tangle of lines and curves confronting us was more difficult to process than the simplicity of the seaside. The more I looked at it, however, the more sense it made until it, like the rest of the environment, bore a normalcy it shouldn't have had.

To complicate matters, the trees themselves bore sharp thorns as large as a human hand and grew close together, creating a veritable forest of immovable blades at odd angles. I took great care to not risk injury and so slowed to a snail's pace. Seth was hastier and paid the price as he received a scratch from one of the thorns across the back of his neck.

"Damn," he said, hissing as he explored the area with his hand. "It barely touched me."

"Let me see." We stopped, and I examined the wound, which was no more than a simple surface injury, not even bleeding. "It doesn't appear to be serious," I said, "but you should slow down. We will get there when we get there, although I would like some time to look around his lair before he returns."

He gestured to the artifact. "Do you really think that's where it's leading us?"

"I have no reason to suspect otherwise. Do you?"

"I suppose not. Check the image again."

I pulled the compass out of my pocket, watching as its surface once more resolved into the cave in a clearing of the wood. I fixed the position of the trees surrounding the tableaux in my mind, and then I opened it. The arrow pointed dead ahead. "We are on the right course," I said. "Just be less hasty."

As the trees continued to crowd in on each other, we picked our way with less confidence, planning our moves well in advance. In this way, we covered no more than a half mile in the next few hours, but determining time was difficult in the solid black atmosphere. I hoped it would get easier.

With great caution, we were able to escape further injury and eventually came to a clearing which looked much like the one on the compass. When I removed the object to compare them, the image—which had been clear the last few times I'd checked—was now scrambled, refusing to re-form. "The artifact appears to have reset itself," I said, "so this must be it."

"It doesn't look like the Lord of the Land lives here."

I regarded him with some skepticism. "The Lord of the Land, is it? Unless I'm mistaken, you've just created a title you now wish to inherit."

"I merely meant it was…unprepossessing," he said with some vexation, his hand going to the back of his neck. "Warner, please look at this again. It seems somewhat irritated."

He bent over and, to my surprise, the scratch had deepened a good deal, perhaps a quarter inch or so. The edges of the wound were now pulled apart from each other. However, no blood issued forth. The fissure appeared dry, crust forming on the very edges of the skin. I described as minutely as I could what I saw to Seth.

"How peculiar," he said.

"It must be some sort of…" I was going to say poison, but I thought it best not to alarm Seth.

She'lath, the voice said, without expounding on the word. Intuiting this was curative in nature, for it sounded soothing, I touched both edges of the wound with my fingers.

"She'lath," I said. Gauging the effectiveness of my intuition was difficult as I could not distinguish colors and so could not notice either redness or its absence, but the edges of the wound drew closer together and Seth began to calm. For a moment.

"What did you say? What did you do?" he demanded.

"I do not know. Truly."

"More of your magic box, I'll wager. No matter. It feels much better. Thank you, Warner. You continue to amaze me." His gratitude was barely noticeable, wrapped in as much jealousy as it was. But even Seth's plain gratitude was somewhat transitory, usually wrought by some feigned motive or other.

"Let's move forward into the clearing," I said. "I would like to stand erect and not have to think about where to place my feet or move my shoulders for a change."

"Why not? He doesn't appear to be home."

I felt marvelously unimpeded as I stepped out of the trees, not caring if Seth was behind me. He overtook me, however, rushing carelessly toward the cave. I hissed him back. "Surely this isn't how you hunt prey?" I said. "Don't be too anxious to claim your throne, my Lord of the Land. You might find a spike or two on its seat." I delighted in his glare.

"After you, then," he said.

He remained behind me as we approached. As grand as Seth's observation was, its accuracy was unerring. The outside of the cave was simple and plain, hardly an abode in which a being of the Old Man's position would have dwelt in the earthly realm. It didn't even have a door and so was open to the elements. Inside, we found nothing out of the ordinary—a bed of straw, a small table, and what appeared to be a naturally vented fireplace. The interior was cramped and crabbed, and we both had to bend over to enter.

"Humble," I said at length.

"Your talent for understatement remains intact," Seth sniffed. "I do not see so much as a scroll, let alone any tomes of magic."

"And why would you be looking for a tome of magic?"

"For inspiration, if you must know," Seth said, puffing out his chest, as if daring me to challenge him. "I hate to admit it, but I have been at a loss to come up with a solid plan for his defeat so far. I sought to find something I could turn against him, but this—" And here he gestured with his arm. "—this paucity of resources is not helpful."

Seth's sneer had barely faded when I felt a luminous presence growing somewhere outside. It filled my consciousness rapidly, and even Seth stopped poking around and listened. "He returns," Seth said.

"And quickly. We should get out."

"Why bother? He already knows we're here."

I felt that as well, so we stayed in the entrance to the cave, our gazes intent at the forest opposite as we believed he would emerge from there. But he simply appeared in front of us. He *wasn't*, then he *was*. He looked much the same as when I'd seen him in dreams—however, those dreams had been, for wont of a better description, in color compared to the blackness in which we were now enveloped. The being in front of me had no shade other than black, yet I saw every detail as plainly as I had in my dreams. As if we had entered a hyper-dimension.

"Welcome," he said in the raspy voice I so well remembered from that night in the Chelsea. I could no longer smell the brine, however, and I had seen the bastard so often in my nightmares, his flaked and withered countenance was as ordinary as my own. "Let me make you more comfortable."

He twitched a finger, and an explosion of color and brilliance suddenly conquered the dark. We stood in the middle of a beautiful, richly appointed dining hall with comfortable-looking chairs surrounding a well-laid table. The smells were tantalizing, but the sight of such vivid colors was too jarring after the unrelieved blackness I was quite longing for at this point. I attempted to shield my eyes with my hand. "Less contrast," I said.

The Old Man smiled, if you could call the upward movement of the tattered skin around his mouth a smile, then the brightness of our surroundings faded until I could see comfortably. As my eyes adjusted, I now saw the Old Man had a hole in his shoulder. It was approximately two to three inches in circumference, its interior jagged. You could, however, see clearly through it.

"My apologies," he said, sweeping past us and sitting at the table. He waved us into seats as well, Seth at his left and I at his right. He also gestured toward several serving dishes and a decanter of red wine. "Help yourselves," he said. "Your journey through the forest must have been debilitating."

I could not stop looking at the cavity in his shoulder. Its effect was as jarring as I'm certain he intended it to be. Nevertheless, I poured myself a healthy draught of wine, and Seth followed suit. "Are we still in your poorly appointed cave?" I said, "or is this an illusion?"

He shrugged, somewhat like Seth. I could see the family resemblance in that respect. "Perhaps my poorly appointed cave is the illusion and this the reality. I see you've noticed my little reminder of our last encounter."

"It's difficult to miss."

"Isn't it, though? The sewer system in New York City is

full of metal appurtancences that jut out at odd angles. My fall impaled me on some sort of girder. Had I not expended so much energy during our battle, I might have been able to recover a bit sooner. I would have vanquished you, you know."

"Perhaps."

He smirked. "In any case, I decided not to heal it. It makes me think of you. Please do have something to eat. It's perfectly safe, I assure you."

"This must be the part of the plot where you're kind to us," I observed, marking my speech with drink, "for whatever reason."

"Oh, you *know* the reason," he said. "You reek of the other shore. Of its magic. But then again I notice it much more readily as I am currently enamoured of it."

Seth had stopped his glass mid-air. "The other…"

"…shore," the Old Man finished for him. "Surely, you didn't think this was the only shore on an ocean of essence, did you? There had to be others—peopled by beings different from us, of course, but essentially the same. Did you meet them in the earthly realm or here, Warner?"

"So, *that's* what's different about you," Seth said, not giving me a chance to respond to our host. "Another shore. Different magic. Of *course.* How could I have been so stupid?"

"Stop talking," the Old Man told him. "You factor little in the remainder of this episode as you were injured on those poisoned thorns. Your time is limited. The wound will grow, becoming deeper and more purulent as it eats its way through your body. At some point you will expire." He shrugged again.

They really were quite alike.

"Warner has cured it," Seth said defiantly, "with a healing spell from the other shore."

The Old Man grinned. "Has he, now? The poison occurs naturally and is not of my making, so I cannot tell for certain. My sense, however, is that he has only slowed its effects. What should have been a quick death might now be slow and more painful. Who can say? Your end may be marginally interesting but no less final."

Seth's face bore a curiously neutral expression. I did not know if he was taken aback by this turn of events or simply disbelieved the Old Man. I hoped he wasn't depending on me to cure him. I felt I should need more than soothing words, but I did not have time to ponder the matter.

Without warning, I felt the Old Man's intrusion into my head. Seth's treatment had been rough, but nothing like this forced entry. The pain was sharp and mighty and all-encompassing. I had never felt anything like it before. I more than winced. I bent over double and nearly vomited the wine I had just drunk. But after a few seconds, it was gone.

Oddly enough, the Old Man seemed to be in as much pain as I was. He gave a loud cry as if he had been stabbed, rubbing his temples and fixing me with a baleful glare. "Damn you," he said with a hiss. "How did you—" He shook his head as if to clear it, then he looked me in the eye and I again began to feel the pain. This time, however, it stopped as soon as it had started. He cried out once more and reeled away, his eyes rolling back as if he'd been slapped. He fairly leapt out of his chair.

"I *will* break you," he said. "I will have your secrets or your life, you miserable wretch. One or the other." He angrily waved both arms in a wide circle and was gone—as were the table, chairs, and other accoutrements. We were back in the dismal cave, or should I say flat on the ground outside its entrance, bound in chains that felt as if they reached to the very core of the land. And I was held as fast as Seth.

"That did not go as I had hoped," Seth said.

"Indeed."

"I hope you can find something to extricate us in your bag of tricks. I feel quite unwell." The poison had once again taken hold, and I could see the wound from the thorn, previously on the right side of his neck, now peeking from the left as he thrashed about. It was suppurating, dampening the ground beneath him. He was paler than normal, sweating profusely.

But Seth's condition didn't alarm me as much as the fact that the voice I had been hearing in my head ever since our arrival at the All-Ocean had fallen silent. I felt bifurcated, as if my consciousness had been secluded in the attic of a house, everyone else on the floor below. I could feel its faint presence and, in my fevered imaginings, thought I heard a muffled sound, but its distinctness, its proximity, was quite far away. Its absence panicked me, and I struggled against my chains for a few moments to no avail. In time, I purposely calmed myself, attempting to assess the situation clearly.

No sooner than I had regulated my breathing than we heard a tearing, wrenching groan in front of us. I raised my head, as did Seth, to find the poison thorn trees unearthing themselves, raising their roots out of the ground as a boy on the beach might free his half-buried feet from the sand. Soil fell from their underpinnings as they moved toward us on earth-encrusted limbs. I could feel the voice in my head, louder but no more distinct. It seemed to be shouting at me, but I could not understand it. I panicked once more.

"For God's sake, Warner, they are coming for us. Is there nothing you can do?"

My panic turned to impatience. "You're the one who's been giving me lessons—is there nothing *you* can do?" If I'd have had my hands free, I would have slapped him, wound or no.

He seemed chastened and sobered by my anger. I could tell he was as frightened as I, but he creased his brow in thought. Five of the damnable trees had uprooted themselves. They marched toward us apace, having a distance of perhaps twenty or thirty yards before they would be upon us. And as they moved, their thorns did as well, sliding from their trunks down to their roots, poised to pierce us.

I looked over at Seth, who grew paler—whether from fear or poison, I do not know—but he stopped thrashing and raised his head slightly. "I can try to slow them," he said. "*Mol'hep toch.*"

His words had no discernible effect at first. The trees continued their journey, their trunks now bare of the poisonous thorns. They had all gathered on the roots, clawing up the ground as they moved inexorably toward us. The trees had covered perhaps three quarters of the distance before Seth's words slowed their speed. He had bought us time, but not much.

Meanwhile, the voice in my head grew more urgent but no more understandable. However, it seemed to have multiplied itself, mounting into a chorus of wild, disorganized sound. The cacaphony slowly metamorphized into a steady rhythm that ebbed and flowed, much like the breath of the Old Man when he tried to suffocate me in the Chelsea Hotel. In my mind's eye, I pictured the voices breaking against the barrier holding them from the side of my brain that would recognize the words, reforming and again crashing against the obstacle.

I tried to picture that barrier weakening, but I was distracted by another part of my mind registering Seth's increased agitation. Indeed, I looked to my side and found him thrashing even more wildly than before. His mouth was open, and I could see his vocal cords straining, but the noise in my head was so loud I could hear little else.

Again and again the voices swelled and broke on the shield, coming back louder and more forcefully with each try. My heart began to beat in the same rhythm, my breath matching both. I looked up and saw the trees were upon us. All I could see was slick, black wood and the tangled roots above us like feet, their thorns glittering deadly ebony as they descended, and the voices reached a deafening pitch. Suddenly, all was silent and the words came to me with crystalline clarity.

I gave no thought but repeated exactly what they said.

"*Ben'ai misch!*" I fairly screamed.

The foot-roots stopped mere inches from our bodies, and the chains that bound us to the ground disappeared. Careful not to scratch myself on their thorns, I scuttled backward to safety as did Seth. We both jumped to our feet once out of range, but Seth's adrenaline rush had expended itself. He staggered and fell.

I rushed to his side, sickened by the smell from his now festering and ugly wound. It was far deeper, eating into his neck and shoulders. I attempted to recall the healing phrase, but he waved me away. "I am beyond anyone's assistance," he said. "I can feel the rot in my body. This will be my end. Our task rests with you. But, please allow me to begin the blaze we had planned. How—or even *if*—you use the fire, is entirely your choice, but I will have my revenge on this damned forest."

I nodded and stepped away from him.

He uttered a rather complicated invocation, and I could not at first determine if he was actually casting a spell or cursing the instrument of his demise. At length, he raised his arms, wincing from the pain in his shoulder, and shouted the last few words. Brilliant arcs of orange and yellow flames burst from his hands, all the brighter as they were the only color visible in the black world to which we had come.

The flames engulfed the five trees that had threatened us. I could hear their crackling roar, but they did not illuminate our surroundings. They were mere streaks across the eternal night. He maintained them for some minutes, such was his anger. His face paled with the effort, though he wore a determined grimace of pain and fury.

When he ceased, the trees remained unscathed.

Seth groaned and fell back. He scooted against the cave wall and sobbed. "I have failed. Failed you. Failed us. Failed myself."

"We may not yet be lost," I said, reaching for the tinderbox in my pocket. I opened it, finding flintsteel, charcloths, and a few matches. I hoped for some words of encouragement from the voice, but it did not even offer instructions. It had been silent since the utterance of the spell which saved us.

I approached the trees warily. They had not moved since our escape, and they remained still, even when I grasped a root and shook it, carefully avoiding the thorns. My hands somewhat shaky, I struck one of the matches against the side of the tinderbox. A blue flame burst from its head, which I then held to a piece of the charcloth, igniting the fabric. The flame gathered strength and when it was finally ablaze, I hung it over a slender portion of the root and grabbed more charcloth from the box.

Before I had even set the second piece alight, the first had caught the root, its bright blue changing to a faint yellow. By the time I had hung pieces of charcloth over the roots of all five trees, the yellow flame was licking the trunk of the first. Presently, I heard a low moan—from where, I did not know. Perhaps Seth.

I closed the tinderbox and looked back at him, still slumped against the face of the rock. His head lolled as if he was asleep, but he straightened as I approached. His eyes grew wide as he beheld the trees. "How..."

Holding up the tinderbox, I knelt down beside him. "This came from the other shore as well," I confessed. "I apologize for the deception, but in your own words, misdirection is our greatest ally."

The stench from his wound was overwhelming. "Indeed it is," he said. The creases of his mouth turned up in a faint smile I could see by the flicker of flames behind me.

I turned back to find all five trees ablaze with a yellow flame that actually pierced the incessant darkness, illuminating their brown trunks and green leaves, all of which were being devoured by the fire. Suddenly, the low moan I'd heard had increased in volume as well as fervor, nearly to the pitch of a scream.

And, in seconds, it rose to just that as the trees which had assaulted us began to move again, this time backing away from the clearing, the blackness returning as they retreated twice as fast as they had advanced. The fire reached the lowest branches of leaves and soon their crowns were incendiary. The screams turned to shrieks as they reached the remainder of the forest, and their blazing branches caught the leaves of the other trees. Mere moments later, we had just the conflagration we had hoped for.

Seth grinned weakly amidst the wailing of the trees. "My revenge," he said. "Thank you, Warner. You have been a far better friend than I ever was to you. I know my apologies mean little…"

I knelt beside him again, suddenly recalling the healing phrase. I put my hand on the wound once again. "*She'lath.*"

The potency of any spell may be doubled by the addition of m'kah, the voice said to my immense relief. It was not gone or expended or depleted or any one of a hundred fates I'd feared.

"*She'lath m'kah.*"

When I took my hand away, the wound was no less deep, but the suppuration had dried a bit. "How do you feel?"

"Somewhat better," he said, mopping his fevered brow with the edge of his cloak, "though I doubt I will be of much assistance to you."

"As usual," the Old Man said from behind us. Seth looked up, and I turned to face him. He stood near the trees, the fire beyond him visible through the hole in his shoulder. "You were never particularly useful when you were a child, and your adulthood is not much different as far as I can see. Warner, on the other hand, has some potential. He seems to have made short work of the forest, in any case."

"Compliments make me uneasy," I said, raising my voice to be heard above the screaming of the trees. "Especially when they come from those who have tried to kill me."

The Old Man cocked his head as if he couldn't hear. He looked over his shoulder with some annoyance, raised his arms, and the trees fell silent. Or at least we could no longer hear them. "We would make a formidable team," he continued. "I felt your strength during our last encounter, and it has only grown with your experience."

I was not about to shout across a clearing. I strode forth, fixing him with a cold glare. "Stop dissembling," I said. "You would say or do anything to obtain the secrets of the other shore. If not for those, I would be worthless to you."

"And yet you would partner with the man who killed your best friend. Or have you forgotten?"

"I forget nothing," I told him as I approached. "And I partner with no one. Seth has much to answer for, and we will have our own battle once this one is complete."

The Old Man snorted. "If you both live. He's nearly dead from the poison thorns, and you are sorely trying my patience. That's close enough. Come no farther." He brought up his palm and raised a shield about twenty feet away. It shimmered, obscuring my view. With a bit of concentration, however, my eyes adjusted, and I saw him clearly once more.

Walk through it, the voice said.

I did so without hesitation, feeling no more than a slight tug as I passed. "You're going to have to do much better than that," I said.

He danced around the edges of my mind but could not enter, and I did not stop advancing on him. I did not know the source of my confidence and surety, only that I felt it in every part of my body. Was it the voice? Was it my cause? No matter its origin, I judged its effect by the uncertainty in the Old Man's cold, dead eyes.

A look of desperation crossed his face, and he cast red bolts directly at my chest. They bounced off as if I wore a suit of armor. He seemed dumbfounded and tried them again with the same effect.

But being dumbfounded was not going to kill him. Although my confidence was high and his magic had no effect on me, I still had no offensive spells to cast and was at a loss to deliver a killing blow.

We are peaceful, the voice said. *No such weapon exists for us. But you have all you need to accomplish your task.*

All I had was the fire.

Take that which he values most—or make him believe you have.

Misdirection. Illusion.

Think it, and it shall be. Be'la mech.

I do not know if I or the voice thought of the plan. I almost felt as if we were one. But as he tried the red bolts a third time, I looked out over the ocean of essence spread out to my right, and I knew what I must do.

"Like Seth, you waste your energy on useless actions," I said to him. "Had you conserved your resources, you might be able to do something like this. *Be'la mech!*"

I faced the ocean of essence and imagined it churning and whirling, forming a whirlpool which then inverted, drawing itself up into a huge waterspout. The ocean of essence rose up in the air, leaving its barren bed a deep, dry welt on the land. It roiled and coiled high above, the wind from its vortex whipping the flames from the trees higher and higher. And then it rushed straight for us, compacting itself, concentrating itself, balling itself up into a sphere no more than a foot across that flew into my hands.

The Old Man's face was a mask of horror. He looked toward the dry bed, as did I, but I do not think we saw the same scene. For I saw the outline of the ocean still there, its whitecaps lapping at the shore—while at the same time, it was gone.

The master of illusion sees both what is and what is not.

The Old Man turned his gaze back to me, open-mouthed. "Put it back."

The illusion spun and whirled in my hand as I smiled at him. "I don't think so," I said. I dipped my hand into the ball of ocean and stepped closer to the glowing embers of the roots, feeling their heat. I threw a handful of liquid on them and heard the hiss, smelled the burning essence.

"NO!" he screamed. "Do not destroy the All-Ocean. I'll... I'll do whatever you say."

"I want nothing from you," I said, "except your death."

Transfixed by the ball of essence, he could not speak although his mouth moved. I glanced back at the cave, curious as to whether or not Seth saw the same thing, but he was no longer propped against the stone. He had disappeared. I could not let that break my concentration, however.

The Old Man's eyes were still on the essence. "But how will we—how will *you* feed?"

I'd been waiting for that question. "I care not. If I perish, so be it."

He groaned.

"You are finished," I said. "Your age is done and another dawns. *Starve.*"

I hurled the ball into the white-hot embers of the fire and, as I expected, the Old Man shrieked and dove into the inferno as if he could rescue it. When he hit the tree, I heard a crack from above. His impact had jarred a half-burned limb loose, and it fell squarely across his back. His screams rivaled that of the tree as he twisted and thrashed. He had managed to turn himself over, and I saw his disfigured, smoking face staring up at me through the flames. His tatters were on fire, but he continued to struggle, heaving upward against the limb, then suddenly I saw his face change.

B'ren mach. It was almost finished. The faces turned slowly at first then sped up, all races blurring into one colour until at last it changed to a very familiar one. Fair, with blue eyes and blonde hair.

Wade.

"Help me, Warner," he screamed. "For God's sake, *help me.*"

I swear by all I hold sacred I lost my head for a moment. It did not matter that he had gulled me with that face before, I put a foot out and tried to roll the log off him. He had nearly thrashed and wriggled himself past the limb, and his *b'ren mach* had ceased with Wade, who was still pleading with me.

"Die, you miserable bastard!"

Seth appeared from nowhere and grabbed him, forcing him back into the heat of the fire. He put his hand through the hole in the Old Man's shoulder and held him down, his own cloak now ablaze. I could smell singed hair and skin as Wade's face was replaced by another and another and another until finally the Old Man turned to ash.

I rushed to Seth's side and grabbed his pants, dragging him out of the fire and turning him over on the blackened ground. His burned and blistering face changed rapidly.

"She'lath m'kah," I said as calmly as I could. I doubted a healing spell would work properly if said in haste, but I had no time to lose. His faces continued their parade. I tried again, this time putting both hands on his body.

"She'lath m'kah," I repeated. As soon as I had uttered the phrase, I felt a warmth stir through my body and out my hands. His b'ren mach ceased, and his face was as I remembered it once again, albeit altered by the fire. He was not conscious, but he still breathed. Another of the burned limbs fell inches from us.

"I've got to get you out of here," I said to no one. I looked back at the cave, which was a cave no longer. It was a respectably large castle, not as ostentatious as I would have thought, but a big enough shelter. Now I knew which was the illusion. And at that thought, I looked out toward the ocean of essence, which was back in place, lapping at the black, sandy shore.

As I grabbed Seth's legs, I looked across his body at the pile of the Old Man's ashes and wondered if I should scoop some up and put them in my pocket. For what purpose? I asked myself, immediately discounting the idea. Taking a souvenir could be dangerous. Better to leave them. Scatter them, in fact. I kicked the ash around. Satisfied they could not recombine in some fashion, I resumed pulling Seth away from the fire.

I took him into the castle, wrestling him onto a divan just inside the doorless entrance. I would find a more suitable place once I looked around. I thought the voice might come again, if not to give me some direction in healing Seth, then to congratulate me for vanquishing the Old Man. But the last was nothing but hubris, and I banished the thought from my mind.

As far as healing went, I had the phrase well in mind and would use that in addition to whatever else I found in the Old Man's lair. I was certain I could glean much from what looked to be a library off to the left. But first, I had to tend his burns and perhaps journey down to the shore and bring back some essence for him to drink. That might help him recoup his strength. Or at least bring him to consciousness. Whatever measures had to be taken, I would take. After all, he had done the same for me. And when he was well?

I would kill him. Just as I had vowed.

THE LORD OF THE LAND

have the most amazing recuperative powers, don't I, Warner?"
Seth asked me one day while we were enjoying a fire and a
snifter of brandy in the library. The Old Man had a very fine
cellar. He bared and lifted his arm. "You'd never know how
badly burned this was, would you?"

I would because I'd wrapped it and bathed it in essence
for the three weeks he was unconscious and the week when he
was awake and grateful. I was less successful with the wound
from the poison thorn, which had healed but left his neck and
shoulder resembling the result of a botched beheading.

However, I said none of this. "How is your research coming?
Have you yet found a way back to the earthly realm?"

He shook his head. "I have found quite a few rare volumes
about our kind, of which I'd only heard rumours, but nothing
helpful. You're certain you have nothing in your bag of tricks?"

"No, I'm afraid not." I remembered what Eddy had told me
about "the vibe," but I was loathe to disclose to Seth that since
the Old Man was dead we might not be able to get back. "You
have tried the spell which brought us here?"

"Yes, of course. It must be a one-way ride."

His constant complaining about the darkness was becoming bothersome. Even more bothersome was the disappearance of the voice, which I had not heard since our battle with the Old Man. Maddeningly, however, I could feel its presence. I was not alone in my head, but that portion of it was silent.

Seth got up and paced in front of the fire. "There *has* to be a way back. How did he buy these most excellent vintages? But this library does not contain a single volume about magic. Surely someone as powerful as he would have a few magical volumes lying around instead of all this history and philosophy. Are you certain this is the only room with books?"

"You are as ambulatory as I. We have been in all the rooms there are and taken inventory. Shall I count them for you? The ground floor has the kitchen, the library, the dining hall—"

"Yes, yes, I know." Suddenly, he stopped pacing and fixed me with a hopeful look. "The *compass!*" he said, more animated than I had seen him in some time. "Do you still have it?"

"Of course."

"Well, fetch it," he said. "I think some experimentation is called for."

I snapped the Emerson I was reading shut, wondering when I'd been pressed into involuntary servitude, and left the library without a word. Seth was becoming more irritating with each passing day. He was haughty, imperious, demanding…I stopped with one foot on the stone staircase and took a deep breath, closing my eyes to collect my thoughts.

Considering how much I had to gain by losing him, I would be wise to use all my resources to help him find his way back. If I occasionally had to suffer some indignity, well that was that.

Once he was gone, I'd finally have some peace. Perhaps the voice would come back. It had not said as much, but I was inclined to believe it never really liked Seth anyway. Thus resolved, I blew out my anger and frustration and ascended the stairs with a measure of calm once again.

I paused on the landing to look out the window. The view of the All-Ocean and the black landscape never failed to fascinate me. It soothed me in a way no earthly vista ever had, for it was not—as Seth said—an unrelieved blankness. It had shading, it had detail, it had movement, it had *vitality*. More's the pity if he could not see it.

I should have killed him. Once he was fully recuperated, we should have had it out. I owed it to Stacks. But I could not bring myself to do the deed, even though he would have killed me had our positions been reversed. However, I had not the heart for it. Stacks. The Old Man. So much destruction. And without his assistance during the battle, the Old Man might have deceived me into freeing him using Wade's face. It would be better if he just left, and I ought to be concentrating my efforts to that end.

I took the rest of the steps with a lighter heart, or at least a thicker skin, reaching the top and crossing to my room on the left. Seth's quarters were to the right, and in the middle was a small sitting room with a few overstuffed chairs, another fireplace we rarely used, and a large oval window with much the same view as the one on the landing. This one, however, showed the burned and ashen forest. But during a recent walk, I noted black seedlings sprouting from the charred stumps, except where the Old Man's ashes were scattered. Nothing grew there.

The compass was in the small writing desk in my room. I

snatched it up and put it in my pocket, feeling the outside face shifting against my palm, never settling into an image until I thought of one. I then hurried back downstairs to Seth, waiting eagerly in the library.

I held it out to him, but he did not take it.

"It's *your* artifact," he said. "It seems to respond well to you."

"Very well," I said. "What am I to envision?"

"A magical book."

"And how am I to distinguish a magical book from any other book on these shelves? They all have bindings and covers and pages. Perhaps the one you seek is decorated with glittery stars and half moons. Shall I fix that in my mind's eye?"

"Your wit astounds me," he said with a glare, tapping his chin with his forefinger. "Perhaps instead of a book, we ought to be seeking a small room. You're right, of course, to think it's nowhere we've looked. It might be a hidden library somewhere. One as cautious as the Old Man would not have kept something so valuable out in the open for visitors to find."

"*What* visitors? We're in a forgotten castle on the shore of some magical realm. It's not like we have Jehovah's Witnesses knocking on the door twice daily."

"Who?"

"Never mind," I said. "So, you want me to think of a small, hidden room with books and papers and the like?"

"That's right."

"I shall try."

"Wait, let's not do it in here. Perhaps we should try it out by the stairs so as not to confuse it with this room. If it points back here, we'll know it's wrong."

I followed him out of the library next to the stone staircase, then I thought of a small, hidden library. No sooner had I the image in mind, than the swirling gold face of the compass resolved itself into a picture fairly close to the one I imagined. I opened it up, and the arrow of the compass pointed to the stairs on the northwest wall.

"Curious," I said. "But the kitchen is on the other side of that wall. There is not space enough for a room." I closed the cover and looked at the image once again—a small room with a chair and books and papers on a small desk beneath an oval window.

An oval window like the one in the second floor sitting room between the bedrooms.

Seth blathering questions behind me, I bounded upstairs and stopped in front of the door to the sitting room. I opened the compass again, and the arrow pointed straight ahead. But the wall beneath the window was blank. "Look at the picture on the compass," I said, ignoring what he was going on about and holding it up for his inspection.

He steadied my hand with his, and I nearly shuddered at his touch. "It's the very same window," he replied, letting go and shoving past me into the room. He began feeling his way over the wall, examining the stones. "It must swing out from the wall—there has to be a catch here somewhere."

In a short time, he'd exhausted the immediate area to no avail. Thinking the trigger mechanism was hidden in plain sight, I looked to the uppermost portion of the wall but saw nothing suspect. When I searched the area near the floor, however, I noted a stone which didn't fit quite right about four or five feet to the left near the sofa. Ignoring Seth, I walked over and nudged it with the toe of my boot.

We heard a click, and a panel in the wall slid up, popping out the small writing desk I'd seen on the face of the compass.

"See?" he said to me. "You have a knack for this sort of thing. You're a very clever fellow, Warner. Despite your shortcomings."

I didn't ask him to elaborate. He had busied himself perusing the spines of the volumes stacked on the small shelf atop the desk. It contained about twenty volumes of varying thicknesses, most of the titles in the old tongue and some barren of any markings on their spines at all. I picked up one of these, a dull brown affair, and as I slid it past its companions, I heard the voice in my head once again.

That was stolen from us.

I was so unused to the sound that it startled me, a reaction that did not escape Seth's attention. "What is it?" he asked immediately, looking up at me. He had taken down one of the books and was examining the index. "Did you recognize something?"

"No, no—not in the least," I said.

"Why did you jump so?"

He must not know it is from our shore.

"Did I? I believe your imagination is taking over." I shrugged and put it back in its place as if it was of no consequence.

"I have no imagination," he said, holding out the volume he was looking at. "This is interesting. The Old Man appears to have written it himself. I recognize the hand."

Seth's words swooped meaninglessly in and out of my ears. I wanted to hear the voice again, regardless of what it said. My heart had leapt up so. I wanted to talk to it, share with it, ask it questions, but Seth spoke so loudly and so insistently, I could not concentrate. And as I wanted to appear normal, I could show no consternation.

Seth snapped the book shut and gathered the half closest to him up in his arms. "Well, come on," he said. "I'm not going to study these in here. Let's take them into the other library where the fire is already laid. Can you take the other half, or shall I come back for them?"

I took the rest of them but feigned an accident, the books falling to the floor in a fluttering of pages. Seth clucked his wicked tongue. "Do take some care, Warner," he cautioned. "These are ancient and may be easily damaged. Now, pick that lot up and come along."

As he strode out, I picked up the rest of the books and stopped in my room, putting both the compass and the brown volume from the other shore in the writing desk. He would never miss it.

CS

knew those books would keep Seth quiet. Indeed, I saw no more of him for the rest of the day. He even declined to walk down the mountain as we sometimes did to feed at the shore. The essence from the ocean was the purest I'd ever tasted. Of course, that meant I would not have to listen to him complain about the darkness, which was preferable. I told him I would make the journey alone.

"Aren't you in the least curious about what is in these books?" he asked incredulously.

"Curious, yes. Obsessed, no. I have not the enmity you have toward this realm. I quite like it, in fact. I find it peaceful and relaxing and have no desire to leave."

"Of course not. You have your friends on the other shore. I'll wager you would not help me even if you knew how. Just leave me, Warner. I will attempt to figure it out as best I can."

Not help him? I spent weeks doing just that. I longed to point out his ingratitude, but what would that serve? Instead, I did as he wished. I left. Getting out of the castle would do me a world of good. I went up to my room to fetch my cloak. Seth had brought the other shore to my mind, not that it was ever far away from my thoughts.

I opened the drawer of my writing desk, took the compass and the book Eddy had bade me return and tucked both in an inside pocket of my cloak. I did not trust him not to search my room, and the book would cause questions and, perhaps, even a confrontation. The time was not right for such a contretemps.

As always, I looked at the backs of my hands as I left the castle and emerged into the darkness of the land. All color disappeared from my flesh and became one with the blackness, yet I still saw the detail: the fine mesh of skin cells, the map of veins, the cuticles of my nails. It was indistinguishable from its background yet differentiated. I found that fascinating and never tired of it. Seth merely found it depressing.

I threaded my way through the burned husks of the thorn trees, already, as I have said, regenerating themselves quickly. The black saplings rising from the stumps even had protuberances of nascent thorns on their stems, and I wondered if this generation would be as deadly as the last. I firmly resolved to stay and find out. Even if Seth should find his way back to the earthly realm, I was finished with it. I would not be returning.

The path down the mountainside was steep at first, but I had long ago gotten used to its incline. I used its solitude and the comfort of the ebony night to search once again for the voice inside my head, but it had fallen silent after it warned me not to reveal the book's existence to Seth. Would it always remain a voice only to be heard for some *reason*, some *purpose*? I devoutly wished to converse with it, to listen to its secrets if it had any, to become at least as familiar with it as I was with Seth's voice—a damnably poor substitute.

Where Seth's speech was nasal and whining with more than a hint of entitlement, the voice from the other shore was calm and honeyed, speaking with the resonance of reason and reflection. It was not a voice of haste or half-measures. But most of all, it was not false, a far cry from Seth's dissembling. It had never lied to me or told me a half-truth.

I reached the end of the trail and stepped onto the black sandy shore of the beach. From there, it was but a short walk to the edge of the All-Ocean. Its heady brine filled my senses. No longer a harbinger of the Old Man for me, it carried the scent of life itself and I marveled at how I could ever have been sickened by it as I was when I could not feed.

As was my habit when I came down to the ocean to feed alone, I simply disrobed and bathed in the essence. The Old Man's tattered and papery skin notwithstanding, I felt it had to be good for me. Though I could see no improvement—it was no fountain of youth, after all—neither did I see harm, and its warmth was a source of comfort to me. I set my clothing and boots on a nearby flat rock and waded in.

My hunger sated and my body nourished, I padded out of the ocean, its moisture only remaining on my skin for moments before it was absorbed. I was dry by the time I reached my clothing, though my hair was still a bit damp. I pulled on my pants and my boots and threw the loose shirt over my head. When I snatched up my cloak, the book from the other shore fell out of the pocket.

Though it remained closed, the edges of the pages emitted an odd blue glow. They had looked gilt inside the castle, but out here was another matter. I picked it up and held it close to my other hand, seeing something close to its flesh color instead of the blackness which surrounded me. Curiouser and curiouser, I thought. The glow can pierce this atmosphere. With some trepidation, I opened it to a random page.

The letters—or characters, for I could not discern their origin or meaning—glowed the same color, brightly enough to illuminate the page itself. But as I looked at them, like the front of the compass, they swirled and jumbled themselves, finally coalescing into what resembled the Old Tongue. I read no more than a few words before they again rearranged their patterns, into English this time. But once they had solidified, they then again changed into the original symbology.

This must be returned this to us, the voice said to me.

"I understand," I said aloud, as speaking the words seemed more like the conversation I wanted to have with the voice, and

Seth was not around to overhear. "But how?"

You must bring it here.

"I would like nothing better, but, again, how? Is there some spell I might use?"

I heard some low rumbling, which sounded for all the world as if the voice in my head was conferring with someone else. At length, it ceased. *The book should have returned itself. It may be fixed, but we are not prepared to unlock those secrets for you.*

"Why? Have I not proven myself?"

Your companion has not.

"Seth is hardly my companion," I said, aghast at the thought they, whoever they were, might believe the two of us were allied now that the Old Man had been dispatched.

We are aware of your differences, but his curiosity is strong and his capacity for treachery evident. We do not wish to leave anything to chance.

"Then we are back to the beginning. How am I to return this to you?"

You will travel to our shore.

At first, I took umbrage at their not trusting me enough. The more I thought about it, however, the more I realized I would relish the adventure. Seth would be too busy trying to find his way back to the earthly realm. By the time he realized I was gone, I might be halfway there. "Is it far?"

We do not know. We have never undertaken such a journey.

"You speak in the plural," I said. "Is someone with you?"

All will be clear in time.

"When should I leave?"

Now.

"Now?" I repeated. The voice was silent at that. Even though I hesitated, I could not think of a valid reason to delay my departure. I had my walking boots on as well as my cloak for warmth. I had no need of food or drink as an ocean of essence was at my disposal, I had the volume in hand, and Seth certainly would not notice I was missing for some time—not that I owed him an explanation of my absence in any case. He would become curious, but I would be long gone by then.

"Very well," I said. "Which way shall I go?"

Left.

And so, I began my journey.

⊛

cannot say how long I walked because the celestial bodies, if that indeed was what those were, never changed position. The faint, suffused light which always shone, for lack of a better word, allowing me to differentiate the shades of blackness was of little assistance in either regard. It came from no specific point and simply *was*, as fixed and unchanging as the ocean of essence or the ebony shore it lapped.

A timepiece would have helped, but I could not recall seeing one anywhere in the confines of the castle. This was in perfect keeping with the solemnity and eternity of this world. To overlay the concept of time here would have been vulgar. Past, present, future, counting the moments, passing the time—all were superfluous and somewhat absurd amidst the constancy of its darkness and the ceaseless, gentle rolling of the waves.

I walked until I was spent, always keeping the shoreline to my left. The land mass on my right rose and fell in some arcane topography. At times, it vanished into a level plain and at others, it rose so majestically tall I could not follow its line as it blended into the eternal darkness of the sky. I saw no creatures, no other souls. When I could walk no more, I rested against either the land mass if it was tall enough or one of the flat rocks that occasionally poked up on the beach.

I had walked and slept seven times before I heard Seth in my head. And that was a peculiar conversation, or rather it wasn't a conversation at all. I could not respond to him. I awoke to the sound of his voice, almost like a recorded message. And I found I could access his words whenever I chose.

So, you've gone journeying, eh? he'd said. *To your friends on the other shore, no doubt. I wish you'd consulted me before you left, but perhaps it was better this way. We were getting on each other's nerves. Not to worry. I probably shan't be here when you return—if you indeed return. I have found many worthwhile spells and though none of them have opened an earthly portal, I suspect something shall turn up. Not that any of this interests you. I have other revelations for you as well, but we shall speak again. Eventually.*

Other revelations, indeed, I thought. And I'll wager he left none of those books for me to peruse. Though, to be fair, he was not certain I would come back. I didn't even know that myself. I began to wonder when I would reach the shore I sought. I tried to ask the voice, but it had again gone silent. I was not about to give up, so my only option was to stay the course.

Refreshed after a morning dip in the All-Ocean, I began the

days' trudging. Hitherto, I had kept a wary eye on the scenery for changes or creatures or anything hinting of danger, but nothing had come my way. The landscape was that beautifully unrelieved blackness, nearly poetic in its ceaselessness. The land mass rose and fell many times before I again slept, nestling this time in a small natural notch in the rocky outcropping.

I felt the sun long before I awoke.

It had, in fact, become part of the dream I was having. I was face up in a field of wildflowers, their colors and scents colliding and clashing as bees droned overhead. Everything was bathed in the brilliant, warm light I had nearly forgotten existed. The change was welcome, the blazing sun stirring my spirit in a way the darkness, though beautiful and stately, could not.

As I came to consciousness, however, I felt the same heat on my cheek and forehead. Instinctively, I buried my head deeper in the wadded cloak I'd been using for a pillow, but then the realization struck, and I opened my eyes.

Luckily, the beach was still very dark sand; otherwise, I would have had to squint much more than I did. Even so, I had to raise my hand to my forehead and shade my eyes. The ocean of essence was a deep azure color, smelling much the same but with a hint of spice I did not recognize. And up in the sky, the sun beamed.

I shifted and looked to the right, where I felt a presence. I saw the sole of a bare foot, crumbed with grains of black sand at the heel and toes. It was attached to a tanned, hairy leg and that leg was crossed over another. I heard a chuckle as I was handed a pair of sunglasses.

"You better put these on, dude. Your eyes ain't used to the

sun yet."

Grateful for the relief, I donned the eyewear and saw Eddy sitting in a tattered lawn chair, his cargo shorts and white t-shirt stirring in the faint breeze. He wore a New York Yankees ballcap over his brown curls along with a pair of shades and a lopsided grin shining out from his beard. He looked breathtakingly delicious.

"Welcome to our shore," he said, gazing out over the All-Ocean, or rather—what had he called it again? The Big Sea. "It's gonna be another beautiful day."

"It's very...sunny."

"That it is," he replied. "It's always sunny. Y'know how your shore is always dark? Well, it's the opposite here."

"But it was dark when I went to sleep and now it's light."

He grinned again. "Tellin' the truth, you ain't exactly in the same spot. You were close to us, so we thought we'd just nudge you a little. Bring you to us." He jiggled his foot, some of the sand falling from it while he dug the toes of the other one in further. "It's cool you could come," he said shyly. "Glad you dusted the Old Dude, man."

"Thank you. If it hadn't been for..." And then I realized his was the voice I had been hearing in my head. Oh, the language was different, but it was clearly his. Calming and restorative, yet forcefully assured. "It was you, wasn't it?"

"What?"

"In my head. During the battle with the emissary and again with the Old Man, feeding me spells and words—and you persuaded me to bring the book here."

His sole jiggled even faster, and his grin got a bit wider.

"Well, yeah. You brought it, right?"

"Of course." I sat up and unfolded my cloak, spreading it across my lap so I could access its pocket. As I grasped the volume, I noted its warmth. It could have been my body heat or the sun. Perhaps it was my imagination, but it seemed… happier? I shook off the feeling and handed the book to him.

"Thank ya kindly," he said. "I got somethin' for you, too." He put the book in his backpack, which rested against the stone on the other side of his chair. Pluto meowed and stuck his head out of the main compartment, yawning and blinking at the sunlight as Eddy rummaged around. "Here ya go," he said, handing me a bundle. "Shorts and a t-shirt—and a Yankees cap like mine. Shake out the cat hairs first. I got a pair of flip-flops somewhere, too. That black outfit of yours is gonna get mighty warm in a couple hours. Figured you ought to get comfortable. You *are* gonna stay a while, right?"

"My mind has been so focused on getting here," I said, "I have not thought much about what I was going to do once I actually arrived. But I see no harm in staying a while. In fact, I'd like that very much."

"Me too. Tell you what—why don't you take your morning dip and then change, and I'll make us some breakfast back at the shack."

"The shack?"

"Well, the cave actually. It's not far. How's an omelet sound? Maybe with some bacon. You're not veg, are you?"

"Veg?"

"Vegetarian—as in you don't eat meat."

He spoke with dizzying speed and processing his words

quickly enough to maintain conversational momentum was difficult at best. I could only hope I'd grow quicker in time, as I found him charming. Challenging, but charming. "How do you know of my morning ablutions?"

"Hell, I do it too. Let's feed, and then we'll eat. Gotta use up what food I have left before it spoils. This essence is a little different from what you're used to, but I think you'll like it. The old dude sure lapped it up." As I stood, he took off his cap, jumped up from his chair, stripped off his t-shirt, and let his shorts fall to the sand. Totally naked, he had a fine, furry body with a prick that, even soft, was large enough to jut out from the mat of hair surrounding it. I felt my own stiffen.

"Admirin' the view, huh?" he said, smiling. "Well, get nekkid and join in." And he dashed away into the All-Ocean, his hairy buttocks disappearing beneath the waves.

I tried to stuff my carnal thoughts away as I struggled out of my boots and shed my black, long-sleeved, full-length garments, which were indeed becoming uncomfortably warm under the hot sun. When I removed my underclothing, I had the most complete sensation of freedom I believe I'd ever experienced.

My appetites had returned, the Old Man was dead, Seth and his malcontented treachery were miles away, and a smiling companion awaited me in a cool surf of pure essence. All the dread and work and plotting and counter-plotting of the past few months had evaporated under a beaming sun. The most genuine smile I can recall since the affair with Wade crossed my face, and I laughed and ran full bore into the essence.

You got to flip it just right," he said, loosening one end of the omelet from its moorings. The spatula slid noisily in the cast iron skillet as Eddy crouched down by the fire, twisting his hairy torso for a better vantage point.

We were out in front of a natural cave some yards away from the edge of the All-Ocean. Unlike the Old Man's disguised abode, however, Eddy's cave had an actual door on hinges, though it did not fit the opening well. But building materials were the last thing on my mind as I watched Eddy from behind. I had cut a piece of my own omelet and speared it with my fork, but I was so distracted I had yet to bring it to my mouth.

"There we go," he said, picking up the empty plate beside him on the sand and sliding the contents of the skillet onto it. He stood up and turned around in such a quick, fluid motion that he caught me staring at him. "Don't wait for me," he said with a smile as he settled into the beach chair next to mine. "Dig in. Wish I had some potatoes or fruit or somethin' to go with it, but the cupboard's kinda bare. Wish I could stock up."

"Where exactly do you stock up?" The omelet— cubed ham, mushrooms, and cheese—was simple but magnificent. I couldn't remember the last time I had actually eaten food, but it had been ages since I had sated any appetite other than revenge. "Surely these ingredients cannot be found around here."

"You got that right," he replied around a mouthful as he scratched the thatch of hair on his chest. "Can't grow nothin' in this sand or on the rocks. And if somethin' does sprout, the sun just burns it up. I used to be able to open up a portal to get to the Von's in San Ysidro, but that's all over now. Gonna have to do without. Don't get me wrong, we're glad the Old Dude's dead, but like I was sayin' back in the Neighborhood Bar, it really fucked up the vibe. Makes things a helluva lot tougher. How's your omelet?"

"It's sublime."

He inclined his head. "Thank ya kindly. It's hard to tell when you're the only one eatin' your cookin'."

"Your companion does not eat?"

"Companion?" He looked around and then pointed to Pluto, who lazed in the shadow of the beach chair. "Him? Well, he gets some scraps once in a while, but that's about it."

"No, no. You often refer to 'we,' and I had assumed at least two of you were together in this land—unless you *were* referring to the cat."

"Gotcha," he said. "It's kinda tough to explain. I'd have to go back to how I got here."

"I should very much like to hear that tale." As I put my now empty plate on the sand, Pluto wandered over and sniffed at it, daintily licking a few morsels from its edge.

"Lemme get rid of these," he said, getting up and shooing the cat away as he took the plates inside.

I turned to watch him walk away. I couldn't see his

rump in those baggy shorts, but I remembered quite well how firm those hairy mounds looked. My member stirred so in response, I had to adjust it. I marvelled at my own randiness as well as how Eddy incited it. He caught me, smirking a bit before he sat down again.

"Lemme see," he said. "We gotta go back to Baltimore, 1849. I was a big shot writer, but I was always broke 'cause I had some problems—namely laudanum, opium, and brandy. I was a mess. Brilliant, but a fuckin' mess. Plus, I was one gigantic asshole. I pretty much pissed off everyone I knew."

"How?"

"They were all no-talent charlatans," he said, lowering his voice in mock seriousness. "And every time I published an article, I trashed a few of 'em. Thing was, I ran out of enemies and couldn't find any worthwhile friends to feed off. Well, there was George Lippard, but he was a bigger asshole than I was. No protegés. My peers all hated me. Wouldn't even talk to me. I used to have to go down to Richmond and feed off the more talented university students. I couldn't get a decent meal."

"Would I have known your work?"

"I'd be damn surprised if you didn't." He cleared his throat and recited. "Once upon a midnight dreary/While I pondered, weak and weary/over many a quaint and curious volume of forgotten lore..."

"*You* were Edgar Allan Poe?"

He nodded. "Your humble servant. Anyhoo—"

"Now, wait," I said, holding up my hand. "I must stop

you and ask something."

"Shoot."

"If you are, indeed, Edgar Allan Poe—and I'm not *disputing* that, mind you—why is your mode of expression so different?"

"Because it's not 1849 anymore," he replied. "I like slang. It's colorful, it gets right to the point, and it's fun to use. See, words are not your thing, dude. Notes are. They're fixed and unchanging. A B-flat in 1849 is the same B-flat as now, but speech is liquid. It's gotta fit the times. It's gotta play to the audience."

I pondered that a moment, but he continued before I could respond.

"It's like when I'm in your head, I use another voice, right? One without slang. One you understand. One you *believe*. It's all in the delivery, bud."

"I see." And I rather did. "But I apologize for the interruption. Please continue with your tale."

He clasped his hands behind his head, the scent of clean musk wafting from his furry pits as the change in the topography of his skin hid his nipples in his chest hair. "Well, see, it was late September, and I was on the way back home to New York City from one of those trips to Richmond. I also went down there to get money to start a magazine, and I was feelin' pretty good 'cause I got some backers and some bucks. Anyway, I got to talkin' with this dude on the boat. Smelled his talent somethin' fierce. Said he worked for the *Baltimore Sun* and had to get back to cover the election. I woulda taken him right there on the boat, but waaaay too many people were around. So, I got off in Baltimore with him."

"Did you feed?"

"Hell, no. I tried, believe me, but my battery was so low, the glamour wouldn't even work. And to top it all off, we both went on the bender to end all benders. Said he wanted to have a couple drinks with the great Edgar A. Poe, but we didn't stop with alcohol. Cocaine, opium, laudanum—you name it, we spent my money on it. Usually, my constitution could take it. You know how it is. But I was weak, and all the partyin' didn't help. From there on, things got kinda fuzzy. I lost the reporter dude somewhere and passed out in the street. Someone found me and took me to the hospital. That's when shit started to get real."

I could usually follow what he was saying through context, but I must confess the last had me puzzled. "Get real?"

"Yeah." He became more animated, unclasping his hands and leaning forward. "I kept going in and out of consciousness, no idea what was goin' on. I know they called for Doc Moran, and I remember him checkin' me over and askin' questions, but I don't even know if I said anything he could understand. Anyway, I suddenly saw this bright light, and I thought *this is it*, right? I'm checkin' out for good. But then this blinding, brilliant white light starts talkin' to me."

"What did it say?"

"It said, *Your work will be immortal, but you have squandered that privilege for yourself through dissolution and decadence. Would you like another chance?"*

He sounded exactly like the voice in my head. "What was your answer?"

Raising his hands palms up, he looked around. "Whaddya *think*? I had to swear my allegiance, though. Make a few promises."

"Such as?"

"Lemme finish one story first, dude. So, as soon as I agreed, a big silver portal opened up. The light went inside, and I followed it. We came out into the blackest night I ever saw. I mean, solid black. But I could still see details, like the waves of the Big Sea. Weirdest goddamn thing I ever saw."

"You have described my shore."

"Yup. But before I could say anything, the light shot past me and set itself up in the sky right where it is now. And the night became day. So, when I say 'we,' I mean me and him. He Who Shines."

"Is that what he asks you to call him?"

"Nah. But it's kinda catchy, innit?"

I smiled. "That's only to be expected. You're a wordsmith, after all. But if I might ask one more question, I promise to stop being so inquisitive."

"Fire away."

"You look nothing like the renderings I've seen of Edgar Allan Poe. Was that image artifice or is this?"

"Good question," he said, rubbing the stubble on his face. "I'm one of those dudes who likes to change bodies every once in a while. Never saw much point to shapeshifting. Takes too much energy, so once I'm in a body, I don't leave it until I change again. Poe's was shot, man. Bad liver, brain tumors, substance abuse. I found this one in San Ysidro. Cali boy. You like?"

"Very much."

"Thanks. You ain't bad lookin' yourself, Dark Man. Handsome, I might even say. I seen you runnin' nekkid into the surf. You got a fine body and one of them long, skinny dicks, don'tcha?"

I am not dumbfounded often, but I could only grin in response.

"I thought so," he said as he stood up. I saw the bulge in his shorts as he stepped over to me, ran his hand over my chin and tipped my head up. "I got a feelin' we're gonna get into some trouble later," he said. He kissed the top of my head.

☙

assisted him in cleaning up after our feast, scrubbing the plates and skillet with black sand, then rinsing them in the All-Ocean. We let the fire go, for the rising tide would extinguish what few embers were left. Even a conflagration did not last long in this atmosphere, no matter whether the realm was dark or light. We carried the cookware and our chairs back up to Eddy's cave.

"Sorry 'bout the mess," he said in apology with his hand on the knob of a standard door with additional lumber nailed to its edge, raggedly sawed off to fit the opening. Mostly. "I don't get much company. Hell, I don't get *any* company."

As he opened the door, Pluto sauntered past us, headed for the All-Ocean. The cat stopped at the shoreline and began to lap at the pools of essence left by the tides. "Is he one of us?" I asked. Anything was possible.

"Don't rightly know. All I can tell you is one day I asked He Who Shines for a companion 'cause it gets pretty lonesome out here with no one to talk to. The next day, Pluto kinda wandered in. Been here ever since. He seems to live off the essence, so maybe? There's some things I just don't question."

He busied himself putting the supplies away while I took stock of the medium-sized room, partially illuminated by the light from outside. I saw a surprising number of acquisitions from the earthly realm, probably brought in before the Old Man's death, efore the Old Man's death had altered "the vibe".

A large mattress on some sort of raised platform took up most of the farthest, dimmest wall. Next to it on the left was a rickety set of shelves holding cookware, utensils, and containers of food Eddy was busy rearranging, his back to me. The opposite wall was host to equally ramshackle shelving with quite a number of books, some professionally bound but most stitched together by hand. Next to this, closest to the entrance, was a desk littered with notebooks, papers, pens, and pencils.

Most of the bound volumes had no writing on them or script too small to read without more concentration. I withdrew one of the hand-stitched ones and opened it to a table of contents in flowing script, reading a few of the titles: "The Crystalline Entity," "The Rubric of Being," "An Ecclesiastical Tale," and "The

Resurrection and Banishment of Roderick Usher" among them. It then struck me that I was looking at Edgar Allan Poe's most recent work, unpublished and unseen by anyone except myself.

"Hey!" Eddy said, snatching it away from me. He regarded me with some distaste for a few seconds, as if he had been violated in some way, then his face softened. "Sorry," he mumbled, returning the volume to me. "It's funny. I used to write to be read. Now, it all seems kinda private, if y'know what I mean. You can read 'em if you want, though."

"No, no," I insisted, putting it back in its place on the shelf. "The fault was mine. I should have asked permission before poking around your private library."

He reached past me, took it out again, and handed it to me. "I'd be honored to have you read 'em," he said, the shaggy smile returning to his face. "Even though I know these'll never see the light of day, I still have to spin a yarn every time I get an itch. Got some new poems, too," he said, stepping over and pointedly closing the open notebook on the desk before putting it away in the center drawer. "Work in progress," he said with a shy grin.

"I totally understand, and I'd love to read your most recent work—tell me, is it written in the language you currently speak, or is it of a piece with your older writing?"

"It sounds like the old stuff. Style is style, I guess."

"From the titles, the subject matter still seems to be the same."

He laughed. "I can conjure up dread on the sunniest of days," he said as he stepped toward me, put his hands on my face and drew me closer. "But there's only one thing I wanna conjure up right now."

He kissed me softly, barely breathing as he caressed the contours of my head with his hands. I could not only taste but feel the spice, the piquancy of his essence. This was much different than that of our shore, and I could see how it could become addicting. But perhaps it was Eddy who was becoming a habit I could not break. Moreover, I had no desire to. It was not merely his essence, however. It was his wit, his charm, his unique outlook; it was how the essence was filtered through his body and through his scent that enticed me more than anything.

I returned his caresses, combing his beard with my fingers. It fascinated me. My own body hair and beard growth was sparse, and I'd always been envious and excited by those who could grow full, lush beards like his. I broke the kiss and pulled away just far enough to begin unbuttoning his shirt and feeling the pelt on his chest.

"You like that, don'tcha?" he breathed in my ear. "That rug's all yours, dark man."

I stroked it gently and then roughly, finding his ample nipples within that forest and tweaking them with my thumb and forefinger. He whimpered softly and hugged me tighter, grinding his fat, erect member into my own hardness as he shrugged out of his shirt and it fell to the black sand. I reached around and dug inside the back of his cargo shorts, running my hands over his fine, furry cheeks before I pulled him closer.

He chuckled gently. "Ass man, huh? That's cool. Got a lotta cushion for your dick to be pushin.'" He groped my stiff member. "Mmmhmm, just like I thought. Long and skinny. My favorite kind."

Eddy sank to his knees, joining his shirt on the sand as he

pulled down the board shorts he'd given me, the head of my cock jutting out and brushing his beard. "Handsome cock," he intoned. "Lookit that big ole head." Without warning, he took me into his mouth, bringing his hand up to caress my bollocks. I ground my toes into the sand and made a concerted effort to keep from expelling then and there, but even at that I could not prevent a breathy groan.

I grabbed his head. "If you don't stop, I will fetch."

He smiled. "Been a while, huh? I get it."

He tongued my shaft instead, which allowed my rise to subside a bit. But he eventually worked his way down to my sack, tickling my thighs with his beard as he again grabbed my cock and began to pump. My rise again built quickly, and I removed his hand gently but insistently.

"I believe it is my turn," I said. "Stand up."

He did so, dropping and stepping out of his cargo shorts. His cock may have been stubby, but it was rock hard and hot, and its girth was tremendous. I could just fit my hand around it, and his bollocks were huge, hanging low. They were delightfully pendulous, and I could not help but caress them with one hand. Unlike me, he was circumcised, and its head was already dripping. I lapped up his nectar, then took him into my mouth, nestling my nose in the tangle of his pubic hair and inhaling his musk while I fondled his balls.

I bobbed up and down on his cock, using my fist for even more friction until he began breathing heavily. I slackened my pace, giving him as good as he gave me until I could sense his rise. "Crouch on your hands knees on the bed facing the wall," I commanded.

"Yes, sir," he said with a smile. "I do love a man who tells me what to do."

I wish that area of the room had been lighter, because the sight on the bed was truly magnificent. Eddy's perfect buttocks, ample and hairy, framed that marvelous hanging sack and his rigid prick, which swung ever so slightly back and forth as he moved. Gods, how I loved that view. Innately masculine yet beautifully vulnerable. I lost my sense of composure, not that he had left me much to begin with, and approached stroking myself.

Kneeling on the rug he had placed in front of the bed, I took his cheeks in both hands and spread them ever so gently apart, exposing his tender, moist hole. I drew closer and closer, marvelling at his hairy skin, and running my nose up and down the crack of his ass, breathing in his tang. When I could hold off no longer, I explored the wrinkles around his hole with my tongue. I sucked and licked at it until I had to unhand myself lest I come too quickly and spoil the fun.

Eddy panted and moaned, backing his hole into my tongue and squirming. "Jesus, I could shoot right now. Fuck me, Warner. For God's sake, fuck me."

He was wet with my spit, but my prick was dripping. I straightened up, making contact with his entrance with the head of my cock amidst our moans. I rubbed up and down his crack until I thought I might fetch, but at last I entered him. He gasped and backed up even more, murmuring unintelligibly, but I needed no words. He was as lost in the sensation as I.

I buried myself deep in his guts, amazed at the tightness and warmth encasing my cock, and then I began to fuck him with long, powerful strokes. It did not take long before my rise started once again, but this time I let it mount. I picked up speed, my own heavy breathing lost to Eddy's guttural groans of pleasure. It might have been five minutes or five hours I was fucking him. Time had become secondary to the come which was surely on its way.

And then it was upon me. I came hard and copiously, never feeling such a release in my life, and after I withdrew, ropes of come were still pumping out of my cock. Eddy flipped over, his prick red and angry. I grabbed it with my hand, still slick with my own seed, and began to stroke him. It didn't take long for him to buck and whine and then he spurted his own semen, which shot forth with such strength, it hit the wall behind him, leaving a trail of come down his beard and chest.

I sank down beside him, still panting with my efforts, as was he.

"That was better than I dared imagine," I said, turning over and covering him with my sweaty self. We kissed for a long time before letting go.

He shook his head. "*You* are better than I dared imagine."

e slept, then made love again, then slept more, not really knowing what time it was or when the day was over since Eddy's realm was constant light and mine was constant dark. Despite the vague cast it gave my life, I enjoyed losing the constraints of modular time. It was very freeing. When we grew hungry, however, Eddy built a fire out of thorn tree logs, and he again made us omelets.

"Gotta use this all up before it goes bad," he said. "This is the last of the eggs, but the ham should be good for a while. I wish I could stock up. I'll miss my food, but it's okay." He patted his stomach. "I could stand to lose a few pounds anyway."

"I assume you've already tried casting a portal back."

He nodded, then stretched out his arm. "*B'emnet ardum to'bach.*"

I looked in that direction, noting a shimmering in the atmosphere, much like the disturbance of a heat wave. A faint outline of an arch coalesced, stayed for a few moments, then disappeared.

"See? It blows," Eddy said.

"What difference would the Old Man's demise have made?"

He dished up our food. "Beats me," he said, handing me a plate. "The best I can figure—and this is just a guess—is that your Old Dude put some kind of global enchantment over this whole world that let us portal out and in. When you croaked him, that enchantment went with."

"It was not so before he came?"

"Dunno. That was waaay before my time. He Who Shines might know, but when he speaks to me, it ain't exactly an information exchange kinda thing."

"Really? What is it?"

His countenance grew serious in a way I had not yet seen, almost bordering on fearful. "I don't think we oughta talk about it," he said. "How's your omelet?"

"It's fine, but…" He silenced me with a beseeching look, and although I craved more information about this being, I never finished my thought. It hung between us as we ate in silence, undissipated until he spoke.

"So, what about you?" he said.

"Me?"

"Yeah. I mean, you know who I am and how I got here. Who are you and how old are you?"

"I am not as old as Seth, whose lineage goes back to Roman antiquity. Did you know his father was the Old Man?"

"I believe I heard somethin' like that, but I'm more interested in you. Did you come from po'folk?"

"Hardly. I was born Henry Grey in 1405. My father was a British Peer, the fourth Baron Grey of Codnor. I took my present appellation when I emigrated to America in…oh, when was it again—the early 1800s, I think."

"Who made you?"

"A handsome but vile creature named Snavely, referred to me by the nearby Vernon family as a tutor for my rather witless namesake, Henry. This was a few years after I returned from the Second Battle of St. Albans."

"A soldier, huh? That where you got your taste for men?"

I grinned. "As we both know, that particular trait comes from birth. I often had dalliances, especially when making war, but I was expected to marry and produce heirs. And speaking of that, history does not record Edgar Allan Poe's predeliction for men," I said.

"Now, you and I both know history ain't what it's cracked

up to be. Anyway, go on with your story."

"Snavely endeared himself to me through our mutual interests in both alchemy and music. I was quite proficient at the lute and dulcimer—any stringed instrument, really. One evening whilst conducting a smelting experiment, he made pretense to kiss me. As I said, he was a fetching fellow, and I did not resist. Oddly enough, I felt more than the usual amount of suction and, even more oddly, he expelled air into me, or rather a sweetness I could not define. Then, he sat back with a smug look on his face. 'You are one of us, now,'" he said.

"He actually said that to you?"

"Indeed, he did. He then proceeded to tell me not only about the 'gift' he had given me, but he also said it was courtesy of the Vernons, with whom I'd had a land dispute long settled in my favour by the courts. I thought him daft and told him as much. Such beings did not—*could* not—exist. He laughed, snapped his fingers, and vanished into thin air."

"Did that make you believe what he said?"

"Of course not. Though his sudden disappearance gave me pause, I simply could not put credence in his words. Surely it was some flight of fancy on his part and his 'disappearance' a misdirection of sorts. But then he missed Henry's next lesson and the one after that. And I began to crave essence, wasting away no matter how much food I ate. In desperation one night after yet another unsatisfying meal, I disguised myself with an old cloak and hat and rode into a nearby town. I located a busker with little trouble. He was not a comely lad, but his talent with the recorder was evident. Besides which, I could *smell* it. I paid the boy handsomely and bade him ride with me to the outskirts of town for a private audience."

"And then you took him."

I nodded. "In all senses of the word. He actually seemed to enjoy the buggery—I suspect he was no virgin in that area— but I'll wager he had not counted on his talent being stolen as well. For my own part, I felt rejuvenated. That's when I knew what Snavely had told me was all too true."

"What did you do?"

"What any man in my position would. I raised an army and sacked the bastards. I turned out all left alive, but Snavely had been gone for weeks. I'd heard a rumour he'd been seen in Nottingham, so I turned my attention there, only to find my admittedly hasty actions censured by King Edward. I never did find Snavely, not even in Ireland, where I later gained a post. And therein lies my sad tale."

"Sooo, you are quite the badass, dark man."

I shrugged. "I *was*. I no longer lust for battle or revenge or pursuits which harm others. Six centuries of at least partial repentence for the sins of my human adulthood have taught me patience and forgiveness among other things."

"Among other things like how to fuck," Eddy said, standing up to take my plate as he ran his hand along my crotch. Again, I hardened at his touch. He was insatiable and I seemed to be making up for lost time.

"I knew how to fuck before," I said with a grin. "I've just had six centuries of practice."

"Amen, brother."

CB

did not notice at the first, and I really cannot say when it began, but our idyllic happiness lasted until the sun began to dim—and with it, Eddy's mood. It started simply, with a sharp word or phrase here and there, but as the light in the sky turned perceptively gloomier, he became subject to bouts of despair, if not outright anger I was unable to cajole him out of. He complained of headaches, and I sometimes observed him walking along the shore of the All-Ocean, seemingly in dialogue with someone, but no one was at his side. Our lovemaking stopped altogether, and we passed the days in tense silence.

When confronted, however mildly, he assured me it was not I who had brought on this change, but new love brings with it a feeling that you and you alone are responsible for even the most subtle shifts in the tenor of your relationship, and so his words went unheeded. This went on for what seemed like an interminable length of time until one day he finally approached me, his backpack over his shoulder.

"I gotta go up the mountain," he said. The sun was so low, the sky looked grey and stormy. Pluto peeked meekly out of Eddy's pack without meowing. Even he had grown silent.

"At this very moment?"

"Yep. Been puttin' it off too long."

"Very well—let me fetch my cloak."

"I didn't say 'we.'"

"You intend to leave me behind? What am I to do in your absence? Surely you could do with the company if your journey is long."

"You haven't even read my stories or poems yet. You could do that without me lookin' over your shoulder. Maybe even check out the *Big Book of Prophecies*."

I must admit to snorting derisively. "Read? If I wanted to read, I would have stayed at the Old Man's castle with Seth. I fail to see why I cannot accompany you."

"Because you *can't*, that's all."

I remained silent, looking at him. He ran his hands through his hair.

"Look," he said. "Remember I told you there was a price to pay for bein' rescued? Well, it's time to do that."

"Fine, but let me go with you. If we are to build a life together, should we not support and assist each other?"

I felt his anger and frustration building. "Maybe some other time, but not now. I ain't used to this new—" And here, he closed his eyes and furrowed his brow as if in pain, nearly doubling over as he raised both hands and clutched his head. "*STOP!*" he cried, sinking to his knees in the wet, black sand. Pluto ducked back inside his pack. He writhed there for what seemed an eternity but was probably only a moment before the fit passed and he again got to his feet.

"I gotta go," he announced. And he headed out toward the mountain without a further word. Me? I did what any jealous lover might do when confronted with such a mystery.

I waited until he was out of sight, then I followed him.

❧

As my supply of essence was unlimited, I could take advantage of our skill at invisibility without worrying about draining my reserves. However, since I did not know if Eddy had the capability to pierce that veil, and the exposed, narrow path up the mountain mirrored the one on my own shore, I also used as much stealth as I possibly could. I moved quietly and quickly, staying at least fifteen or twenty yards behind my quarry.

At length, we reached the top of the mountain, finding—as I had suspected—a forest of thorn trees. Eddy, however, was far better prepared for this eventuality than were Seth and me. He put down his backpack, moved Pluto aside, and retrieved a small hatchet he then used to chop the thorns away. He was careful and methodical, making sure to remove the lower and middle ones especially before proceeding.

This made following him less difficult as his concentration was on the removal and avoidance of the thorns rather than whether or not anyone was following him, not to mention my own ease in moving through the thicket. In the interim, the sky had grown dark grey, and a chilly wind I had not yet experienced began to sweep through the area. I was glad I had thought to grab my cloak.

Eddy had no such protection, but the wind did not seem to bother him in the slightest. He simply kept chopping his way through the thorns until we at last reached a clearing. As on my own shore, at the far edge of the clearing was a cave—or rather two of them fairly close to each other. I was certain the larger of the two, off to the right, hid a castle similar to the one Seth was residing in at the moment, but the second, smaller cave was a puzzlement. It was this one to which Eddy headed.

He made no hand gesture or spoke any incantation before entering, so my guess was that it was not spelled in any way. My curiosity was aroused at the thought that the end of our journey was only a cave, but I waited a moment before crossing the clearing and gaining the entrance. Clinging to the edge of the cave as the wind battered me, I peered inside.

Eddy was lighting candles and placing them in sconces on the walls, slowly illuminating its interior. I heard a trickling noise and smelled essence, eventually seeing a stream flowing through the cave, disappearing under the rock close to the shore edge. When the sconces were all full, I saw in the center of the room an oblong stone platform with arcane symbols unfamiliar to me decorating its ends and sides. Silver handcuffs on chains were affixed to all four corners of the platform. The manacles were open, glinting meanly in the candlelight.

My stomach became unsteady at the sight, but fairly turned over when I looked straight ahead at the far wall of the cave, for it was not a wall. At least it was not made of stone. It was a grey substance I could not identify but which moved and swirled much like the outside of the compass I carried. It did not resolve itself into any kind of picture, however. It undulated restlessly, rippling from corner to corner. At times I thought I could see through it, but it thickened and obscured itself again without rhyme, reason, or pattern.

Eddy then stood before the moving wall, taking care to place the right manacle to the very edge of the platform, as if to reach it easily. He began to recite something in a low voice I could not quite hear. As I ventured in a bit farther to improve my position, a gust of wind came from behind and blew me off balance. I clutched the edge of the cave, dislodging some stones which clattered to the ground.

"Who's there?" Eddy said, turning toward the entrance. He peered my direction for an uncomfortable length of time before speaking again. "Warner?"

I stayed silent—and invisible.

"It's no good, dude. I can see you. Goddammit, I told you I had to do this by myself. You were gonna stay on the shore and read or somethin.'"

"No," I said, becoming visible. "That was your plan. Mine was to solve this mystery which seems to have come upon you so suddenly, and I could do it no other way than to follow you."

"It's not a mystery," he insisted. "I told you I had a price to pay for being rescued, and this is it. That's all."

"That is *not* all. This price of yours is obviously taking its toll, and I might be able to help or at least assist you in carrying the burden." I expected an outburst but instead received a weary shake of the head.

He spoke quietly. "I got enough on my conscience—I ain't draggin' you into this too." He paused for a few minutes, looking at me solemnly. "Well, if you ain't gonna leave, don't try and stop me. I wouldn't be doin' this if I had a goddamn choice."

"Agreed," I said, but I could feel my brow furrow in confusion. What was all this about?

He resumed his position before the swirling wall of grey and started his recitation anew. As he spoke words I had no hope of understanding, the grey darkened to black and then seemed to become transparent. I saw the moon as well as Orion's Belt and other constellations I recognized. It was the earthly realm. A dim figure on the other side of the transparency suddenly snapped into focus, and I saw a man standing there.

As soon as the man became visible, Eddy reached through the barrier and grabbed him, bringing him through to the cave. Eddy screamed and cursed, his hands and arms smoking as the stench of burnt flesh rapidly filled the small space. I watched his skin blister and pucker as he wrestled the struggling man toward the platform and snapped his wrist in the silver manacle he'd placed closest to the edge. Once that had been accomplished, Eddy ran to the stream of essence and plunged his arms into the flow. The man continued to struggle like a fly caught in a spider's web until Eddy turned his attention toward him once again. "Shel'bach!," he said over his shoulder.

The man stopped moving and stood there motionless, appearing almost catatonic. I realized then this was no ordinary man. He was one of us—a young man of perhaps twenty or twenty-five with long, blond hair. He was dressed in a t-shirt and jeans, and I could tell from the dark rings around the hollowness of his eyes that he was newly made and sick from never having fed. He sniffed the air and began to shamble toward the essence, straining silently against the silver handcuff holding him to the platform.

Eddy turned his head once more. "Shel'bach m'kah!"

And the young man again stopped.

"Where did he come from?" I said. "How—"

"I don't know," he said, holding up his hand, now healed from the essence, to silence me. "They're just there when I'm ready to pull 'em through. Don't say anything until it's finished."

"There's more?"

He did not answer, or rather he answered through his actions. He sat the young man, now as silent and compliant as a rag doll, down on the platform, laid him out spreadeagled, and chained up both his arms and legs. After testing all the manacles to make certain they held, he walked toward me.

"Let's get out of here before that spell wears off."

"Are you just going to leave him like that?"

"He won't be like that for long."

Eddy made a circuit of the cave, blowing out the candles. He breezed past me, and I followed him out as we paused in front of the other cave. The sky was an even darker grey than before, and the chill wind whipped my cloak about my head. I shivered, but it was not from the icy blast alone.

He spoke the reveal spell and, just as I thought, a castle similar to that of the Old Man appeared. This castle, however, was also graced with a large black stone obelisk a few yards from its entrance, the object bearing the same runes I'd seen on the platform. I could recall no such fixture at the Old Man's castle.

"*Hey!*" cried the boy from the cave. "*Where the fuck am I?! Lemme out, goddammit!!*" The chains rattled and clanked.

"Let's get outta this wind," Eddy said. He opened the door, but I paused on the threshold. He looked back. "Don't even think about gettin' him out. There's no key for those manacles, and I don't know what would happen to you if you tried. C'mon upstairs."

He wearily mounted the steps, I right behind him looking out over the first floor of the castle. It was exactly the same as the Old Man's, and so was the second floor, with an alcove at the landing and rooms off to the left and right. Eddy turned left, entering a room with a bed, a small desk with a pen and sheafs of paper, and a fireplace with a cradle of thorn tree logs nearby. He crumpled some of the paper, took some kindling and a tinderbox from a shelf near the mantle, and laid a fire.

"I know you got questions," he said, his back still to me as he lit it. "I can feel 'em burning in your head. But it ain't over yet." He didn't turn around until the fire was blazing and he had thrown on some wood.

The wind howled outside a head high window, sounding bitterly cold, but the fire had the room cozy in no time. He approached me, taking off his shirt and shorts and standing tantalizingly naked in front of me.

"I'm pretty sure I disgust you right now. I mean, I disgust myself, but I hope you can find it in your heart to get in bed with me. I ain't in the mood to fool around, though. Just hold me, okay? Could you do that?"

I nodded, not trusting myself to speak. We disrobed and climbed into the surprisingly roomy bed. I cradled him as we both stretched out, his breathing becoming regular as we snuggled into the bedclothes and his warmth covered me. He closed his eyes and was soon asleep

Despite my weariness and the now drowsy warmth of the room, I could not stop thinking about the boy. Who made him? Who was he? And what was to be his fate? Most likely, he was a sacrifice. I could not decipher the runes I had seen, but such are the ways of some creatures. Sacrifice to what god, though? The obvious answer was Eddy's rescuer. This is what he must do to maintain his existence here.

The decision I had was whether or not my feelings for Eddy could allow me to overlook the necessities of his servitude. Could I be complicit in them? I sighed deeply enough that he moved his head. I already was. And as much as I despised the thought of again sentencing someone to the end that young man was bound to meet, I knew I would assist in the endeavour if Eddy asked. In that instant, I realized my heart was lost. Whatever protestations I might make to convince myself otherwise would be of no avail. The realization was both a relief and a burden, as most realizations are.

I have always been pragmatic, even in matters of the heart. There, especially, one has a duty to face facts and not let delusions interfere with reality. And the question for me was how far I would go to assist him, for this would surely be required of me sooner or later. Weighing multiple factors, I was lost in thought for the longest time until I heard a faint noise from without.

The low hum of a human voice emerged, sharply rising to a scream and then something beyond sound, signifying terror of the utmost magnitude. It came from high in the sky and right next to the window at the same time, first appearing here and then somewhere else, whirling around until I could no longer tell from which direction it originated.

I had no doubt whatever dreadful ritual he had been preparing that boy for was now taking place. Eddy slept, undisturbed. I craned my neck a bit to see more of what was happening outside, but I saw only grey mist, though it was darkening steadily. A stray thought seized me, and I reached for Eddy's arm, draped across his belly.

His hairy skin bore no sign of scarring or trace of trauma.

His fingernails, cuticles, and rough elbow skin all looked exactly the same. As I marveled at the change from the blackened, smoking mess I had seen in the cave, the screaming outside cut off mid-syllable, ringing for a moment in the sudden silence. I looked out the window and found the mist beginning to recede, clearing until I could nearly see the All-Ocean. By the time I settled back to close my eyes, the refreshed sun was peeking above the horizon, and the day already felt hot.

awoke alone in Eddy's bed, sweating lightly. Through the window, the sun bore down upon me like a heat ray. I started, wondering where he had gone, but then I smelled bacon and knew I'd find him downstairs tending to breakfast. Stretching as I got up, I dressed and went to the kitchen. He was toiling shirtless at the firepit with his back to me, the muscles moving under his skin as he stirred the bacon. My member stiffened.

Time enough for that, I thought. Explanations now, though I was certain I'd already figured out his predicament. As if sensing me, he drew his head up and turned around, clutching the fork he used to turn the bacon. He wiped his hands on his camo shorts. I could smell the bacon, but I could also smell him. His anticipation. His musk. Maybe they were the same.

"I thought we'd have a little breakfast before I...uh...have to clean up," he said. "There's not much in the larder here, but I found some bacon and some bread. I guess you probably figured out what went on last night."

"Indeed I have," I said. "For some time now the sun has been growing dimmer and you have been more and more anxious, so the being who controls it—the one who rescued you—required a sacrifice. As I lay holding you last night, I heard screams as if from one in torment. When they ceased, the sun appeared once more on the horizon, and I fell asleep." I nodded toward the fire. "The bacon is burning."

I don't know if my words or the smell startled him, but he seemed to jolt awake. I crossed and stood at his side. He frowned thoughtfully as he turned the strips. After some time, he faced me, his expression difficult to read. "So, you're good with this?"

"'Good' might be an overstatement, but if I understand the idiom correctly, you mean to ask if I find it permissible."

He nodded, removing the bacon from the fire.

"Let me approach this a different way," I said. "I have given my heart to you, and you have won mine. As we are two complex beings, parts of each of us are bound to be somewhat distasteful to the other. This is something you must do, as you have given your word to this being. To renege on this promise would dishonor you. May I ask you something?"

"Sure."

"What would happen to you if you disobeyed?"

"The screaming you heard last night would happen in my head. And worse. I've tried, and it nearly drove me crazy. I couldn't eat, I couldn't sleep, I couldn't feed—I couldn't even think."

"There you are, then. Not only would disobedience

dishonor you, as I said, it would harm you as well. So, I cannot blame or fault you in any way for avoiding such a consequence."

"Even if it means taking a life?"

I pondered how to explain this. "This being only feeds on creatures such as ourselves, is that correct?"

"Yep. Fresh ones."

"You do not turn them?"

"Nope. They come to me that way."

"Then their lives, such as they know them, are already forfeit. You may be the instrument of their demise, but unless you actually kill them, I might even call that into question. Make no mistake, I have a great respect for the sanctity of life, and you may be called to account for it when you meet your maker—if that deity truly exists—but I certainly have no right to judge you or your actions in the meantime. Will I participate in this process? No. I will not. I am bound by no such promise. My curiosity has been satisfied, and I understand why you must do what you must do." Here, I reached out and caressed his face. "It does not change my love for you."

He began to sob uncontrollably. "Th-then you don't think I'm a m-monster?"

I gathered him into my arms. "You are my Eddy. That is all I see."

The poor man wept as if he was inconsolable, and I had never felt as happy or fulfilled in all my existence as I comforted him. When he seemed under control of himself, I rubbed his back and let him go. "Is the bacon ready?" I asked.

"Probably cold by now," he said with a smirk. "I'll make us some sandwiches before I go clean up...uh...out there." He wiped his eyes and nose on a greasy towel he had wrapped around the handle of the skillet and set about constructing huge triple-decker sandwiches out of bacon and the last of a gaily wrapped loaf of Wonder bread—the only wonder being its classification as bread. We sat down at table in two rather uncomfortable wooden chairs and, whether from emotion or true hunger, we ate heartily and quietly.

"Perfect," I said when we had finished.

"Yup. Sure hits the spot." Somewhat more grimly, he eyed the door. "Now, I gotta be gettin' out there to clean things up."

"I can assist you if you like. I have nothing to do in here."

He hesitated. "I dunno. It's kinda grisly. Maybe you better stay here."

"Nonsense. I'm not some sheltered schoolgirl to be horrified at the sight of blood. If I help you, we can start down the mountain sooner and be away from this place."

"Okay," he said. "I could use the help."

Thus resolved, Eddy picked up his shirt from the back of his chair, and we left the kitchen. By the time I retrieved my cloak from upstairs, Eddy had Pluto in his backpack, which he plopped in the doorway of the castle. When we walked outside into the bright sunshine, I immediately smelled the stench of gore coming from the cave.

"Okay, strip," Eddy said, letting his shorts fall to the ground and throwing them over by his backpack. "You don't want to get your travelling duds bloody. Hey, what happened to the shirt and shorts I gave you?"

"I left them down the mountain as I had no idea where you were going or how far. Besides, the absence of the sun left me chilled. I wish I had brought them now."

"Well, we're gonna do this nekkid. It's easier, but don't be gettin' no bright ideas when I bend over. This ain't the place or the time."

"Right," I said. I could not help but smile. This was the brash, confident man I loved, not the gloomy one who had trudged up the mountain.

"And put 'em over by my backpack. There's a natural slope comin' downhill out of the cave, so they'll get wet."

I toed out of my boots and padded over to the threshold of the castle, where I disrobed and folded my garments, wrapping all but my boots in the cloak. As I placed the bundle near Eddy's knapsack, I glanced at the sleek stone obelisk. If both castles were the same, as indeed the floor plans and their manner of being hidden indicated, why did the Old Man's not have this feature? My curiosity drew me closer. The sun glinted off the shiny black surface. It was chock-a-block with symbols—combinations of lines and circles and triangles I'd also seen during my brief glances at the platform inside the cave. Did it have something to do with the sacrifice, then? I reached out.

"*DON'T TOUCH IT!*" Eddy screamed from the cave, running over and taking my hand away from it.

"Whyever not?"

"You'll fuckin' disappear. Pluto did that once. He put his paw on it, and then he vanished—just for a second, but it scared hell outta me. Outta him, too. I couldn't get him out of the backpack for three days."

"But it has the same symbols on it as the platform does. Surely it must have something to do with the sacrifice. Aren't you the least bit curious?"

He shook his head. "There's some shit goes on in this realm I don't need to know about. Like this." He nodded toward the cave. "Let's get to muckin' this out so's we can go home." I followed him away from the obelisk and into the cave.

The smell of congealed blood was overpowering. However the being feasted, it was certainly thorough. Nothing remained of the boy we had chained up last night except half a shoe I found over in the corner. I gave it to Eddy, who pitched it far into the thorn trees. Blood covered the platform and was splashed halfway up the side walls, through not the swirling grey one.

I took one of the two wooden buckets by the stream of essence and, as Eddy did, dipped it in the flow to wash down the walls and platform. Again wondering at the connection between that and the obelisk, I ventured to touch it while Eddy's back was turned. Nothing happened. I thought he might have been mistaken about Pluto's disappearance, but then again I considered anything might happen in this realm. He was probably correct. When the platform was cleaned, I turned my attention to the walls. Again, I noted the tumultuous grey wall. It had not ceased moving. I drew closer to it, feeling a bit of a pull.

"Don't touch that, neither," Eddy said. "Goddammit, Warner—do I gotta tie your hands behind your back?"

"I might like that."

He chuckled. "No doubt. We can try that later."

"So, what *is* this wall?"

"Beats me. Nearest I can figure, it's a thin spot between this realm and the earthly one. Things can get in, but we can't get out. Least *I* can't. You saw what happened to my arms, and as best as I can tell, there ain't no stream of essence on the other side to heal 'em up again. I'm thinkin' you wouldn't get too far before it turned you into a crispy critter, but I've only done it a few times. It's all kinda new to me since the portal spell don't work no more."

"Is that how you obtained your sacrifices before?"

"Yep. Used to make a day of it. Portal down to the beach at San Ysidro, catch some waves, hit the Von's for groceries, and then go to this club called Falana's where the other creatures like us hung out. She'd have somebody fresh turned, spelled, and ready to go."

"What was this being's hold on her?"

"No idea. I'm tellin' you, it don't pay to be too curious around here. Anyhoo, then I'd bring the sacrifice through the portal. It took a lot of concentration to get me and another person through at the same time, though. Sometimes they'd be too slow or lag behind, and the portal would snap shut. Lots of 'em lost heels or fingers or whatnot—let's get a couple buckets on this floor here, and I think we're done. Throw 'em toward the entrance."

I followed his instructions, washing the faintly bloody essence his direction at the cave opening until the floor was clean. "Will that do?"

"Looks good," he said, glancing up at me. A smile started to break out on his face, but it aborted itself, replaced by a confused expression as he drew closer and stood by my side. "What the…"

I looked back at the grey wall to find it swirling faster than normal, a strain of black added in. The amount of black grew until the grey was nearly all gone, and the waves had clearly coalesced into the black outlines of the stars in the All-Ocean's eternal night sky. My nightworld. After the unrelenting sunlight of this place, how comforting it grew as it solidified.

I gripped Eddy's arm. "Do you not see it?" I breathed. "My world."

"I see it. I don't believe it, but I see it."

Once the black was in place, we saw the beginnings of a bright blue moon heretofore not in my wor—no, no, *not* a moon. A portal. A deep, bright blue portal. Seth stood beside the portal, and within its parameters, five distinct figures took shape, those individuals stepping onto the shore of the All-Ocean one after another.

"Welcome, gentlemen," Seth said grandly. "Welcome to Nepenthe, the land that Time forgot. Your rooms have been prepared, and it is but a short walk to my estate, a perfect way to acquaint yourself with your new surroundings. We will, of course, have excursions to the lands around my castle so that you may pick your own locations and begin to lay in your workers. But all that comes in good time. Follow me, gentlemen—oh, one more thing. When in this realm, I beg of you to address me as 'milord.' I do so love the old customs."

At the end of his speech, my world and the blue portal vanished, replaced by the undulating, maddeningly blank grey surface. I longed for more information.

"What the fuck was that?" Eddy aloud wondered for the both of us.

"I have no idea," I said. "Does it usually show you visions?"

"Sometimes."

I couldn't help but sigh. "Wonderful," I said. I was growing weary of magic walls and sacrifices and battles and artifacts and the like. I just wanted to be with Eddy and eat burned bacon sandwiches on artificial bread.

"But hang on a minute. A couple things don't make any sense here. Lemme try somethin'." He walked outside the cave and raised his arm. "*B'emnet ardum to'bach.*" Again, the atmosphere shimmered, and the outline of an arch appeared, but nothing solidified, and it vanished once more. He nodded. "See, the wall showed your boy casting a portal strong enough for five people to walk through. Now, if *I* can't do it, *he* damn well can't. Plus, blue portals are only for travel in this realm. Travel to the earthly realm is a shiny silver motherfucker. Best not to believe visions you see on walls, my dark man."

"Perhaps the wall, like the scene the emissary showed Seth and myself back in the earthly realm, signifies something that might be. One possible outcome rather than a certainty."

"Now you're talkin'. That makes more sense."

"But even the possibility bothers me tremendously. Before I left, I had the impression Seth fancied himself a lord who wanted to rule over a land. He nearly said as much. It is not such a great leap to imagine him importing a population to subjugate."

"So? Let him. If your land is anything like mine, there's plenty of room. You could stay here with me."

"The issue is not space. Seth cannot be allowed to install himself as some high and mighty ruler. No good will come of it for me or for any of those under his dominance. You know as well as I he is not to be trusted."

"Did you just totally ignore the part about staying here with me?"

"I cannot," I said, regretting the finality of those words and their effect. But I did not have a choice. Seth could not gain this foothold. "I have a duty to my shore. Surely we have a mutual understanding of the necessity of doing what must be done considering our recent joint effort."

His face was as mercurial as the artifact by which I told directions. It stirred and swirled until his features finally settled on understanding resignation. "Don't you even regret going?"

I smiled with some wryness. "If you were half the mindreader you believe yourself to be, you'd know the answer to that question. I will be back, my Eddy. Perhaps sooner than you think."

"Smart ass," he said, some joviality returning to his blue eyes. "I'm gonna miss you."

"And I, you." We embraced, kissing for the longest time. "But we are immortal," I said when we broke for a breath. "Time is simply an inconvenience. I will be back. But may I not hear from you while I am away? Were it not for your telepathic guidance, we could hardly have defeated the Old Man. Your advice and company would be welcome this time as well, though I understand you cannot accompany me in body."

I had expected a heartier assent than I received. He gave my back a final pat, and we separated. "You know I'll do what I can," he said, "but I might be a tad distracted. I think I have a mission of my own as long as you're gonna to be away."

"Oh?" I was intrigued. "Does it have something to do with

the necessity of sacrificing one of our fellow creatures?"

He rubbed his beard. "You're readin' my mind," he said. "Maybe that's a contract that needs to be renegotiated. Tell you what, I'll walk you back to the border."

"The border?"

"Between your shore and mine."

"I remember no border," I said.

He rubbed his beard again, this time scratching around the back of his neck. "I sorta dragged you across while you were sleeping, remember?"

"Ah yes. How were you able to do that, anyway?"

"Oh, a little glamour to keep you asleep—and you had our book, so you passed right through."

I suddenly didn't like the uncertainty of this conversation. "I *can* get back to my shore, can I not?"

"Yeah, sure," he said quickly. "I mean, I don't see why not. I get burned when I stick my hand through, but I'm not *supposed* to leave. It probably won't happen to you."

"How encouraging."

"It's the best I got."

I sighed before I knew I had done so. Once again, I was overtaken by weariness at undergoing yet another new and excitingly novel experience when I preferred my Eddy, a cozy fire, a book, and a rainy night. Perhaps a dog, but Pluto would do. "Shall we, then?"

"Right now?"

"Why not?"

"Well, we *are* nekkid."

I could scarcely believe my own inattention. I had been so

focused on the vision and what it meant that I had forgotten we were still undressed from our cleaning duties. I took a step toward the pile of clothing on the ground and bent over. Eddy slapped my posterior with deadly aim, and I nearly fell.

"Damn, lookit that ass. I'm gonna get me a piece of that yet."

As I straightened up, he ran his hand down my chest and fondled my balls while my member stiffened. His was already hard.

"You sure you don't wanna poke me once or twice before you go?" he asked.

"I dare not," I said, rubbing the pelt on his chest and watching his cock bob up and down, an essence-laden pearl of ecstasy already forming at its tip. "I might never leave." I kissed him long and deep, and we fell into each other's arms, grinding our members together. "We must get dressed," I said.

He sighed. "If you say so."

⊃⊂

That's the border," Eddy said.

After several days of grey, cooler weather, the sudden heat and burning sun both going down the mountain and walking to the border had made me queasy. Looking at the demarcation between our lands didn't help. It wasn't so much a border as a black wall that stretched up the mountain to the left and as far out on the All-Ocean as I could see, yet its surface moved and rippled.

I sighed. Were there no *solid* walls in this land? As I continued to stare at it, I found I could discern familiar shapes within the black—the continuation of the mountain as well as the shore on the other side.

"Weird, huh?"

"Quite," I said, taking a few steps toward the foreboding obstacle. As I neared, I felt its cool pull. The ripples migrated to a point directly in front of me, the remainder of the wall growing stiller and smoother as they moved. They began converging at the foot of the wall, slowly building upward in a roiling mass about two feet wide until it formed a doorway of sorts.

The rest of the wall looked quite firm by now, though I had no intention of touching its surface that moment. I could still see through it clearly, but the doorway was another matter. The waves and pulses crashed into each other with ceaseless abandon, obscuring anything on the other side. They appeared ready to scald me if I even got close, despite their chilly feel.

"Is this what burned you?" I said to Eddy. He did not respond, so I glanced back to ensure he was still there and saw him staring at me. "Did you hear me? I asked if this doorway was what burned you. Did you attempt to go through it, or were you injured by something else?"

I was growing impatient by the time he actually spoke. "I've never seen it make a doorway before," he said. "Okay, first the sacrificial cave wall turns into a drive-in movie once you showed up, and now the border goes all fucknutty right where you're standing—no offense my dark man, but what *are* you?"

"I am no longer certain," I said as the ripples reached out from the wall and engulfed me without warning.

I do not know if my feet touched the ground—if, indeed, ground was beneath them. I neither stepped nor moved ahead, but was propelled through an atmosphere which felt both solid and liquid but allowed me to breathe. I felt a pull from all directions, as if unseen forces were attempting to sway me from my path, yet I saw nothing but the ripples.

After an interminable amount of time, my vision cleared and I beheld my beautiful night shore once more. I felt the essence in the air caress my face, and I rushed eagerly forward but went nowhere. The back of my body seemed to be mired in whatever I had crossed. Impatience took over, and I began to panic and struggle, but that effort merely seemed to sink me back into the mass. I went still and waited a moment. Finally, it spat me out like a wad of phlegm, and I stumbled a bit, falling onto the black sandy beach.

I rested thus a moment, catching my breath from my exertions as well as the bizarre journey through the barrier. I felt weak and groggy, as if I'd completed a full day's hard labor instead of merely crossing a border. I shook my head and tried to gain my footing, but as I lurched and swayed, a blast of noise shouted its way into my brain.

"—CKING CHRIST, WARNER! WHERE DID YOU GO!? I CAN'T—AAAGH, GODDAMMIT THAT BURNS!!"

"Stay where you are," I said in a firm, soothing voice I hoped would override the panic I felt from him. "I am fine and unharmed on my shore."

What happened? he said inside my head.

"I haven't been able to answer that question with any certainty for some time now," I said aloud. Speaking the words helped me speak in my head. "All I know is that the damned thing grabbed me, passed me through, and spat me out like a gobbet of spoiled beef."

But you're okay.

"No worse for the wear. Did you burn yourself attempting to follow me?"

It'll heal. So, what now?

The course seemed obvious. "I must sort out this situation with Seth. I would appreciate any advice or assistance at your convenience."

I'll try to check in as often as I can, but I might be kinda busy with He Who Shines. Dammit, Warner. We didn't even get to say goodbye. I was kinda hopin' you'd grab my ass one more time before you left.

I couldn't help but grin. "I would have added a goodbye kiss," I said.

Just one? Piker. I love you, dark man.

"And I love you, my Eddy."

And then he was gone. But his residue remained—a whiff of irreverence carried on a masculine breeze. I would have that to treasure as I faced what was likely to be a grim task ahead, as was his. Although I keenly felt his loss, part of me knew he was a distraction I didn't need. Not when dealing with Seth and whatever he'd gotten up to in my absence. We were free to turn our minds fully to our respective matters at hand.

Having mostly regained my senses, I decided to strike out on my journey immediately. I could see no sense to lingering at the border, which gave me a distinct feeling of unease. But before I made too many footprints, I wanted to see what Seth was thinking. I was sure I could do it and not draw his attention. If I could but make my presence unobtrusive enough, I might be able to find out more about not only the portal I saw but the beings he brought through. I was unsure which worried me the most.

Thus resolved, I sat down a bit farther up the beach so as not to be interrupted by the tide swelling over my lap. I could not march boldly into his thoughts or risk detection, so stealth was of the utmost importance. I intended, then, to begin with visualizing the castle and proceeding carefully inside, guarding my own thoughts against his intrusion.

I decided to attune the compass to the castle for no other reason than the sake of completeness. Anything to improve my chance of remaining undetected. I pulled it out of the pocket of my cloak, its outside face the usual moving, swirling fog. As I pictured Seth in the library, the castle began to take shape on the outside of the artifact. When the scene settled, including the now waist-high thorn forest, I opened the compass. It pointed east, the only direction I could go.

I snapped the artifact shut and returned it to my cloak. I cleared my head and began to reconstruct the Old Man's castle in my head, complete with lighted candles in the library window. I focused on the window, eventually crossing its sill to see Seth sitting at the table.

Various books both large and small lay open and scattered everywhere, some in precarious piles and others face down with their spines cracking. I needn't have worried about attracting his attention because I could feel how distracted he was. Words and disconnected phrases swirled so thickly in his head, I imagined a jumble of fonts rushing by on an unseen current of pages.

Richly intoned syllables murmured all about me, rising and falling as they repeated themselves with different inflections. All were too fast or too indistinct to decipher, but they were all in Seth's rather nasally voice. I had never seen him so flummoxed, the words whirling faster and louder. When they had reached a crescendo, Seth stood up and swept the books onto the floor, where they whispered quietly, creased and cowed. He sank back down, nearly blowing the candle out with his sigh.

The answer lies here somewhere. It must. *But I want it too badly to be able to see it. This is where I need Warner's cool eye, but where in blazes is he? Off studying with some strange being of the other shore, no doubt learning of things I should know. Perhaps even this portal business. Damn him. Well, then, I shall be a model of patience and prudence. He will return. He considers me unfinished business, and his thoroughness is uncanny. But no matter how formidable he is, I will have what he knows.*

I am loathe to admit it, but my ego swelled at his opinion. He had never expressed such admiration in person. Perhaps he saw that slight mental motion, for he again stood up and cocked his head, remaining stock-still as if listening for something. I shrank further into myself, drawing my cloak almost to a close. I felt his mind's eye pass over me, lingering too long for comfort. I dared not even think about what I'd just heard. His scrutiny bore down on me like a great weight.

Welcome home, Warner, I heard.

Cß

The journey back to the Old Man's castle did not seem as long as the journey away from it had, but then again, I was comforted by the dark. As much as I loved my Eddy, I had always distrusted the sun. It could not keep secrets, which is why I much preferred the night and shadows. And knowing this particular sun only shone because a life was taken made me even less keen on the idea. Perhaps he could come to some compromise with the being to whom he had made his promise. I would have wished him luck had our parting not been so sudden.

During the trip back I also resolved to keep my own counsel regarding Seth. He needed to know nothing of Eddy and certainly not of the vision in the cave. Seth understood me all too well, and no good would come of revealing too much too soon—if, indeed at all. Those cards would have to be played very close to my vest. I would not show my true feelings and instead, muster as much joviality and friendliness as I could stand. We still had a score to settle about Stacks, and perhaps that is what he would think on should circumstances catch me being occasionally shirty.

At length, I finally reached my destination only to be greeted by an interesting tableaux. Seth was high up on the shore, close to the beginning of the narrow path up the mountain. He was seated at a small table with an empty chair for myself. A decanter, probably of his favorite port, was also on the table with another glass. He waved at me as I drew closer.

"Welcome, my friend. You're just in time for a bit of the Old Man's best port. An infernal being, to be sure, but he had exquisite taste in vintages and had laid in quite a supply before his demise at our hands. May I pour?"

"You may indeed," I said, sitting and sipping once he had filled my glass and refreshed his own. "This is most excellent, especially after a long journey."

"I'm sure. Have you then finished your course of study in the other land? Ready to best me, are you?"

"How many centuries have we known each other?" I said, shaking my head. "Competition is your speciality, not mine. And who says I undertook any such study? I traveled to that shore because I was bored, and you were busy with your own work."

"You also went to return a certain book missing from the Old Man's library, one referenced in his personal diaries but absent from the shelf."

"Honesty has its own rewards."

"Doubtless," he said. "but such discussions are best reserved for when you are fresh. Your rooms will not take long to ready, and this damnable night chills me. Why don't we go up the mountain to the castle? You can avoid telling me what you've been up to. I also have something to propose which you might ponder before answering me in the morning." At this, he glanced around. "Such as it is."

"Must we walk?" I said, tongue half in cheek. "I would have thought by now you would be able to transport us with the nod of your head."

"Hardly," he said with a rare, self-effacing snort. He drained his glass and encouraged me to do the same. I followed suit, and we began our trek up the mountain.

"After long study," he said, "I actually found the portal spell, but I must confess that I lack the skill or power or gravitas or whatever to successfully cast it. Observe." He halted and raised his arm. "*B'emnet ardum to'bach.*"

As when Eddy tried, I saw a shimmering in the atmosphere, then the faint glow of a portal that winked out as soon as it appeared. If this was truly the extent of his powers, the scene Eddy and I witnessed on the cavern wall must have been either the future or a possible future. Perhaps I had been notified in order to return to stop it, but I did not feel comfortable mulling over the situation at the moment. Seth was too close and much present in my mind.

He looked at me sheepishly. "I was hoping you could do better," he said.

"Oh, I rather doubt it. You yourself know magic is less my forte than it is yours."

"You could at least try."

"Seth, if I could cast a portal, do you think we would be forced to walk up this mountain? I've been walking for days. I'd be in bed by now."

"You could," he repeated, "at least try."

"Very well." I raised my arm. "*B'emnet ardum to'bach.*" To my surprise, I was able to produce the very same shimmering, but mine flickered out of existence even faster than Seth's had. "See?"

He raised his eyebrows, then they fell again. "Your facility with the Old Tongue has grown, my friend," he said. "Your inflection was perfect after only hearing the spell once. How commendable. Unless you are holding something back."

"Yes, I am holding something back—I flunked Advanced Portalling."

Seth's eyes grew wide, then he threw his head back and laughed long and heartily, bending nearly double in mirth. "Oh, the *cheek*," he said at last. "I have missed you terribly, Warner. Terribly indeed." He was still chuckling by the time we gained the top of the mountain and entered the thorn tree forest.

"Mind your ankles," he said. "The thorns are presently spikes at the base of the trees, but they are beginning to grow again. I have but one or two things left to tell you, and, of course, I shall require your assistance."

"Of course," I said, minding my ankles. "However, I must be honest with you. I learned no magic and gained no knowledge of the other shore except that its sun is as pervasive as the night is here. Beyond that, I know little." I could tell this truth forever, and he'd still not believe me. "If the assistance you require demands more than that, you will have to seek it elsewhere."

Instead of disappointment, I saw dismissal on his face. "If our lives were in danger, you would use whatever means at your disposal whether or not you were keeping it from me. It's a matter of self-preservation. But as it happens, all we'll need to complete our task is your artifact and keen mind."

"I do so feel warm and wanted."

"As well you should." He picked his way carefully through the saplings, and I followed. "Your suspicions and sarcasm aside, I need your help to find an amulet—or a ring, perhaps. I am not sure of its setting, but I seek a stone."

"A stone? What type of stone?"

"It will allow me to focus my admittedly meagre abilities and create a doorway back to the earthly realm. As I'm sure I've said before, this damned darkness oppresses me so that I can scarcely breathe sometimes. I know you love it, and you are welcome to stay here, but I must get back to my former life."

I doubted that was his only motive. "What else can it do?"

"Do? It does nothing by itself. Its power lies in amplifying those attributes the user already has."

"And how do you know of this stone's existence?"

"While you were off on your retreat, I was also seeking knowledge. Among other, less positive attributes, the Old Man was an excellent archivist. Many of the volumes in his library are in his hand, and one of them tells of a battle between himself and another being who ruled a piece of this land."

"*Ruled.* As if one could rule the night."

"You might if you could change it to day."

I had the most curious sensation of Eddy's presence lurking in my mind. He was just on the outer edge of my consciousness, but I felt him nonetheless. He wasn't even trying to remain hidden. I was concentrating so hard, I nearly missed Seth's explanation.

"In any case," he continued, "the Old Man was victorious and hurriedly interred his enemy in *cha'lan*. He overlooked this artifact in his haste but did not consider going back for it because it has no inherent properties of its own. It merely amplifies."

"How did he know he'd overlooked anything?"

"The item was listed in the being's journals and not found

among his other belongings."

"So, you need my help to go grave robbing, eh? What jolly adventures you conjure, Seth. Will you be Burke or Hare?"

Seth sniffed. "Don't be asburd, Warner. They killed people. This one's already dead—or as dead as possible."

"Ah well, there's a comfort, then. Can you give me one serious reason I should support this lunacy?"

I can, Eddy said inside my head.

Seth stopped, regarded me for a moment, then silently resumed his path through the trees. He didn't speak for several seconds, but Eddy did.

He's gonna do it anyway. At least you can be there to keep an eye on the situation. If he goes off and finds it by himself, who knows what else he might bring back from the dead? You gotta go with him.

"You know how I loathe being here," Seth finally said, turning back to me. "This damnable night suffocates me, depresses me beyond words. I miss my other life. My home. And we are not friends, Warner. We were allies, but that's where our bond ends. You would rather I not be here, either. Admit it."

He could not have been more right, yet I knew he was lying. "If you do not want to stay, far be it for me to prevent your departure. Consider me and my artifact at your disposal."

"Very good," he said. "And very well-timed, for the castle is straight ahead. I'm grateful for your assistance, but I must say your sudden acquiescence makes me wonder if you have some other motive."

"My motives are as pure as your own," I replied as we emerged from the thorn saplings into the clearing before the castle. I looked toward the spot where the black obelisk had been at the other castle and noted this one had been broken off at the base. I wonder how and why the Old Man had done that. "Now, if you'll excuse me, it's been a particularly trying day, and I am unused to conversation with others. I'm assuming my rooms are still free? You haven't started renting the castle out yet, have you?" I grinned broadly at the last, wondering where the barb would land.

If it embedded itself anywhere, Seth didn't let on. "They're as you left them," he said, opening the door and heading for the library. "I need to check a few things before I retire. *If* I retire. Rest well. We shall begin in the morning—although when that is in this cursed land is anyone's guess."

⁂

The room smelled musty despite the open window and the constant temperate breeze, but I was too weary to care. The day—or however long it had been since I last rested—had been draining. Waking up in Eddy's land, still reeling from the events of the night before, the mysterious summons on the cave wall, being sucked through the gelatinous border, and now Seth's latest quest. I longed for some respite from it all.

Though I felt more at ease in the darkness than I did Eddy's sunlight, I must confess I longed for Eddy and, were I being honest, the creature comforts we enjoyed. His company had whetted my appetite for other people. Solitude, after all, must be chosen to be fully appreciated. And if I helped Seth create his portal, I thought as I undressed for bed, we could get something to drink other than the Old Man's rancid port.

But Seth desires to import a fiefdom, and I cannot stand by idly and let that happen. I don't object to others in this realm. The land is vast enough for many of us, and perhaps *should* be a habitat. A place of retirement. A reward. It's our birthright, after all. But that birthright should not have fealty to another attached. Seth would find a way to subjugate those newcomers and extract money or loyalty, though he needs neither except as manifestations of power.

I crawled between the sheets, once again feeling weary and resentful at being forced to go off on yet another expedition. Petulance took over. *Let him find it himself. I have no need of it. And who is to say my stewardship of such an artifact would be better or worse than his?* But even before I finished the thought, I knew the answer. And I knew I had to go, no matter how much I disliked the idea. I would do it for Eddy.

I bristled at the sheer inconvenience of it all. Had my time with Eddy in that paradise not been cut so short by the vision on the cave wall, would I have even come back? Once again, I have been cheated. And again, by Seth's ambition. Had the Old Man not said in the Chelsea that getting rid of us was a preemptive strike to rid himself of Seth's threat? And he still has not been brought to account for Stacks' death. As I tossed and turned, one inescapable conclusion faced me: Seth must be dealt with.

Even as I was resolved to finally commit the deed or at least begin to hatch the plot, the memory of the Old Man's death blazed in my head. I felt the heat from the damned fire, saw the struggle for life on his face, and felt his resignation when Seth pulled him back into the flames. Seth had saved my life. Certainly, that was not his only purpose in ensuring the Old Man's death, but I could not overlook the fact that I still lived because of him.

Perhaps my conclusion was not so inescapable after all.

I had, however, wrestled with the demon long enough and could think no more about it. I fell into a deep yet unrestful slumber and awoke some time later. I dressed quickly and went downstairs, suddenly remembering I had no way to break my fast other than a dip in the All-Ocean. I missed having breakfast with Eddy even if the custom was still relatively new. I felt a pang of loneliness once more, followed by the previous evening's anger.

"Are you finally ready?" Seth asked from the door of the library as I came down the stairs.

"Have you slept?"

"Not since I came to this infernal land. Who can sleep in eternal darkness? I need the light for balance, for performing all those activities which make sleep necessary. Even the starlight would be welcome over this dreadful pall of night."

"I'll take that for a no then, shall I?"

He rolled his eyes at me. "You do tax me sometimes, Warner. I hope your artifact is as keen as your skill at repartee."

I bowed with mock solemnity as I approached. "My artifact is at your disposal," I said, taking the compass out of the pocket of my cloak. It warmed my hand with a most pleasant sensation, its cover swirling and roiling as always. "What does this stone look like?"

"It's green."

I waited a moment, but he did not continue. "And?" I prompted. "How is it cut? Is it set in something? A ring? An amulet?"

"I have no idea. I told you that yesterday. Why do you never listen?"

"Because listening to you fills me with despair." I rubbed my forehead and had a sudden thought, rushing past him into the library. I glanced about but had no idea what book it was in, so I appealed to him for help. "Let me read the passage about the stone myself. Perhaps I can glean a clue from it. You said it was in the Old Man's diary, if I recall correctly." Seth did not move, so I purposely began to scatter his carefully arranged piles.

"Have a care, Warner," he said, snatching up the volume in my hand as he eased his way between the table and my person. I stepped back a notch. "Don't be so hasty. Is this really necessary?"

"Perhaps not, but what would be the harm in it? Unless something is in that passage you'd prefer not to show me."

He sniffed. "Don't be absurd." He put down the book I'd held and grabbed a smaller one from the stack. It appeared to be bound in some sort of leather, its surface devoid of any markings. "But as this is his personal diary, there are family…er, details I'd rather be kept private. It took me a moment to think, but I don't believe this bit bears any of them. I'll just find the correct bookmark."

Fumbling with the various ribbons and slips of paper stuck in the top, he finally opened it and scanned the pages until he put his finger up. "Ah, here it is. At the top of the page. The reference is not long."

>"...and at last he was overcome. Once he ceased breath-
>ing, I looted the body, obtaining a number of interesting
>artifacts along with some baubles. All were most ordinary,
>including a green stone that seemed to be of some import
>but it ultimately proved useless. As I was far from home
>and did not wish to be overly burdened, I buried it with
>him in cha'lan, the head several miles from the body. May
>his decoration serve him well in Hell."

Seth had now moved behind me, reading over my shoulder.
"You see?" he said. "A green stone. Is that not what I told you?"

"Yes, but I had forgotten about the body being in *cha'lan*.
I told you I was weary yesterday. Knowing that, I can give the
artifact a clearer picture of the scene than I could just imagining
a green stone."

He murmured something, but I waved him away and tried
to fix the image in my mind—a headless body and a green
stone in a glass coffin. When I felt sure of the vision, I closed
my hand around the compass, feeling its heat and motion next
to my palm, like an army of ants anxious to form a picture. I
opened my fist and saw the surface in motion, roiling until it
finally settled into the image of a headless torso in a box with
an oval object resting on its chest. When I opened the compass,
the needle read north.

"Due north," I said. "Inland."

Seth snorted. "Inland? Well, of *course* it's inland. It's not
going to be buried in the All-Ocean, is it? Your compass seems

to do well with the obvious."

I could not help but sigh, which I'm sure he delighted in. "We found this castle with it, did we not? It's an ancient artifact, not Google Maps. Surely the direction will change during the journey."

"Inland," he muttered once more. "And what lies inland?"

"I have no idea."

"You're the traveler. Did you learn nothing on your retreat?"

I didn't rise to the bait. "I only traveled along the shore. My notion of what lies inland is as vague as yours, but we'll never find out if we stand here bickering. Shall we begin?"

"The sooner—"

"Stop," I commanded, holding up one hand. "Before you issue yet another sharp retort, allow me to make an observation." He said nothing, so I continued. "I realize we have our difficulties with each other, but I've agreed to join with you in your effort to leave this realm. The very least you—or I, for I am also guilty—can do is be civil to each other. Whatever lies inland, we will be far more effective meeting it as allies. As the Old Man would attest were he here." I extended the hand I held up.

His countenance went blank for a moment, then he sighed deeply. "The fault is mine," he said, shaking my hand. "This atmosphere oppresses me so, I sometimes quite lose myself. You are right. Despite our differences, we make a formidable team." He smiled widely, almost genuinely. "Let us begin," he said, turning for the door. "Perhaps you'll even grace me with some discourse on what this world is like on the other side of that border."

I followed him, trusting and not trusting. "Perhaps," I

replied.

☙

had no preconceived notions of what this realm might look like farther inland, but I was determined to keep an open mind. If there was other vegetation as deadly as those thorn trees, we would need to keep our wits about us. The ones in front of the Old Man's castle—for I still could not think of it as ours—had regrown rapidly, and I was loathe to wonder what else might cross our path.

As we exited the castle, pausing at the entrance, I saw the only barren patch among the plants—the place where the Old Man had burned to death. Although the spot had no recognizeable form, I remembered well enough how the body fell and could almost see it in flaming repose. I only realized I was standing still, staring at the spot, when I felt Seth's gentle pressure on my arm.

"Some sights are best forgotten. Come. Our journey awaits." I followed him to the opposite edge of the clearing. "I have learned some tricks to bend these plants to my will," he said. "Though I fear the effects are temporary, they should afford us safe enough passage."

He planted both feet firmly on the black, sandy soil. "*Bem noch.*"

While the thorn trees did not exactly part, they rather shrank out of the way, leaving us a narrow path to navigate.

The poisonous prickles themselves seemed to turn their points downward, becoming less hazardous. I wondered why he had not spelled them such yesterday, but I held my tongue and complimented him instead.

"This is marvelous," I said. "Was it in one of the Old Man's spellbooks? How long does it last?"

"Yes, and I have no idea. We should, however, be able to go some distance before having to forge another path ahead. You first, Warner. You have the compass."

I pulled the device out of my cloak to check it one last time. The face remained the same, as did the indicator when I opened the piece. "Still north," I said. "Off we go."

Though the path was clear, it was still narrow and overgrown with roots, so the walking was not the easiest. However, we managed to cover more than a few leagues before leaving the area that had been burned, and the vegetation again began to close in.

"I think your assistance is required," I said. "I can't see the way forward."

He stepped wordlessly in front of me, and as he passed I saw his obvious agitation. He was pale and sweating, and I didn't believe either of those to be from exertion. "Bem noch," he said, and the trunks leant to either side.

"How are you faring?" I asked as I opened the compass and checked our bearings.

"Not well. I long to be away from these trees. This darkness is suffocating enough, let alone their damnable crowding. I feel trapped, and their old injury to my neck and shoulder throbs as if they are calling out to it. This can't be all that's inland, can it?"

"I have no idea. I see no trees in the scene on the face of the compass, for as much or little as that may mean." I put it away once again. "Have we any choice but to proceed?"

"I suppose not," he breathed. "March on."

I wished he had not mentioned the proximity of the trees, for I myself had felt some discomfort. His words only exacerbated the problem, but I tried as best as I could to tamp my feelings down. We continued in this fashion for many miles more. I began to weary, and Seth was sweating so badly he was removing pieces of soaked clothing. His breath was growing ragged.

There was, however, no place to rest. If we tried to sleep on the trail, the trees would close in. We had to see this through to the end. As I thought on whether or not to broach the subject with Seth, a solid wall of thorn trees blocked our passage.

"*Bem noch*," he barely breathed. He cleared his throat and tried again. "*Bem noch!*"

The wall of thornwood remained immobile, its prickles threateningly sharp.

"Have you any spells of movement or dislocation?" he asked me.

I closed my eyes, opening myself up to Eddy's presence. I could feel him in my mind, as I always did, but I sent all my desperation into that space, hoping he would reply.

The border's magicked. Your 'bem noch' won't work anymore.

As I turned to warn Seth, I saw him bent at the waist, breathing heavily and rapidly—and as he respired, I swear the atmosphere around me moved against my skin as if he drew it in and out of his lungs. I don't know how long it continued because I was fascinated by the sensation. Suddenly, he drew his body up straight and roared a one-word incantation so loudly I could not understand it. He raised his arm, and a burning blue ball of flame appeared in his hand.

He hurled it at the wall of thornwood, but the wood did not burn. It sputtered and puckered, and the vegetation withered and fell, but it never caught fire. The blue flame ate through the barrier, the flame and the hole becoming larger and larger until at last I could see beyond the trees. I again turned to Seth, but he had fallen, sprawled backward on the path.

By the time I had tried and failed to get him to his feet, the flame had eaten a substantial portion of the trees away, enough to provide passage for both of us. I gathered Seth in my arms and carried him beyond the forest, carefully putting him down on the black sand. I took the cloak from around his waist where he had tied it and loosened his collar, anxious until his breathing evened out. At length, he opened his eyes.

"Let us not make a habit of this," he said, sitting up and wiping the sand from his palms. "Sand. Just like the beach back at the castle except we have a forest of thorn trees where the All-Ocean should be." He narrowed his eyes, a disgusted look on his face.

"Perhaps this is not real. See if you detect any deception, Warner. Surely your friends must have taught you some—" He stopped. "Sorry."

I was touched. I'd never known him to censure himself. I cast a reveal spell, but our surroundings were as real as anything I'd encountered. "This all appears genuine," I said, pointing ahead, "including the large outcropping of rock ahead with the plainly worn trail that looks exactly like the one we're already acquainted with."

"Care to wager on more thorn trees and a castle in a clearing?"

I held out my hand and helped him to his feet. "For your sake, I hope no more trees. How are you feeling?"

"Fine, fine. I was not prepared to feel so…closed in. It was most unpleasant, but I have taken some preventative measures. Let us proceed warily, though. This all seems familiar, but who can tell?"

"True enough." Before we began, I checked the compass. It did indeed point toward the rock face. Seth behind me, we trudged through the sand until we reached the beginning of the trail up. As we ascended, I occasionally glanced out at the vista we had just left. I could not do so frequently, as I was also trying to be wary of my steps, but the sight was jarringly similar.

As always, the darkness was so pervasive, color or detail was immaterial. All was reduced to outline and movement, so the landscape had fewer waves and more spikes than the previous one. It was clearly different yet felt the same. Suddenly, I knew we were not being deceived—or, rather my nose knew.

"I cannot smell the All-Ocean," I said, stopping so short Seth nearly collided with me.

"Neither can I. Let's see what awaits us at the top."

The ascent gradually leveled out, ending at yet another thicket of thorn trees. These, however, were not as tightly grouped as the forest from which we had emerged. I opened and checked the compass. "I'm afraid we have to go through," I said.

Seth smiled and stepped forward. "*Bem noch mer.*"

The trees not only parted, they moved away from each other, clearing a path large enough for us both to walk abreast.

He grinned and took my arm, suddenly in the greatest of moods. "The spell needed refining," he said. "Come, let us get to the clearing while I tell you what I just remembered."

I nodded and walked with him. "Yes?"

"I don't know why I didn't think of it before because it caused me quite a bit of puzzlement when I read it. One of the Old Man's books speaks of a series of waypoints throughout the land, but the remainder of the reference had been torn out. I have no idea where or what they are, but it is not inconceivable for them to be in similar sites."

"Such as inside disguised castles."

"Or outside them. On break from my studies, I often wandered around the somewhat limited castle grounds. Off to the far left, I found the base of what seemed to be a stone obelisk, the rest of which had been destroyed by some means. I often wondered what it was and what happened to it, but I never put the two together until this very moment."

Ah. He had noticed it as well. What was it Eddy had said? Pluto had disappeared when he touched it with his paw. For a moment, I considered telling Seth, but I did not. Such information would undoubtedly lead to questions I was unwilling to answer. Instead, I posed a question of my own. "But why would the Old Man destroy his own waypoint?"

"Perhaps he did not want to be on the route, so to speak."

"So, you contend we should be seeing a clearing shortly along with a castle disguised as a cave."

"And a stone obelisk or similar structure," he said. "I am

certain of it."

In a few more feet, we saw the clearing with the cave on the right side of the clearing, but no obelisk. "This is surely a different clearing than ours," I said, "because the death shadow of the Old Man is not here."

"'Death shadow,'" he said with a chuckle. "How vivid. You really are quite the wordsmith, Warner. But where is the obelisk?"

"Perhaps if you unmask the castle, the obelisk will be revealed as well."

"I knew I had a reason for bringing you on this quest," he said. "However, you should probably do it while I ready something in case things are not what they seem."

"Very well. Ready? *Toch'nem.*"

The cave vanished, the doorless entry of a looming castle just like the Old Man's appearing in its stead. From what I could see inside, the arrangement of the interior seemed exactly the same—so much so that I once again checked the clearing for the Old Man's outline. Nothing was there.

A suspicion grabbed me. "*Toch'nem,*" I said, directly at the spot where the body would have been.

Nothing appeared. The ground was unmarked.

Seth's look turned quizzical. "What on earth are you doing?"

"Checking," I said, turning back to him and noting for the first time the obelisk over his shoulder. I nodded toward it. "And there is your waypoint."

It looked just like the one in Eddy's land—triangular and as black as everything else in the landscape. Its base was one or two feet across, tapering up to a fine point just above waist-high. I could even see the same runes. As we approached, I wondered what sort of force the Old Man could have brought to bear to break such a structure off at its strongest point.

The nearer we got, the more Seth's eyes gleamed with excitement. Perhaps he had known of this all along. It might have even been the purpose of the trip, but I could do little now except keep my wits about me. A delaying tactic might serve me well, for Seth was rushing headlong toward the object. When he reached it, he extended his hand.

"*Stop!*" I said as forcefully as I could. "Do *not* touch it! Are you mad? You have no idea what it can or will do."

He withdrew his hand. "Of course," he said with some reluctance. "Experimentation is called for."

"Indeed, but not right now. At the moment, we are going to take advantage of these lodgings and rest. We've just come through a thorn forest that took at least a day and a half. We should get as much sleep as we can and approach the thing refreshed. If you were thinking clearly, you wouldn't even be as close to it as you are now."

Sighing, he stepped back a pace and nodded. "Again, you are right," he said, joining me some feet away. On the threshhold of the castle, however, he stopped short and looked at me. "Why do you bother?" he asked.

"Bother? I don't understand."

"Saving me. Twice today alone. You carried me out of the thorn forest and now just prevented me from doing something foolish. I may be your ally now, but I have been a mortal enemy—well, you know what I mean—for centuries." He rubbed his shoulder. "I'm surprised you didn't let me die when you had the chance. Why *do* you bother?" he asked again.

"I don't know, really. I suppose I do it more for myself than you."

"How curious." He looked at me a moment before clapping me on the shoulder and striding ahead. "Well, let us poke around and see what we can find. This one is laid out exactly like ours." I saw a new thought in his eyes. "I wonder if it has a hidden library as well."

Rushing up the stairs, he stopped at the landing halfway and faced the circular window. "*Toch'nem*," he said as I came up behind him. The air shimmered and a doorless entry to a small room appeared. We stepped inside, but the table was bare save for a lone candle, and the shelves held nothing.

Seth frowned. "*Toch'nem*," he said again, expectantly, as if the books and papers themselves would have been spelled. They weren't. Obviously frustrated, he swept his arm over the table, raising nothing but dust. "Damn," he said.

"Maybe they weren't readers."

He regarded me reproachfully. "I have not been snide with you in some time, Warner."

"My apologies. Perhaps you'll overlook my hastiness when I tell you I have spotted a difference between this castle and the Old Man's."

"What's that?"

I started back down the stairs, indicating he should follow. "I saw a doorway as I rounded the corner here at the bottom of the stairs on the left. The Old Man's castle does not have this feature. Doubtless you would have discovered it sooner or later."

Although I called it a doorway, like the other entrances

on both castles, it had no door. This was merely a squared-off opening in the face of the stone wall. Had the visual atmosphere been the same inside the castle as outside, I wouldn't have noticed it, but as with the other castle, what was ebony without was normal within.

Seth stepped forward into the square. A second later, he snapped his fingers and lit a torch on the wall inside, snatching it from its sconce. "A stairwell leading down," he said. "And do you smell that?"

"I do, indeed." Essence, but not solely the type that came from our part of the All-Ocean. I certainly recognized the spicy scent of the All-Ocean from Eddy's world, but I also noted a third, unknown component.

"It smells like essence, but…what is that strange odour along with it?"

I refrained from asking which one.

We had descended perhaps forty feet, the scent of essence growing stronger and the atmosphere more humid, when a feeling suddenly seized me. I had been here before. Not here, exactly, but in a similar place. Then I hit upon it. I grabbed Seth's shoulder.

"Douse the torch," I said.

Even in the flickering firelight, I could see the incredulous look in his eye. "Are you mad? You *do* like the dark, don't you?"

"I perceive a glow from below us. Stealth will do no harm."

He peered down and frowned. "A glow?" He snapped his fingers twice, and the torch snuffed itself, a whiff of sulphur in the air as we stood on the stairs in the dark.

"Let your eyes adjust," I said. At length, we saw a faint,

bluish light on the walls of the stairwell.

"Incredible," Seth said. "But how…I mean, is there danger?"

"I sense none. Do you?"

"No," he replied quickly. "Let us proceed." His step, however, was cautious and tentative.

We went down about another twenty feet, the blue glow getting stronger until we at last saw a doorway to a much larger chamber and heard the echo of water lapping against stone. Seth did not falter at the last step but entered the chamber without prompting from me. He stopped dead ahead, looking around with his mouth agape. I nearly had to shove him aside to enter.

The huge room we stood in felt exactly like Eddy's sacrificial cave, but the swirling wall here was a glowing deep blue and held neither an altar nor sconces on the wall. Was this yet another thin spot between the worlds? If not the worlds, between what? I questioned Eddy in my head, but he was silent.

The wall, however, had spoken to me before. And I nearly trembled fearing it would do so again. What would it say this time? Would it repeat Seth's deed or add an entirely new revelation to the mix? Or would it remain silent?

"Why do you look at the wall so?"

Damn his observant hide. "Well, it's glowing for a start."

He shook his head. "There's more in your eyes than that," he said. "But as you seem to be in the habit of saving me, you may keep your own counsel. I'm assuming we're not in danger."

"No, no danger."

"Have you been here before?"

"No."

"But you've been to a place like it?"

"Yes."

"Feel free to add detail whenever you deem it appropriate," Seth said with more than a little exasperation.

I wanted to. Another's insight might be well worth my while, but I dared not tell him anything that happened beyond the border. Who knows how he might use that information? It was safer in my head than out in the open. I would, as Seth himself had suggested, keep my own counsel.

"No detail is necessary," I replied. "It's merely another piece of the puzzle fallen into place. If this is a way station of sorts with temporary lodging, it stands to reason some sort of refreshment might be provided as well. Hence, the somewhat mysterious access to the All-Ocean, or whatever part of it this is."

"And the place you were in?"

"It was similar."

We regarded each other for a very long time, our expressions unchanging as I felt his expectancy harden into resigned disappointment. "The fact that I have been unable to gain your trust chagrins me," he said. "Still, I hope one day to convince you I mean less harm than you think, and I have some deep regrets about what I did to your friend, Stacks. I know that still bothers you, as well it should. Perhaps we should retire and be alone with our thoughts," he said, heading toward the stairwell. He snapped his fingers to relight the torch. "Are you coming?"

As he turned back for my answer, I saw the hurt look in his eye and felt a pang of remorse. Had I not known what a master of the ruse he was, I might have been taken in. The urge to divulge what I knew was strong enough, never mind

Seth's manipulations. I could not wholly doubt his sincerity but neither could I entirely believe it.

"Yes, of course," I replied, taking my leave without looking back at the walls.

ॐ

"Have a care," I said to him when we had rested and were once again standing around the obelisk. "Stand back before you throw it."

As we were outside the castle and could only see outlines, I had to imagine the frustration in his eyes. It wasn't difficult.

"I can only stand back so far before I will be unable to hit the obelisk," he replied quietly as he gripped the rock in his right fist. "I am not proficient at games." He brandished his left. "Why can't I just touch it with the branch?"

"Rock first. Trust me."

He sighed and tossed the stone. When it first struck the obelisk, it flickered once, then began a short journey down its incline, disappearing every time it was in contact with the surface. It finally clattered to the bottom where it rested fully visible in the sand.

"Fascinating," Seth said, moving closer and picking it up. "It remains unchanged. I wish I could understand these damned runes." Without saying anything else, he extended the branch until it was nearly touching the obelisk.

"Stop," I said. "Do you feel it pulling you?"

"No," he replied after a few seconds' hesitation. "All right then, I'm going to fit the branch to the surface."

As he did so, I saw the damned thing vanish.

Seth withdrew a bit, and the branch was once again in his hand.

"Could you still feel it between your fingers?" I asked.

He was examining the branch and did not respond. "It appears unchanged as well," he said quietly, apparently more to himself than to me. Throwing the branch aside, he suddenly stepped up to the obelisk. "Hang caution!" he said, and he touched it with the palm of his hand.

He vanished instantly.

I rushed forward and searched the area with my hands—carefully so as not to touch the stone—but he was gone. Just as panic began to rise, he reappeared nearly on top of me, stumbling backward and falling in the sand. He scrambled to his feet and went into a crouch, whipping his head around. When he saw me, he straightened up and seemed to relax.

"Extraordinary," he said.

"What did you see?"

"See? I saw damn little before the wind blew me away from the obelisk. I have never felt such force, never mind the electrical charge in the air. It is definitely a citadel of power. My God, it fairly *crackled*." The intensity of discovery fired his eyes. "You *must* see it!"

"And so I shall, but what about the little you saw before you lost contact?"

"I glimpsed other obelisks forming a circle on either side of me, but I could not tell how many. I seemed to be perched on a ledge, at least I sensed space behind and below me." He stepped up to the stone once more. "I suggest grabbing the top with both hands and holding on. Likely we'll have sufficient purchase to withstand the wind and look around more." Before I could question him further, he did exactly that, vanishing as before.

I had no choice but to follow him. As I approached the stone, however, I saw an indentation on the rear which provided a grip. Seth probably hadn't seen it from his angle. Very well. I breathed deeply and grasped the obelisk.

The wind was as fierce as Seth had promised, but I was able to hang on as I had been forewarned. I also felt the atmospheric power which had impressed him so, and it was forceful indeed.

Seth stood to my right. He was also looking around, taking in his surroundings. His hands were at the top of the obelisk, directly above my own. I could see them as clearly as I could inside the castle. Was the ebony atmosphere artificial or was this? Interesting, but larger questions were at hand.

I felt a space to my immediate left, and beyond that saw another obelisk. Indeed, I counted three—including the one to which we clung—equally spaced approximately two feet apart. The absence to my left was most likely the obelisk the Old Man had obliterated, which brought the total to four. I saw neither sky above nor ground below, just a dimness where they should have been. I could not even determine what we stood upon. There must have been a light source, but it was not immediately apparent.

We must speak, Seth said inside my head. *Release the obelisk.*

I let go and found myself standing right in front of the

castle where we had been, Seth reappearing a few seconds after.

"Forgive the intrusion," he said, "but I could not make myself heard over the wind. I'm keen to hear your observations."

"I have more questions than I do observations," I said. "Off to the left, I saw the empty space where the Old Man's obelisk should have been. I counted three, including ours, but were we inside? Outside? Between worlds? What were we standing on? Why is that atmosphere different from this? Who is responsible for this system? Or who even uses it?"

"More to the point, *how* does one use it?" he added with some consternation. "How do you let go of one and grab another if you return to the point of origin once your hand leaves the surface?"

A thought seized me. "Perhaps you don't," I said. "The obelisks are within an arm span of each other. What would happen if you were to keep hold of one with your right hand and grasp another with your left?"

"And hold both simultaneously," Seth said, smiling. "*Brilliant.* We must try it." He made for the obelisk again, but I halted him.

"We should check the compass first. Remember the object for which we are searching. If, indeed, that is the reason for our search."

Seth sobered. "I don't like your implication," he said, "but your logic and infallible tendency toward caution outweigh my likes and dislikes. For the time being." He pointedly looked away, down the vast stretch of black sand beyond the castle. "I thought you were going to consult your artifact." he said at last.

I must confess to being distracted by Seth's pique. I had

known him to dissemble, of course, but his outrage at such times always rankled of hollowness. This seemed too genuine. My natural inclination was one of regret and apology; however, he appeared to brook neither presently, so I withdrew the artifact from my pocket without further word.

As we had not yet reached our destination, the cover of the compass remained fixed with the image of the headless corpse in *cha'lan*, an oval object on its chest. I opened it, the needle on the compass still pointing north. "Still inland," I said, snapping it shut and putting it away.

When Seth next spoke, his voice was maddeningly neutral. "Well, then. We would appear to have two courses of action. We either attempt a shortcut with the obelisks or go the long way around. I believe we ought to try the shortcut. We are, after all, looking for something glowing beneath the sand, and I see nothing—"

I grabbed his shoulder. "What did you say?"

He seemed confused for a second. "I…what *did* I say?"

"You said we were looking for something glowing beneath the sand. That was not in the passage you showed me."

"It wasn't? No, no it might not have been." He extricated himself from my grasp. "Studying the Old Man's documents was an interesting experience," he said, weariness in his voice. "Occasionally, I would read something—a portion of a spell, for instance—then have necessity to refer to it a few seconds later and it would be gone, vanished from capital letter to period with the surrounding text undisturbed. Yet, I would still *know* what it said. Oh, I don't blame you for looking askance considering your continued mistrust of me, but I cannot tell you how many candles I burned straining my eyes trying to replace words I remembered seeing but could no longer find on the page."

"I believe you," I said. "Magical text that disappears once read is no madder than what we've already seen. And it's not that I mistrust you, exactly..." I was not sure, however, *exactly* how I felt.

He regarded me without expression for a moment, then he sat down in the sand and bade me sit beside him. "We have some issues to discuss. Rather, I have some things I should tell you."

Seth must have seen the concern in my face because he continued hurriedly.

"I'll freely admit to being derisive and dismissive of your more humane approach to hunting and feeding in the past— indeed, your entire compassion-based philosophy—but since we allied against the Old Man, I've come to understand it a great deal more. I never had a facility with compassion. Oh, I could feign it when necessary, but the genuine article was quite beyond me until I began to study your behavior."

"*My* behavior?"

"Of course. Particularly during your recovery period when you could no longer feed. And before you mistake my rescuing you for actual compassion, let me be clear--my ulterior motive was to involve you in my battle with the Old Man. At least that's how it started."

"And now?"

"You have saved me so many times, it's embarrassing," he said. "I would dearly like to call you a friend and an ally, yet you believe I am misleading you about the purpose of our quest.

You seek to find fault with me, but I suppose it's not difficult to understand why considering we have had enmity for each other for hundreds of years. And I murdered your best friend."

Stacks. I felt guilty. I'm sure my face reddened. Seth, of course, noticed.

"You should not feel shame for forgetting grief," he said. "And you have had much to occupy your mind since his death. If it is any consolation, he died peacefully. In the end, even I could not make him suffer."

"He looked anything but peaceful."

"Artifice," he said. "A postmortem glamour contrived to enrage you and 'Wade'—a habit of mine in those days, though I doubt you believe me at this point. You will recollect no one else seemed to notice anything out of the ordinary."

Oddly enough, I believed what he said. Although importing a fiefdom was not beyond Seth's ken, upon deeper reflection, it was altogether more work than I could envision him willing to do. And for the first time, I wondered why the vision on the cave wall had appeared to me and where had it come from. Perhaps all was not as it seemed.

"Is your silence from anger or careful thought?" he asked. "Unless several hundred years of acquaintance misleads me, I believe careful thought is the correct choice."

"You know me well."

He smiled. "Well enough to realize you come to no decision of any magnitude rashly. My deeds will mean far more to you than my words, so I'm not even going to ask if you believe me or not. I would rather have you regard me henceforth in a different way, as I have you of late. Perhaps if you see me in that light long enough, you will come to change your mind."

"You have given me much to think about, and I swear I will do so."

He actually grinned. "Then I am assured, for I know how you value your word. Let us speak no more of it for now. Now, let us proceed to the shortcut. What does your artifact say?"

When I opened it, the arrow still pointed in the same direction. "According to this, we are headed in the correct direction, which means we should probably choose the next waypoint heading north. My guess is that it's the one immediately to our right."

"How did you reach that conclusion?"

"Well, if the broken one is to our left, that's the Old Man's castle, which would put us back, so forward must be to the right."

"Eminently logical, my dear fellow. Let's try that." He stood up, strode to the portal and reached out with both hands, looking back at me as he grasped the stone and disappeared.

Damn him. Whatever happened to caution? We had no idea this whole affair worked as we assumed. Never mind. I knew the plan well enough. I could still see the indentations of his boots in the black sand. I stood alongside them, positioning my hands a bit lower in case he was still clinging to the obelisk on the other side. With a deep breath, I touched its surface and was taken to the windswept place.

I had been looking at my hands when I transported, Seth's left hand appearing above my own as the first gust of wind buffeted me. I had expected to see it—indeed, had allowed for it—but I had not expected it to be arcing blue and red sparks.

I followed the line of brambling bolts down his arm and saw next to me a veritable Vitruvian Man of glowing, crackling, blue and red electric discharges spanning from the obelisk we were grasping to the next.

But the colors were quickly overcome by a sudden whiteness that intensified until I had to squint and turn away from him. I concentrated on the hand above my own and watched it glow, burning brightest just before it disappeared altogether, leaving me alone in a maelstrom of darkness. My eyes had to adjust to the dim lighting I remembered from our first excursion here before I could figure out how to follow him. I calmed my breathing and waited as the wind whipped around me.

At length, shapes began to emerge. I cast my gaze to the right and saw the recently vacated obelisk. I looked down and discerned a railing on which I stood. It appeared to be solid, and it reached to the other stone. Seth had been correct in its proximity—about an arm's length away. I moved my hands up to the slimmer part of the obelisk for a better one-handed grasp.

Ever-mindful of the gusts of wind, I inched my foot along the railing until I felt sure of my balance. My left hand in position, I waited for a moment of stillness then let go with my right, shifting my weight as I grabbed the other obelisk. The wind immediately ceased.

An indescribable warmth swept through me like a fever as I looked at my arms. Blue and red sparks began to pop from them, spreading until they covered me like a neon tattoo. My torso felt—and I can only approximate the sensation with language—as if it were *loosening,* as if the matter sticking my molecules together had suddenly vanished. I again had to squint against the white glare, this time from my own chest, and I knew *I* was the illuminated Vitruvian Man.

The railing seemed to disappear from under my feet, and I felt like I was falling, landing on my back in black sand. I looked around, but the obelisks and the entire contraption was gone, replaced by a landscape similar to the one I'd left. Except Seth was sitting cross-legged in the sand about ten feet away.

"What took you so long?" he said, grinning. He was so satisfied with himself, he even chuckled.

I should have upbraided him for his haste, but I was so relieved to see him—and myself—safe and sound that I chuckled as well, and soon we were laughing uproariously. My sides hurt and my throat ached, but still the spasms of laughter rocked us both. Seth pounded the ground with his fist, sending a wash of sand into his own face, which made me laugh all the harder.

At last, breathing heavily through the remnants of our mirth, we paused and lay back on the ground looking up at the night sky. Well, the usual dark sky in any case.

"Just think," Seth said, "the last person who used that might have been the Old Man himself. Or the being whose *cha'lan* we seek."

"I hope we have not been altered in some way by this journey," I said.

"Why *would* we?" he said. "Although I admire your caution, it leads to looking for consequences instead of experiencing the marvel. Consider what just happened to us. What a wonder! Our molecules were rearranged and transported some distance away through some magnificent, arcane power. Who built that mechanism? From where did those obelisks come? How did whoever built it discover the power?"

I raised my head and looked at him. "You almost sound interested in this place, yet we're on a mission to find something that might allow you to leave it."

"Of course," he said, obviously not spotting a contradiction. "Outside of the fact that this darkness is monstrously oppressive, the waypoints absolutely fascinate me. I need to do research in all the arcane libraries of the earthly realm. Surely there must be more about this world somewhere other than Olafsson's diary, and I don't think I'll find it here."

"Unless this castle has a library as well."

"Yes," he said, sitting up. "And it very well may, but I must confess weariness threatens to overtake me. That was quite a ride. Perhaps we should rest ourselves for the night before we continue." He looked up at the sky. "Well, you know what I mean."

We helped each other up, and Seth said the words of unmasking. The castle appeared behind the stone obelisk. It looked much the same as the others we had seen, including a library on the second-floor landing. This one, however, was undisguised and held but a few books. Seth immediately began looking through them while I set about laying a fire with the wood generously stacked near the hearth.

"These seem to be duplicates of what I've seen in the Old Man's library," he said, "but we can look more closely once we've rested. Is that a decanter of port I see on that table?"

It was, and we dragged two long sofas from either end of the room and stretched out in front of the fire, glasses of wine in our hands. A few suppositions and a stray plan or two later, I believe we both dropped off mid-sentence.

೮ఎ

When I awoke, Seth was already up and poring over a volume at a table in the room, two more at the ready. Another was face down. "Have you gotten any sleep at all?" I asked him.

He looked at me. "Actually, I only awoke a few minutes before you did. I wanted to try something out."

Seth was one of those annoying people who are not only awake in an instant, but are heedless of those who take a bit longer to come to full speed. "Which was?"

"Remember I told you about text disappearing once I read it? Well, I thought the missing words might be in one of these duplicate copies. Unfortunately, they are also missing here."

"It was a good thought. Are the books all duplicates?"

"Every blasted one of them," he said, closing the volume he'd been looking at and gesturing toward the near-empty shelves. "The Old Man obviously raided the place and left only the dregs."

"Unless another library exists. Have you tried the unmasking spell again?"

"Not yet. I was waiting until you awoke. After all, I might say it wrong."

I had been perusing the shelves from a distance, but I looked sharply at his words. He wore a half-grin, and I saw I was being teased. "I think you have that one mastered."

His grin spread, and he nodded.

He spoke the reveal spell, but nothing appeared.

"I know of no double-masking spell," he said, "but I get no sense that anything else is here. Do you?"

"None. I think this is a dead end. Shall we go down to the cellar and feed while we resume discussion on what to do next? This castle must have its own access to the All-Ocean as well."

"Excellent idea. The door is probably even in the same spot."

And, indeed, it was.

The saline tang of the All-Ocean hit me about halfway down the stone stairs, sharpening my hunger. I could not remember the last time we had fed. But I remembered the light that began to fill my vision as we neared the bottom. And, as I suspected, I saw another stream of essence as well as another glowing blue wall.

"What in the world *are* these?" Seth said, approaching it.

I stepped in his way. "For God's sake, don't touch it. It will burn you."

"How do...oh, of course. The last glowing blue wall was also familiar to you, but you fobbed me off rather than be clear about it with me. Two glowing blue walls in a row. What are they?"

"I do not know exactly, but I have seen things in a wall of this nature on the other shore."

"What?"

"It does not matter."

"And how do you know it burns?"

"I was with someone it burned."

"Who were you with?"

"Again, it does not matter."

He was silent for a moment, merely observing me. Then without warning, he screwed up his face with an intense anger I had never seen in him before. "It *does* matter!" he bellowed. "It matters very *much*!" He stopped, walked a few feet away, then turned and faced me once more. Any illusion I had of his being calmer disappeared the moment he spoke.

"You have kept me in the dark from the very beginning," he said, "pulling spells I did not know you knew out of some trick bag somewhere, but I abided it because those little revelations usually saved us. It galls me that I can be so honest and plain with you and not receive the same consideration. It does not matter? Of *course* it matters. Any information you have that I do not matters because we are in this together. Unless, of course, we are *not*."

He was right. But he gave me no chance to acknowledge that. He began to pace as he continued to chide me.

"You have been off on your adventures, gaining knowledge through experience while I've been in the Old Man's library reading. We should pool those resources instead of hoarding them. Still, you obfuscate and ignore and tell me it doesn't matter. And while I'm about it, let me make an observation. You apparently have questions about what you experienced in the other land. Have you ever considered that discussing it with someone else might be beneficial? I might have read something that sheds a light—not that many lights exist in this damnable darkness. So, you must tell me what happened. All of it. From when you left to when you returned. Now."

And, after an apology, that's exactly what I did. I relayed everything to him, from my initial meeting with Eddy at the coffee shop where he installed my little muse right up until I returned to Seth. I left out the details of our lovemaking, but that was the only item I didn't discuss with him. I made special note of his reaction when I mentioned the message that came from Eddy's grey wall, and he seemed genuinely surprised.

"Perfidy," he said dismissively. "Though I must admit 'Lord of the Land' does have a lovely ring to it. I wouldn't mind it as an administrative title, provided I did not actually have to do anything. The rest of it sounds like far too much work. You should have known better. Well, you were obviously lured back here. But for what purpose, I wonder? Are you sure you have been completely honest with me?"

"I swear."

"And Edgar Allan Poe? Really? Do you believe that?"

"I have no reason not to."

"And you slept with him, I suppose."

"Ummm...yes."

"Of course you did," he said with a chuckle. "The only available celebrity in this entire realm, and you find your way to his bed. I knew I liked you for a reason. But to see the sun again," he sighed. "That would be something indeed."

"Perhaps not what you think. That sun is warm and provides light, but it feels artificial and does not nurture. Nothing grows there except these blasted thorn trees, but I have no doubt whatsoever that it would burn you to a cinder. Eternal daylight, however, is just as disconcerting as darkness. I find more comfort here."

"I find *no* comfort here, but I probably would not find it in the sunny land, either. I miss the earthly realm and all its dubious charms. That's why I assure you I have no intention of claiming any part of this land. It does, however, fascinate me. It appears so ancient. Someone other than Olafsson has to have written about it. I already have several book merchants in mind to approach when I get back. *If* I get back."

"We will do our best," I said. Seth followed me over to where a log separated the chamber from the All-Ocean. A few earthenware bowls for feeding were stacked nearby, and I took two. I dipped them into the essence and handed one to Seth. "And speaking of our best, what is our plan for getting this jewel?"

"First we have to find the *cha'lan*."

"Then what? Do you know how to open it?"

"Not really. It's constructed from the immensity of the crimes the imprisoned has committed, so I know some are thicker than others, but the literature does not mention a way to break it." He drank from his bowl.

"I see. Suppose we do manage to open the *cha'lan* and retrieve the jewel? Can we reconstruct it, or are we then stuck with a headless body in an open grave? And what of the head? How far away is it buried?"

"I do not know."

I drained my vessel and refilled it. "So far, this plan sounds remarkably like the one we had for confronting the Old Man."

"And we were victorious, were we not? We improvise brilliantly."

"I should like a bit more structure for stealing magic jewels from headless corpses," I said, "but I suppose we must work with what we have." Seth handed me his bowl, and I refilled it and gave it back to him. "Once you have the gem, do you know how to use it?"

"Not as such, no," he said. "The Old Man's personal papers claim it focuses concentration and aids in 'disturbing the surface of place,' as he put it. That it will enable me to concentrate hard enough to go through the portal I open is supposition. But I'm willing to take the chance."

"Why would he leave such an artifact behind?"

"He did not realize he had. Again, according to his papers, he believed it was in his pocket when he cast the *cha'lan*, but the shell had already formed by the time he realized it was inside. He worried it might interfere with the spell, but it apparently didn't."

"Unless it did," I said. "We will have to be far more wary than we have of late."

"Is that a rebuke?"

"Yes."

"Fair enough."

"Why did the Old Man cast the *cha'lan* in the first place?" I said. "Was there enmity between these two beings?"

"With whom did he *not* have enmity? He had few friends when he was mortal, and I can't imagine his ascension to immortal being would have increased his popularity. When I allude to his papers, I mean an inventory of his books and spells, more or less. There are a few personal notes in the margins, but nothing as to what caused this battle. Indeed, he wrote precious little about this realm at all, including what we experienced yesterday."

"Do we even know this being's name?"

"Sadly, no. History is written by the victorious, and the Old Man never said who he was."

"I may know one of his names. 'He Who Shines.'"

Seth cocked an eyebrow. "The being to whom your friend made the sacrifice? But this one is in *cha'lan*. He has no need of sacrifices."

"Perhaps the Old Man did not vanquish his foe as thoroughly as he thought. It's just a notion. Probably wrong."

He stood up and took my bowl, placing them both on the ledge. "Anything is possible in this land," he said, giving me a long look. "I can't imagine you actually taking part in a sacrifice."

"But I didn't participate in—"

"The mucky part, yes, but I'm shocked you did not attempt to stop it. Still, it was for your Eddy. I suppose I understand, but love amazes me."

"Your amazement notwithstanding, we have work to do. Shall we?" A thought struck me, and I reached back to grab the bowls. "In lieu of shovels," I said.

He smiled and put his arm out to stop me. "We are not gravediggers. I have a spell of unearthing that will do quite nicely. We should get to it, unless you'd like to look around a bit longer."

"I don't think so. Who knows how long we'll have to travel." We went upstairs to the main floor, and I pulled out the compass as we reached the front of the castle and stepped outside. It pointed in the same direction as before. "To the left,"

I said, turning in that direction.

Surely enough, an eerie beam of blue penetrated the eternal ebony landscape, shining like a searchlight. It didn't seem far away, but its appearance gave me some pause, for I could not recall seeing it earlier. Granted, I had been focused on chasing after Seth, so I could have missed a bright blue beam shooting up into the sky. But I didn't think so.

"Did you see that light when you were transported here?" I asked.

He seemed lost in thought a moment. "No," he said with some finality. "My distaste for this darkness is such that I would have noted any relief."

"I suspected as much. So, this is either some bizarre natural random occurrence..."

"...or someone is trying to draw our attention."

I hated his finishing my sentences, but that seemed to be the likeliest explanation. "Well, they have it," I said. "Let us finish this."

He smirked with silent determination and started forward.

We fell into step easily and began our journey in silence. I was going over what I'd told Seth to ensure I did not omit anything. Trusting him after all these years seemed rather strange, but it felt right under the circumstances. We were each other's best chance for survival at this point. Obviously, whatever lay ahead of us knew we were here and figured out the best way to lure us. For what purpose is anyone's guess. The inevitability of the battle seized me. Neither we nor this creature would rest in this land until the other had been vanquished. I felt it as surely as I had ever felt anything.

I had been thus ruminating for some time, not paying attention to our surroundings until I noticed Seth looking back once or twice, as if in confusion. "We have been walking for a while now, haven't we?" he asked. "I can no longer see the castle, but then I see damn poorly in this dark."

I also looked back. "We are well away from it by now."

Seth pointed ahead. "Then why do we not seem closer to our goal than before?"

I put out a hand and we both stopped. In truth, the beam of light seemed to be as far away as when we started.

"I would say it was a trick of the light," Seth said, "but there *is* no light."

"I'll wager there's a trick nonetheless." A thought seized me, and I sat down in the sand.

"What on earth are you doing?"

I gestured to the sand beside me. "Sit down and rest yourself. If we cannot reach our destination by walking, perhaps we should try being still."

Seth's frown betrayed his skepticism, but at length he sighed and sat down heavily. "How long must we wait?"

"Let me consult the timetable," I said as dryly as I could.

We were not seated but a few moments before the distant beam of light grew larger. I could not plainly discern its movement, but it was no illusion. Whatever it was drew closer. Sight alone did not lead me to this conclusion, however. As it neared, I began to feel an emanation of immense power.

Seth had been slouching in the sand, but he sat up straight, looking around. "Do you feel that?"

"I do."

And amazingly enough, in the time it took for me to glance at Seth and answer his question, the beam of light was upon us, no more than ten feet away.

"Our destination has arrived," Seth said with a half-grin.

I withdrew the compass, which had cleared itself. "Indeed it has," I said, putting the artifact back in the pocket of my cloak. "I believe you said something about an unearthing spell."

"Right."

For some reason, I thought a reveal spell similar to the one we used to find the castles might be more appropriate. But I was loathe to correct Seth. He seemed so proud of that unearthing spell.

He gestured grandly at the finish, and we both stared at the black sand illuminated by the blue light. In a moment, it began to roil and undulate. The motion grew more and more violent until finally the sand fairly flew upward, leaving the blue beam to shine down an oblong hole. We both edged closer to it and peered inside. It was empty.

Seth toed the perimeter and looked down as far as the light would pierce. "Nothing," he said. And as he spoke, sand rushed in from some unknown source at the bottom, the level quickly rising until the hole was once again full.

"I have failed."

"What do you mean? Did you not see the *cha'lan* outlined by the cloud of sand you created? It's right in front of us. A simple reveal spell will probably do the trick."

"You...you *saw* it?"

"Well, I saw an outline. What else is going to be out here under a blue beam of light surrounded by eternal darkness?"

His eyes gleamed. *"Arren'ta bemchi mesch."*

The blue light—which seemed white now that we were inside it— shimmered slightly, its folds wavering until the *cha'lan* was fully in view. I had never actually seen one before, and I was unimpressed with the reality. My dreams and imagination had conjured the vision of a crystal clear sarcogaphus, ornate gold filigree bordering the edges and corners, with an impeccably dressed headless corpse resting comfortably on a bed of pastel satin. Tasteful. Elegant.

That is not what appeared before us.

Once the shimmering had settled, we beheld what appeared to be a solid, oversized cocoon floating about three feet off the ground. The inside was murky, but I could determine some sort of figure in repose and a green spot atop said figure. As we continued to stare at it expectantly, the murk began to clear itself away.

The body was garbed in a tattered tunic whose rips and burn holes spoke of either many battles or the one, presumably with the Old Man, which finally put him in *cha'lan*. His boots were scuffed, with large gouges up the sides, and his short neck stump looked moldy and vile. Resting on his chest, however, was the object of our search.

It was a smooth, oval stone of deep emerald green, thicker at its center and tapering to clean edges. It looked as if it would fit neatly in the palm of one's hand. In fact, my own palm began to itch at the sight of it. My fingers twitched in response. I glanced quickly at Seth and saw his fingers were making the same gesture.

The more I regarded the stone, the more I wanted it and

the less I could look away. I could almost feel its cool slickness soothing the hot itch in my palms. I suddenly wanted it more than anything I'd ever wanted in my life. All I had to do was to reach out and let it know who to come to, but I throttled that feeling. This was a trick of the stone. I steeled myself against all like impulses.

"You want it too, don't you?" Seth said.

"That is the stone talking—or the being holding the stone." On the brink of suggesting a blocking spell, I turned to Seth and saw his eyes widen. When I looked back to the *cha'lan*, the stone inside was clearly hovering above the body. "Do not move," I said. "Be on your guard."

We both remained rooted to the ground, but the stone took no such advice. It continued to rise until it tapped against the inside of the *cha'lan* with a hollow, sterile sound. The taps were not rhythmic, but they *were* insistent, growing louder and faster by the second.

"We should step back," Seth said.

I agreed in principle, but neither of us moved. For my own part, I was mesmerized by the agitation of the stone. It was frantic by this time, both tapping and rocking back and forth until it finally dropped an inch or two, then slammed upward hard into the *cha'lan*. This was followed by a low vibration that intimated—and I can only describe it as such—the thing was *burrowing* out of its confines.

The vibration increased in intensity and volume until at last the belly of the oval stone crested the surface of the *cha'lan*. We watched in fascination as the artifact worked itself out, slowly tipping one way and then the other, the action accompanied by the vibrating hum and then a grinding noise that had me on the threshhold of plugging my ears with my fingers. The edges were now clear of the *cha'lan*, and it began to tip faster and faster as the lower portion began to emerge until it silently popped free.

Into my left hand.

I shrieked and dropped it in the black sand.

And then it was in my hand again.

I felt its cool surface slide into my closed fist. Oddly enough, I sensed no magical charge of any kind. An artifact capable of emerging from a closed *cha'lan* or simply appearing in one's hand should emanate some magical force, yet it did not. This seemed to be a simple stone—a stone I could not rid myself of, to be sure, but nothing beyond that. I opened my hand and looked at it, motioning for Seth to come closer. We both peered at it.

"You saw me drop it?" I asked.

"I also heard you scream like a serving wench."

"My scream notwithstanding, you did not see me pick it up again, did you?"

He shook his head.

"Yet here it is in my palm," I said, holding it out to him. "Take it."

Hesitating, he looked at me.

"Take it," I insisted. "This is *your* quest."

"It seems to prefer you," he said. "And who wields it is probably less importan—"

"*Take it.*"

Seth sighed and reached out, grasping the stone and easily removing it from my grip. He closed his hand around the oval, the tentative fear in his eyes vanishing as he also sensed its lack of overt magical powers. "It's so cool and smooth," he said, "but it feels just like a—"

And it was back in my hand.

"I suspected as much," I said, opening my fist once again. I put my arm straight out in front of me and turned my hand over, palm open to the ground. The stone remained affixed to my hand. I shook it a few times but could not dislodge it.

"Your power is probably greater than mine," Seth offered. "I could feel nothing from it."

"Neither can I. I just can't get rid of it." I tried a few times to switch it to my right hand, but it preferred my left—the one it originally attached itself to. The stone was easy enough to pick off my palm with the fingers of my right hand, but it pulled insistently back to my left. If I closed it in my right fist, it simply vanished and appeared on my left palm once again. I was thus occupied in experimentation when Seth spoke.

"Warner, do you see what I see?" he said, pointing. "Off to the north. There's a white beam of light moving toward us."

I saw a vertical white stripe in the distance and in a few seconds, I could also tell it was in motion. Rapid motion. "What is that?"

"Probably the other part of the *cha'lan*," Seth said. "The head."

"Isn't that usually buried closer?"

He sighed. "With beings of great power, the farther away the head rests from the body, the more difficult it is for them to reunite."

"They can *reunite*?"

"So the legend says. We're apparently about to find out for ourselves."

"I should have researched his quest more thoroughly."

"I hope you've researched your blocking spells," he said. "We will need them before long."

Seth was right. My estimation of such things is woefully inaccurate, but even I could tell the vertical beam of light was advancing at an alarmingly rapid pace, zigzagging through the landscape with no seeming pattern or direction except toward us. Or rather, toward its body. We were merely in the way.

"I'm not certain we can prevent this from happening," Seth said as he held out both arms. "*Mech'da mord.*"

An impressive pair of white bolts of light jetted out from Seth's hands. As they cut through the darkness, they spread and widened, forming a translucent wall a good distance away.

I began to repeat his spell, but before I could finish, the *gem* raised my left arm and opened my palm, emitting a single ray triple the size of Seth's. It was not brighter, but the wall it formed was more substantial and extended farther. If Seth's spell was impressive, this one was formidable.

"Must you keep showing off?"

"I have precious little to do with it," I replied, "but it seems to be having an effect." The beam was skirting around the wall. I shifted my arms, and the wall moved correspondingly. The beam reversed direction, and so did I. After a few of these feints, the light skittered wildly back and forth before the wall a time before stopping.

"Perhaps you've tired it out."

As if reacting to the possibility, the light glared a bit brighter and as it did so, I felt a curious burning sensation—well, I'm not sure *where*, actually. Was it in my fingers? My arms? My head? "It's…resisting me," I said to Seth.

"Then stop blocking it. We can't hold it off forever, so don't waste your energy."

That advice seemed practical, but for a brief moment I doubted my ability to shut the spell off. I could feel its power coursing through the gem embedded in my palm and feared it would not respond. However, the spell ceased on my command with no noticeable aftereffects, and my hand was once again under my control.

The obstacle removed, the light proceeded toward its goal—slowly and a bit tentatively at first, but finally building back up to its previous speed. It would reach us within minutes. "What do you think…" I said pointlessly. Even if I could have finished a thought, Seth would not have had an answer. We just stood in silence as the thing approached.

Finally, it cleared the last small rise before us, perhaps a half-mile away, and then began to slow as it drew closer. I braced myself for its impact, though I had no idea what would happen when it joined with the body in front of us. If, indeed, that's what it was going to do.

The light dimmed as it approached, as if in consideration of our eyesight. It slowed to nearly a crawl before it connected with the *cha'lan*. The light extended through the oblong structure, bathing the entire area in a not unpleasant warm glow that increased in intensity until both of us had to look away. When we again focused our eyes on the spot, in place of the *cha'lan* stood a monstrosity.

Now that the figure was upright, we could clearly see the toll the battle with the Old Man had taken. Its shapeless robes were gashed and split, hanging in tatters. Its left hand had been severed at the wrist, and a hole dug deeply enough in its chest for its heart to have been extracted, that organ being essential to the *cha'lan* ritual.

The head had been bashed in from the left, its right ear and cheek torn away, and both of its eyes gouged out. The mouth had similar trauma, and I'd wager its tongue had been removed. Newly attached to the body, it seemed to balance precariously on its thick neck, wobbling as the creature looked about and went into a crouch, peering around.

Where is he? I can smell him, I heard in my head. Seth started, and I knew he'd heard the thing as well. Just then, it stopped whipping its loose head around, looking—as it were—in Seth's direction. I could swear he was sniffing the air. *You are his kin, but you are no danger. You do not have the power to wield it.*

He then turned to me. *It is you,* he said. As the words entered my head, my left hand rose of its own accord and opened, displaying the gem. *Ahhhh, there it is.*

"You're welcome to it," I said, shaking my hand in a vain attempt to dislodge it. "I don't want the damned thing."

He chuckled low, the sound reverberating through my brain as he raised the stump of his left hand. *I have nowhere to put it.* He hissed, as if he had just realized something. *You vanquished my foe, did you not?*

"We did," I said.

I fear you did not give him the death he deserved. He stole my artifact, rendering me unable to use it even though I stole it back before my prison was fully formed. He cut off my hand so I could not summon the magic, then he removed my tongue so I could not speak the spell.

"Why don't you use your right hand?"

"Don't give him any ideas," Seth said.

Did the gem affix itself to your right hand? Had it preferred my right, I shouldn't have need of your services.

"Are we doing you a service?"

Of course. Do you believe you came here of your own accord?

I sighed without intending to. "I'm not sure I've done anything of my own accord since we came to this land."

"What do you ask of us?" Seth said.

Ask? I ask nothing. I shall tell you what is required of you.

"You are unaccountably imperious for someone who needs assistance," I said, raising my voice along with the stakes. "But nevertheless, make your request, and it will be taken under advisement."

The creature emitted a long, inhuman hiss that seemed to echo in my head so that it was nearly indistinguishable from the words that eventually followed. You must open a portal to the earthly realm.

"Impossible," I said. "We have tried."

It waved its stump at Seth. He has tried. And failed. But he has neither your gift nor the gem. It will succeed. It must.

"Indeed, why must it?

The hissing began again, louder this time with its anger evident. Look at me!, it said. I must be made whole once again.

"An ocean of essence lies but a day's journ—"

I am beyond your ocean of essence. There is only one way to

restore myself. I must get back to the earthly plane and become one of the Blood Brethren.

Become one of the Blood Brethren? I thought. Combining the traits of both ourselves and the Blood Brethren would create a being of inestimable power.

You will open the portal now.

I shook my head. "I cannot. Unleashing a creature such as yourself on the earthly realm would cause incalculable damage. How many of us would you kill? How many of the Blood Brethren? And how many innocent humans? No. I will not have such destruction on my conscience."

As satisfying as using my foe's kin to persuade you would be, he has no hold over you. I have another servant in reserve, but your assistant should be boxed up in case he begins to suffer delusions of adequacy and attempts to interfere.

It nodded its slack head at Seth, its eyes wobbling a bit. Suddenly, Seth was encased in what appeared to be a veritcal *cha'lan*, only clearer than that in which we found the creature. He barely had room to beat his fists against the surface, so tightly was he enclosed. His mouth moved, as if attempting to cast a spell, but I heard nothing and the *cha'lan* remained intact.

You will open the portal now.

"I will not. I cannot."

As you wish.

He nodded again, and a figure appeared at his feet, curled up into a tight ball. It was dressed in a very familiar Hawaiian shirt and a pair of cargo shorts, but my darling Eddy was so emaciated, I could hardly recognize him. Where there was once meat on his bones, there was only gristle. The strong arms which had enfolded me so safely that night we heard the screams of the sacrifice were now thin and slack of skin, and his once lush beard was patchy and sparse. But he recognized me. He lifted his head and smiled.

"Warner," he said hoarsely. "My dark man. My love."

Punishing this one is no longer amusing, the creature said. *He has outlived his usefulness. I could restore him for you, but the portal must be opened.*

Eddy sat up, his voice stronger but the sight of him no less pitiable. "You can't," he said to me. "You can take him. He's weak—hasn't been fed for two cycles. But I'm toast. I can't hear anything but screaming now. I'm finished."

But if he was finished, then *we* were finished, and I could not let that happen. All I could think of was how content we were and how content we could be again in each other's embrace by the All-Ocean. I knew he detested the dark, but we could spend an equal amount of time in both his realm and mine. We could be together for eternity in such a fashion, Seth be damned. The world, in fact, be damned.

That thought loomed large in my mind. What care I for the fate of others? The earthly realm had treated me barbarously, turning me into the undead creature I was—indeed we all were, Seth and Eddy included. Why *shouldn't* it be punished? Perhaps it deserved the terror it was within my power to unleash. Why should I think of humanity when humanity had never thought of me?

Such thoughts were foreign to me, and I detested the feeling that accompanied them, but contrary to both my will and my nature, I found myself believing them. My right arm raised itself, the gem revealed as I opened my hand and pointed. *"B'emnet ardum to'bach."*

A beam of colorless light shot forth from my palm a few yards away from the tattered being, opening a silver, shining rift that coalesced into the familiar shape of a portal. I heard both Seth and Eddy screaming, but they sounded as if they were somewhere else. I was barely aware of anything except the energy flowing through me and the creature's voice, which I heard more clearly than all else.

Very good, it said, taking a few hesitant steps toward the portal. Its gait was halting and awkward, as if it had forgotten how to use its legs. *You have done well.*

I tried to break the beam off, but my will was no longer my own. I could not make myself respond. Seth and Eddy cotinued to cry out, but their words were distant and indistinct although they grew louder as the creature jerked toward the shimmering portal. The *cha'lan* holding Seth suddenly burst apart, and he threw himself at me, trying to force my arm down. I felt the scratches and heard the rending of my garments as he snatched and clutched at me, but I was immovable.

The being inclined his head in my direction, dislodging Seth. I felt enclosed, as if settling into a warm bath. Seth stood a few feet away and began reciting spells I didn't know. None of them had any effect on me, however, and the creature lurched inexorably to the portal.

He was almost upon it when Eddy clambered onto its back, riding its shoulders as he dug his heels into its chest, looking for all the world like Sinbad's Shayk al-Bahr—the old man of the sea. Now off balance, it tottered even more unsteadily, reeling as Eddy batted it about the head, grasping its skinny, malformed neck in an attempt to wrestle it away from its path. But it continued, now mere steps from the portal.

"We must break his concentration and close that damn thing," I heard Seth say as if from miles away. He kept throwing ineffective spells and projecting scenes from the past into my mind—the Old Man as Wade, the Old Man as his true self, our battle with his henchman—all richly detailed, some with sound and odor, but none could shake me.

"We gotta do it *now*," Eddy cried.

The being had stepped one foot through, half in and half out of the portal. Eddy grunted and forced its head back into our realm. "Warner!" he said. "I love you! I wrote a poem for you! My last poem." The following cut through the fog and the warmth, as clear as crystalline:

"*From night's Plutonian shore my dark lord came*
Stern looks that god nor angel e'er could tame.
Yet I, with patience, practiced Raphael's skill
And seeds did sow; his darkness I would still.
If Stygian souls can loving seed empower
Or ebon shoals provide a means to flower
I do not know, nor have I hope to find,
For dark my lord has left, leaving dark behind.
Yet well I know a blossom sweetly rose
In me, despite what hell and heaven grows."

My tears began to fall, and the warmth which had enveloped me turned cold. My hand again became my own, and I closed the gem in my fist.

NO!! the creature screamed, but it was too late.

The portal snapped shut, severing its head from its body once again. Its stumbling trunk and most of my beloved Eddy fell back, vanishing from view, but the creature's head and the arms with which my love had once held me fell to the ground. The eyes on the head blinked as it changed faces rapidly. The *b'ren mach*. It was nearly done. Eddy's arms writhed for a moment, losing contact with the head seconds before they all became piles of ash on the cold, black sand. I opened my hand and poured out the gem, also turned to dust.

And then, all was blackness.

ॐ

awoke in the same cavern where I had made my confession to Seth what seemed like eons ago. I was lying on a makeshift bed of blankets and pillows while Seth was sitting at a table closer to the log separating the chamber from the All-Ocean. He was reading a tome he must have found somewhere, but he looked up as I stirred.

"Warner!" he said, smiling and putting the book aside. "I was beginning to think you'd never snap out of it. I've nearly driven myself to distraction trying to find a spell that would bring you around. How do you feel?"

"Beyond weary." I tried sitting up and felt better momentarily, but my head began to reel and I sank back down again. "Did I just awake from a dream where we did battle with a being in a *cha'lan?*"

"That was no dream," Seth said. "Look the palm of your right hand."

I opened my hand and saw a raw, rough, oval-shaped scar. It looked ugly and painful, but it did not hurt when I touched it. "What happened to the gem?"

"Do you not remember? The *me'bach* turned to dust."

"It had a name?"

Seth nodded. "So did the creature in the *cha'lan*. He was Adnoch, the last of the Elders who populated this realm. This is his castle."

"How did we get here?"

"We walked—well, *I* walked. You shambled."

"You seem to know a good deal more than the last time we were in this room."

"I came upon Adnoch's library."

"How? We searched the entire castle for it, unless I am mistaken."

"You are not mistaken. However, I added directional words to the reveal spell. It's on the south wall of the great room upstairs. I'm sure you will find it worth the trip once you are yourself again." He got up and filled one of the jars with essence from the All-Ocean, handing it to me. "Here, drink this. I've tried to nourish you, but I fear I've spilled more than you've consumed. Seriously, my friend, it is good to have you conscious at last."

I took it from him and drank nearly half of it before I paused. The liquid burned but felt good in my body. "I am not so certain I will enjoy consciousness at the moment," I said. "I have lost my Eddy."

"Ah, yes. My condolences, Warner. If it is any consolation, Adnoch would have won the day had it not been for the sacrifice of your Eddy—who, despite my previous misgivings, may indeed have been Edgar Allan Poe. In Adnoch's writings, he mentions rescuing one of our kind, a rather dissolute early American writer of fantastical tales, from certain death to be his servant in this world."

"He was so thin and wasted," I said, tears springing to my eyes. "I shall never forget the sight."

"If you were able to understand our speech while you were engaged by Adnoch, you might have heard him say he had not fed his master for two cycles. My assumption is that he was somehow punished by the creature and perhaps could not renew himself in the All-Ocean. That is the only conclusion I can draw."

I sighed, dried my eyes, and drained the jar of essence in lieu of crying. "It seems to be a logical one."

Seth was silent a moment, perhaps in respect. "Forgive my asking," he said at length, "but my curiosity overpowers me. I could not break your concentration no matter what I conjured. What finally did it?"

"Eddy."

"How? Was your bond that strong?"

"Yes, but..." I felt foolish for a moment, like a lovesick schoolboy. But then I realized there was nothing foolish about it. And Seth should know anyway. "He sent me a poem. A love poem. It was beautiful."

Seth raised his eyebrows. "Indeed?" He smiled and shook his head. "The world is precarious and turns on such small details. Can you recall it?"

"Every word," I said, closing my eyes. I saw it exactly as I had when Eddy put it in my head, in cursive on an ancient-looking piece of vellum. "But it is for me alone."

Pursing his lips, he nodded.

I extended my hand. "Could you please help me up?" I asked. "I feel unsteady, but I need to get out and see the dark sky. It comforts me."

"Of course." He assisted me and, with the help of another full jar of essence, I managed to mount the stairs, even walking the last few steps out of the castle by myself, Seth's hand steadying my shoulder. I heard the hum of the dark all around, the textures and layers of sound rendering the landscape in vivid noise.

"I think I should like to go back to the Old Man's castle," I said. "I prefer being by the shore of the All-Ocean rather than inland."

"We shall leave as soon as you are stronger," Seth replied. "If you don't mind me accompanying you, that is."

"Absolutely. If you can leave your books."

He smiled and shrugged. "What I haven't read I can take with me. It will be a pleasure to walk with you once again. We have much to discuss."

O ur journey was most pleasant, if a bit wearying as Seth was more interested in lecturing rather than discussing. Nevertheless, I listened to the plethora of information. Much of it, I confess, went in one ear and out the other, but what seemed applicable to me stuck, and it was an agreeable enough way to pass the time.

Once back at the Old Man's castle, for I still could not yet think of it as our own, we settled in to a comforting routine. We read or I tried to instruct him in the art of seeing in the eternal darkness—but he was a far more willing teacher than he was a pupil. Still, he began to get the hang of it eventually.

I strolled along the shoreline, either by myself or with Seth, sometimes in discussion but often in silence. I, of course, had no desire to return to the earthly realm and even Seth stopped searching for a way back, becoming more and more involved in writing his own comprehensive history of this world.

A life of quiet contemplation seemed to be the ticket for the both of us. He occasionally left to add to his ever-growing library of books from all three of the other abandoned castles, often gone for long periods of time.

He had just returned from one such sojourn, and we were walking along the shoreline of the All-Ocean when we spotted something in the distance which had apparently washed ashore. Such debris was unheard of since, of course, the All-Ocean is not an ocean, *per se*. It is an extraordinarily large pool of life-giving essence which does not host seafarers and, therefore, contains neither flotsam nor jetsam.

Intrigued, we picked up our pace, debating what might lie ahead of us. As we neared, my heart skipped a beat in my chest. I saw a scrap of Eddy's Hawaiian shirt. I began running toward the as-yet unnamed pile, leaving Seth far behind.

Closing in, I slowed, knowing what the tangle was. It was Eddy's armless body, his bare legs still in cargo shorts, wrapped around the neck of Adnoch. He was, however, no longer desiccated. He was full and plump, looking as normal as when we said goodbye at the border of his land so long ago. Adnoch, however, was much the same as when the portal had decapitated him. I heard Seth behind me and felt him put a hand on my shoulder.

"What happened?" I said to him. "From all I know or have been able to assume, the bodies should have fallen on the other side of the portal, not into the All-Ocean. Is that not correct?"

"I wish I knew," Seth said, "but, in truth, I have no idea." He brushed past me and put his head to Eddy's chest, feeling his neck. At length, he sighed and straightened up. "There is no heartbeat or pulse. Your Eddy is gone."

"Could we—"

He held up his hand to stop me. "I could, perhaps, reanimate him but he would be walking dead. He would not be what you knew, and such desecration would not respect his memory. I'm afraid we must bury him, no matter how alive he looks."

I wept, though I knew what Seth said was true. "Let's inter him near the base of the mountain. What shall we do with Adnoch?"

"I do not know," he said. "However, let's get them ashore."

The question of Adnoch's fate was presently solved as we pulled and tugged and dragged the fused bodies farther away from the All-Ocean. It disintegrated, leaving a trail of bone fragments and slimy rags until nothing was left and all we bore ashore was Eddy. Luckily, it was not far to the base of the mountain and at last, we put him down on the black sand.

"If you would rather stay here," Seth said, "I can fetch something to dig with from the castle."

"No. I can do nothing more for him, and you'll need some assistance. Let us finish this as quickly as we can."

Without speaking much beyond the necessities, we hurried up the mountainside to the castle, found what we needed, and carried the implements back down to where Eddy's body lay. Amazingly enough, Pluto rested quietly on top of Eddy's chest, purring as I picked him up and petted him. "Where did you come from?" I asked, receiving little answer.

"What manner of being is this?" Seth asked.

"It's a cat," I replied, echoing what Eddy had said in the Neighborhood Bar.

The sand was soft, and the work did not take long. Had I skill in poesy, I would have been able to come up with some final words for my love, but art of that nature is simply not within my grasp and I did not want to recite what he had written to me. That was mine alone. We folded him into the hole and covered him up.

We shouldered our spades and began trudging up the mountain once more, Pluto following behind me. Seth was never the sentimental sort, and I figured he had just about reached the limit of his sobriety. Before long, I saw him cock a small yet insistent sidelong grin at me.

"You know, Warner, outside of this fine and marvelous soul we have just interred, your taste in men has always been abysmal."

I could have rounded on him, but what, indeed, would that gain? Seth was as he had always been. I chose to respond in kind. "You're still by my side, aren't you?"

"My point exactly."

ACKNOWLEDGEMENTS:

t may not take a village to publish a book these days, but it does take some fine friends and excellent professionals to get the job done right. Thanks go out to Sven Davisson and Joseph Campbell at Rebel Satori/Queer Space for putting this out into the world for me, Matt Bright at Inkspiral Design for the snazzy cover, and Louis Flint Ceci for whipping my poem into shape. Kudos also to my beta readers, 'Nathan Smith and Stephen Graham King, as well as Lee Thomas and Tom Cardamone

And speaking of 'Nathan Smith, he deserves special thanks for listening to my endless plot rehashes, trying to alleviate my imposter syndrome, and talking me down from the Ledge of Despair when necessary. A truer friend you'll never find (and he's a damn fine writer, too).